PRAISE FOR BIKING UPHILL

Women's fiction at its best! Excellent pacing, vividly drawn characters, friendship, emotional turmoil, humor, and my favorite part—setting. Some authors have a gift for creating a special time and place; Ms. Williams has done it here. The locations she draws for us are rich with detail and emotion, so much so that closing the book left me with the sense that I had just left home. The author shows us the many ways to build a home, and reminds us how important it is to find our place and nurture the relationships that are dearest to us. *Biking Uphill* is an enjoyable, quick read that also offers a necessary look at the lives of people who matter, people who otherwise would be forgotten, or worse—never known to us in the first place.

—Sarah Martinez, author of *Sex and Death in the American Novel*

From the moment that Antonia's desperation was disclosed, Carolyn was hooked—and so was I. *Biking Uphill* is the story of two women who meet and master tragic circumstances by weaving a transcendent community of courage and love. Through this community, and the power of a magical teapot, author Arleen Williams delivers a captivating perspective on one of the most important and difficult issues of our national life: immigration policy. This book is a unique combination of charm and challenge. It was so easy to read, but its cultural and political themes are not so easy to put down. I will appreciate this eye-opening book for a long time.

—Susan Little, author of *Disciple: A Novel of Mary Magdalene*

Biking Uphill is a touching story of three women, born on three continents, who find family through friendship and discover the true meaning of love. This is book two of Arleen Williams's Alki Trilogy and focuses on Carolyn, whom we met briefly in Running Secrets. In the gripping opener, we travel to Carolyn's past where, as a college student, she sheltered a homeless migrant girl, Antonia. The two meet again, years later, when Antonia registers for an English language class taught by Carolyn. The rekindling of their friendship is hindered by the weight of Antonia's secrets, Carolyn's family history, and the guilt they share over their mutual past. Gemi returns to the series like a dear friend, striving to bring Carolyn and Antonia together, knowing it will bring healing to them and their families as well. In her second novel, Biking Uphill, Arleen Williams takes the reader on a journey of self-discovery, friendship, and restoration.

—Gayle Bellows

Antonia was grateful for what life had given her and also for what it had taken from her. This story of fear and courage, of setback and success plunges the reader directly into the world of today's immigrant to America. In a swirl of friends and enemies, Antonia learns that people are not who they seem to be. Her American friend Carolyn has her own problems and confusions. As the plot thickens, we see that for all of us, life is about learning to use the power of truth—how to tell it, how to time it and how to take its consequences.

—Kit Bakke, author of *Dancing on the Edge*

Arleen Williams has proven again her talent as a storyteller in her second book of the Alki Trilogy which started with Running Secrets. This time the empathy, support, and understanding between the characters walk us through their lives in a way that touches our souls and makes us join them in their triumphs and sorrows. It's a captivating story of women's resilience and friendship. The plot moves with ease and keeps the reader engaged from the beginning.

—Clara Ines Arango

Author, Arleen Williams has done it again in *Biking Uphill*, the second book in the Alki Trilogy. She has woven authentic characters into a compellingly human storyline to create can't-put-it-down read. Williams finds moments in the everyday when cultures collide and moments of kindness result. In the case of *Biking Uphill*, that kindness results in friendships that change the course of one woman's life. I'll be anxiously awaiting the release of the third book in the Alki Trilogy.

—Jennifer L. Hotes, author of *Four Rubbings*

BIKING UPHILL

ARLEEN WILLIAMS

Booktrope Editions
Seattle WA 2014

Copyright 2014 Arleen Williams

This work is licensed under a Creative Commons Attribution-Noncommercial-No Derivative Works 3.0 Unported License.

Attribution — You must attribute the work in the manner specified by the author or licensor (but not in any way that suggests that they endorse you or your use of the work).

Noncommercial — You may not use this work for commercial purposes.

No Derivative Works — You may not alter, transform, or build upon this work.

Inquiries about additional permissions should be directed to: info@booktrope.com

Cover Design by Loretta Matson

Edited by Katrina M. Randall

This is a work of fiction. Names, characters, places, brands, media, and incidents are either the product of the author's imagination or are used fictitiously. Any resemblance to similarly named places or to persons living or deceased is unintentional.

Print ISBN 978-1-62015-349-9

EPUB ISBN 978-1-62015-374-1

DISCOUNTS OR CUSTOMIZED EDITIONS MAY BE AVAILABLE FOR EDUCATIONAL AND OTHER GROUPS BASED ON BULK PURCHASE.

For further information please contact info@booktrope.com

Library of Congress Control Number: 2014905753

*For the real Antonia who inspired this story,
and for sanctuary seekers worldwide sharing similar struggles.*

"An estimated 43.3 million people ... were forcibly displaced due to conflict and persecution ... children constituted 46 percent of the population."

"Every minute eight people leave everything behind to escape war, persecution or terror."

—United Nations High Commissioner for Refugees
(UNHCR), 2013

Los Arboles, California
1996

One

THE NORTHERN CALIFORNIA HILLS were spring green as they sloped to the Pacific. I rode through cool morning fog and coasted to a stop at the far end of Front Street. After chaining up, I wandered amongst the white canopies lining the long street that curved through downtown Los Arboles as vendors set out their fruits and vegetables, pastries and flowers, arts and crafts for Sunday Market.

Delphinium, iris, and poppy crowded five-gallon buckets, the fragrance and color calling to me. I wanted to fill my arms, my cottage, my heart with their beauty, but I had rent and tuition to think about. Cut flowers didn't last.

I moved on through the long rows of booths with nothing but time to spare. I fingered silver earrings and dangling crystals. A rich blend of aromas teased my senses: fresh baked breads, tacos and tamales, candles and incense.

The crowd was thin. The tourists still snuggled between warm sheets in beachfront hotels. The vets and hippies still in the hills deciding if this Sunday they'd come down and face the world long ago abandoned, a world gone sour. The students still home, far away, with families and friends and lovers. Not me.

Place is only part of the equation of love and home and family. Place doesn't fill all the holes in the heart. I was better off in Los Arboles. A full-time student, full-time resident, full-time outsider.

As I bought a few apples, a carton of strawberries, some mushrooms, I wondered if any of this produce had felt the warmth of my students' hands. I smiled at the thought: me with students. At the end of fall quarter, I'd started a class for migrant farm workers two nights a week in the living room of their simple apartment. The men gave me gifts of produce. The women cooked. And what food! I'd never tasted such wonderful food. At home in Mound City, I had never been allowed to eat with the migrant workers or to join the children's games in the sweet shadows of the apple orchard. In school, we had never been in the same classes or social groups. Now I imagined one of my students picking the deep green romaine I stuffed into my backpack.

Then I saw the pottery.

It was a jam-packed booth, the tables covered with soft Indian prints, the interior lined with shelves loaded with heavy pottery in reds, yellows and browns. I'd never been drawn to pottery, but there was something special about this work. It seemed to pull me into the booth by an invisible string.

"Come on in, Biker Girl. Take a look. A touch."

I had no idea where the voice came from. It floated disembodied through the air. "Hello?"

"Come in. Look about. Take your time."

I stepped between the shelves and tables, looking, touching, fearing. I couldn't afford to break anything. Not the most graceful, this I knew about myself.

"You look like someone in serious need of a teapot."

"Excuse me, but where are you?"

Just as the words left my mouth, I saw a small figure sitting on a low stool in the shadows at the back of the booth. Our eyes met.

"You think you might help an old lady to her feet?"

I gave her my hand, but the woman rose with little need of my help. Spry and strong, she stood to my shoulder in a long peasant skirt, a university sweatshirt, and wooly socks in Birkenstocks.

"That's better. Now let's see what you need, young lady."

"Nothing. I mean, I love this work, but I can't afford anything."

"Let's forget that for a moment and see what calls to you."

"Calls?"

"Yes, calls. The work calls to you, tells you what you need, what it has to offer."

"Whose work is this? Who made all this stuff?"

"Well, I did, of course."

I stared at the tiny, old woman with snowy white hair pulled into a braid that hung to the middle of her curved back. I could see her leaning over a potter's wheel shaping clay into teapots, bowls and platters. I could see the mud and water. But I struggled to see her lifting the heavy trays in and out of the kiln.

"The kiln's gotten a bit difficult these days," she said as though reading my thoughts. "But my son helps me out. Comes by, he does, to help me load and unload. He sets up the booth each Sunday morning and takes it down at the end of the day. My grandson used to help, but he's off at school now."

As I listened, my hand slid over the round, plump curve of a teapot. I glanced down and gasped.

"That's the one." The old woman smiled as she picked up the sunflower yellow teapot.

"But I don't even know how to make tea," I said.

"Then it's about time for your first lesson." With a firm hold on my arm, the old woman led me to the back corner of her booth. Next to her stool, a small table held an electric kettle and a sky blue teapot, the blue of the distant horizon where it reaches down to the Pacific Ocean.

I stood and watched as the woman plugged the kettle into an extension cord tucked under the canvas wall. Then she struggled open a square tin and spooned some loose tea leaves into the blue teapot. A few minutes later when the kettle whistled, she poured hot water over the tea leaves, put the lid on the teapot and wrapped it in a colorful dish cloth.

"There now, you see. It's not so difficult. Hot water, tea leaves, and a magical pot. That's all you need."

"A magical pot?"

"The magic of love, of attraction. Like the sunflower yellow that pulled you into my booth. The pot is for you and you are for the pot."

"I'm really sorry, but I can't afford a teapot."

"Have a cup of tea with me, Biker Girl. Then we can talk about what we can and cannot afford in this brief life of ours."

I accepted the steaming cup the old woman offered me. I couldn't think of anything else to do. I had nowhere to go, nobody to see, nothing to lose. I settled into a canvas director chair next to the old woman's stool and then jumped to my feet, sloshing tea on my khakis. "I'm sorry. You take the chair. I can sit on the stool."

"Young lady, I've been sitting on this stool since long before you first saw the light of day. Nobody sits on this stool but Mama Lucy."

"Mama Lucy? Is that what you want me to call you?"

"That's right. Now what's your name, Biker Girl?"

"Carolyn. Carolyn Bauer. How do you know I ride?"

"Small town, dear Carolyn. A student, I suppose."

"Yes."

"But not a happy one."

"Not so much, I guess." I stared at the cup I was holding. "What is this? It tastes different from any tea I've ever had. It's wonderful."

"Glad you like it. It's my own blend. Mostly chamomile with a bit of lavender and rose hips."

I turned to the sound of shoppers. A middle-aged couple in plaid Bermuda shorts and matching windbreakers moved through the shelves of pottery. "I should let you go. You have customers."

"Never mind them. They're not going to buy anything."

I looked at the old woman's watery, blue eyes. "But how do you know, Mama Lucy? How do you know they won't find something they want to buy? And what makes you waste so much time with me when I can't afford anything?"

"Ah, my dear Carolyn, wipe your tears. You'd be surprised what an old woman knows. Now come, let's wrap up that teapot of yours."

"But I told you, I don't have enough money. I could give you about half today, but I'd have to wait for my next paycheck to give you the rest. And really, I shouldn't. I have to pay rent and food and …"

"I don't want your money. I want you to take your teapot and make hot tea every evening. And I want you to come back next Sunday for another cup of tea with Mama Lucy."

With a slight shove, the old potter pushed the wrapped teapot into my arms.

"But I can't just take it," I protested.

"Of course, you can. Now off you go on that bicycle of yours. Wear your helmet and be careful. I'll see you next Sunday."

With a gentle, but firm hand in the small of my back, Mama Lucy guided me out of the shadows of the booth and into the bright midday sun. Blinking back tears, I turned to the old woman and gave her a quick hug before joining the growing crowd of Sunday shoppers. Little did I know months would pass before I returned to visit the old potter.

Two

I MOVED THROUGH the busy market, backpack slung over my shoulder, cradling the wrapped teapot in my arms like a newborn baby, fearful of the jostling shoppers, the random skateboarders, and the not-so-leashed dogs. When I reached my bike, away from the busy market, I loaded the padded teapot into my backpack. Once certain it was secure, I unlocked my bike and took off.

The hill lay ahead of me, steep, daunting, and always a joy. Biking was a passion, had been for as long as I could remember. A passion born of necessity, but still a passion. Back home I had no other form of transportation. There were no buses. There was no way to get into town, no way to get away from the orchard at all. If I wanted to go anywhere, I rode. When I was finally old enough to get a driver's license, Dad wanted it so bad, I decided I didn't want it all.

So here I was in California, still without a license or a car, still pedaling wherever I went, still keeping in shape climbing hills. I sweated and puffed and groaned, but it felt great. The best part, besides that it was cheap and I wasn't closed into a nasty, packed bus, was that I noticed things from a bike people speeding by just plain missed. The heady scent of spring, the birds chirping, and the breeze rustling the leaves.

Every now and again a carload of frat boys would slow down, trail me with their catcalls and dirty invitations, make nasty comments about my legs or butt or boobs. But most of the time I felt safe and healthy and even a bit virtuous pedaling a hill that I knew none of those damn jocks could ever climb. That day it was a quiet ride home from the market. The hill led to the university and the university was deserted. Spring break.

The road curved and leveled a bit, serving as a breathing point, a place to psych myself up for the final challenge. On one side of the road, the hill rose above me with only a few homes scattered here and there. On the other side, the hill dropped into a deep eucalyptus grove and I could catch the distant tinkle of a stream, one of many that fed the river running through town and out to sea.

Something caught my eye in the heavy shade of a large eucalyptus tree a few yards off to the side of the road. A shape, a movement maybe. I slowed for a better look. Behind the tree a small figure huddled. Although she had her back turned towards the road, the curve of her body and the long jet black curls told me it was a girl. There was something in the girl's position under the tree, the way she was rolled into a lonely little ball that pulled me to a stop.

I walked my bike off the edge of the road and through the tall grass towards the tree. As I moved closer, the girl scrambled to her feet, startled by the sound of my bicycle wheels moving through the grass and leaves. As she spun around, I saw her tear-stained face. She snatched a bundle and bolted towards the woods.

"Wait. It's okay. Can I help you?"

The girl stopped. Her shoulders drooped. For a brief second, her dark brown eyes met mine. I stopped, respecting the distance between us.

"It's okay. Do you need help?"

"I no speak English."

Crap, I thought. All those useless Spanish classes. *"Ayudar,"* I managed. *"¿Yo te ayudo?"*

I smiled and hoped I looked safe. To my surprise, the girl sank to the ground, covered her face with her hands, and sobbed.

I moved closer and saw the girl was really no girl at all, but a young teenager. She was thin and petite with huge dark eyes, but she was no child. She looked like she hadn't eaten well in a long time. Her clothes were little more than dirty rags and there was a faint, unpleasant smell. Nothing I could identify.

I laid my bike on the ground and pulled off my backpack. The yeasty sweetness of fresh-baked bread floated between us as I dug the loaf from the pack. I tore off a large hunk and held it out to the girl with the word, *"Comer."*

The girl looked up and met my eyes, her own still moist. With a dirty sleeve, she wiped her face. Then she snatched the bread from my outstretched hand. Like a beaten dog, she scrambled a short distance to wolf down the food.

I waited, awareness of the girl's pain and deprivation creeping up my spine. The girl–for I couldn't think of her as anything but a girl–was alone and hungry. Where was her home, her family?

As she ate, I spread my sweatshirt on the ground between us and pulled the rest of the food from my backpack. I laid out the bread and cheese, apples and strawberries. The girl watched from her distance. I saw her glance towards my bike.

"That's what's missing. Water." I pulled two water bottles from their racks and offered one to the girl. "Are you thirsty? Go ahead. Water. *Agua. ¿Sed?*"

Again the girl came forward, but this time she didn't dart away. I saw the gratitude in her eyes as she reached for the bottle and drank long, greedy gulps. I sat down and waited. When she finished drinking, I motioned to the food. "Let's eat."

The girl moved closer and finally sat opposite me.

I looked at the apple and cheese, then rummaged through my backpack again. When I pulled out my knife and snapped the blade open, the girl jumped to her feet. "Oh," I gasped. "It's okay. Look, it's for the apple. I won't hurt you. I promise."

I sliced an apple in half and then in quarters and cored each quarter. Then I took one of the quarters, peeled it and took a bite. I smiled at the girl. "See, it's good. Yum. *Bueno.*"

I peeled another quarter, set down the knife, and offered both a peeled and an unpeeled quarter to the girl. "Which do you like better? I hate the peels."

The girl stepped closer, reached for the unpeeled quarter, and then moved away again to eat the piece of apple at a short distance. I quartered another apple, then sliced the cheese before I stashed the knife back in my backpack. Then, I looked up at the girl and motioned her to sit down. "Come. Eat with me. I won't hurt you," I repeated.

The girl stepped forward and sat down.

"Try this cheese. *Queso.* It's good with the apple." I put a piece of cheese and apple together and popped it into my mouth.

Instead of copying me, the girl took a small piece of bread, laid the cheese on top and put it in her own mouth with the trace of a thin smile around her eyes. I laughed and the girl's smile widened.

"My name is Carolyn. What's your name?"

The girl remained silent.

I tried again. "*Me llamo* Carolina. *¿Cómo te llamas?*"

The shy smile spread across her face. "*Me llamo* Antonia."

"Antonia. What a beautiful name. *Qué bonito nombre.*" Again, the girl smiled. "What? Is my accent so very funny?"

"Oh yes. Very funny."

We sat and talked, or tried to talk, for what seemed like hours under that old tree. We pointed at things and named them, first in one language and then in the other. Whenever we got stuck, Antonia pulled a tiny, battered dictionary from her pocket, and we searched for the words we needed. It didn't take long for me to appreciate Antonia's English was far better than she let on and definitely far better than my Spanish. I lost track of time until I saw her shiver and realized it was getting late. The sun was already starting to sink on the horizon.

"I need to get going," I said. "Home. It's time to go home."

Antonia sat still as I gathered the remains of food into my backpack and zipped it closed. Then I stopped and took a long look. "What about you, Antonia? Where is your home? *¿En dónde vives?*"

Antonia looked down at her lap and said nothing.

"Come on, Antonia. Where do you live? Where is your house? *¿Tu casa?*"

"*No tengo casa.*"

"Where do you live?"

Silence.

"Where are your parents? *¿Tus padres?*"

"*No sé.*"

"You don't know?"

"*No. No sé.*"

"Where do you live?"

Again, silence.

"*¿Antonia, por favor, en dónde vives?* Where is your home?"

"No have home. Live here." She opened her arms wide to encompass the woodlands surrounding us.

"Here? *¿Aquí?*"

"*Sí.*"

I knew I should ask again about her parents, but it was getting late. I also knew that what I was about to do could get me into trouble, but I couldn't leave her there to fend for herself. "Come, Antonia," I said. "*Vámonos.*"

She didn't move.

"Come to my house. *Mi casa*. Come and rest. Take a bath. Wash your clothes. We'll figure out what to do tomorrow."

I stood, lifted my bike, and began to push it towards the road. Glancing over my shoulder, I motioned for her to follow me.

Three

ANTONIA WAS AFRAID to stand, afraid of the blood soaking through the tank top stuffed in her panties, afraid the flow would track her inner thighs. But she didn't want this Carolina to leave without her.

She thought of the restroom with the small sofa on the first floor of Ferris Hall. A warm restroom with hot water nobody seemed to use. The students had bathrooms in their dorm suites. The first floor restroom was for guests. And she was a guest whenever she could slip into the building unnoticed.

But now the dorm was locked. She didn't know where all the students had gone. They seemed to have disappeared overnight and all the buildings were locked up as soon as they had left.

Ferris Hall was her favorite because she could spend the night on the sofa if she snuck in after the janitor did his rounds. She also liked the small basket full of Tampax next to the sink. She never emptied it, only took three or four each visit, tried to build up a supply so she was ready when the blood came. But this time she miscalculated. This time she ran out. This time she washed her panties and ragged tank top in the stream and waited for sun to dry them enough for another day.

She remembered the first time the blood had come, nothing more than a few stains on panties so old she almost missed noticing. It was the feeling in her body, a thickening, a heaviness, a sense something had changed, that made her look. And there they were. She knew what the stains meant. She'd heard the women in the fields talk of their *reglas*, watched them sneak away to do whatever it was they did, saw the shame on their faces when someone whispered of the telltale dark spot that spoke of waiting too long. Her mother had told her she would soon become a woman and need to deal with her *menstruación* too. But her mother was gone, taken away before Antonia's first blood. When it happened, when womanhood arrived, she had been alone in the woods above campus, surviving on dumpster food and river water. The arrival of womanhood, this monthly flow of blood, saddled Antonia with a new set of problems.

One night, while she snuck through the large campus searching for food, she had seen a sign. She understood the first word: Women's. She'd learned it from restroom doors at gas stations on the migratory route from the Texas border to the California shoreline. She wasn't sure what that little line and the "s" meant and couldn't find it in her dictionary. The second word was Center. So much like Centro, anybody could figure it out. What puzzled her was what a Women's Center might be.

A few months after the first stains of womanhood, when the blood came thick and red, when she knew she needed to do something more than stuff tissue in her *chones*, she'd decided to take a risk and find out what the Women's Center was all about.

She'd seen some students on campus that didn't look American, who were speaking languages she knew weren't English. Maybe she could pretend to be one of them. First, Antonia knew she had to look more like them, so before daylight one morning when she could go unseen, she snuck into the Ferris Hall restroom and soaked her extra tank top in liquid hand soap. Back at the stream, she stripped bare and washed her clothes. She laid them in the sun and washed her body in the cold water. She scrubbed under her arms, over the tiny hard buds she guessed would soon grow into breasts, and between her thighs, intrigued by the tiny wisps of dark hair sprouting there. She felt her bony rib cage and protruding hip bones. "*El cuerpo de mi madre.*" She spoke the words aloud and the tears flowed into the stream, her pain so intense she no longer felt the cold of the water biting her bare brown skin. The touch, the feel, the smell of her mother now lost to her.

She had dried as well as she could in the midday sun and forced aside the thoughts of her mother as she dressed in her damp clothes. Her long curly hair twisted into a knot at the base of her neck, she headed to the campus Women's Center.

"Hi. Can I help you?" the woman at the desk asked.

"*Sí*," she said. "Yes. I have *problema*. Blood come."

"Blood?"

"*Sí, menstruación*. Woman's blood."

"Oh, your period. Are you a student here?"

Antonia gave a slight nod and said nothing. She knew it was better when people thought she understood less.

The woman walked around the desk to a large file cabinet. She pulled open a drawer. "Pads or tampons?"

Antonia said nothing. The woman shrugged and gave her two boxes. "I'm not supposed to do this, but just take both, okay? Do you need anything else? Maybe some wipes? Here, take these."

Antonia had recognized the word on the boxes, seen among her mother's things in the world of a childhood long-ago lost: Tampax. She almost cried out, the pain of loss cutting bone deep. "*Gracias*. Thank you," she said and hurried out the door, the boxes clutched to her chest. Alone outside, she hid them in her backpack and headed for the woods. There she tried to make sense of the instructions folded inside the boxes. She looked up each new word in her tiny dictionary, studied the diagrams, and taught herself the secrets of womanhood.

But now, this month, she was unprepared, now the blood came heavier and longer, now the campus was closed. She had nowhere to go for supplies and no money to buy what she needed. She could stay by the stream until the blood stopped. She was no longer hungry. She'd eaten enough for a few days. She'd be okay. But she was so very tired. Tired of hiding, of searching, of trying to survive alone. Tired of living out of dumpsters, consuming the scraps of excessive capitalistic materialism. Her father's words rattled in her head, made her unsure, worried about whether to trust this nice *gringa*. But she was bone tired and dirty and smelly and she didn't want to go back to the stream in the woods. She didn't want to be alone, to bleed alone. She wanted to follow Carolina. She wanted a hot bath, a soft bed, warm food.

Carolina was at the street when she stopped and looked back. "Come with me, Antonia," she said. "Please come with me."

Antonia followed.

As they walked along the side of the road, Antonia felt exposed. With each passing car, she ducked behind the taller woman, hiding herself as best she could. With each step, she felt the soggy wetness between her thighs. She pulled a sweatshirt from her backpack and tied it around her waist, grateful her blood was not yet dripping down her legs.

Some distance before the entrance to the university, Carolina turned off the main road and entered a maze of side streets Antonia didn't recognize.

"We're almost there," Carolina said.

"There?" Antonia asked.

"Home. *Mi casa*," Carolina said. "*Mi casa es tu casa.*"

Antonia watched the wide smile warm Carolina's face as she laughed. She wanted to relax and trust this new friend, but slowed as they approached a huge house. It was tall and yellow and the lacy wood trim was soft white. The home of aristocracy. That was what her parents would tell her. The home of the *imperialistas*.

"*Ey, no. No puede ser.*" She turned to bolt, but Carolina was quick and strong. She grabbed her arm and spoke a rapid-fire mix of English and Spanish.

"It's okay, Antonia. I live behind. See the path, *el camino*, there." She pointed to a narrow trail along the side of the property. "We go behind the big house. *Detrás.* Come. My house is very little. *Muy pequeña casa.*"

Carolina's Spanish was horrible and her accent even worse, but it was enough, just enough to make Antonia listen. She showed Antonia a small, almost hidden path along the fence line and motioned for her to follow. A tall hedge lined the path to the left and a row of cypress to the right. Antonia's curiosity got the better of her. She couldn't resist the temptation to follow this secret path to see what was at its end. She followed Carolina as she pushed her bike along the trail of matted grass and packed dirt.

The trail seemed long but wasn't more than the length of a large, urban lot. Antonia could catch only glimpses of the big yellow house through the cypress. The path opened to a large overgrown yard. At the back stood a tiny cottage hidden under the tallest fir tree that Antonia had ever seen. The cottage had once been painted yellow with white trim like the house, but now the paint peeled and the front porch sagged. To Antonia's delight a porch swing hung from two chains and swayed in the gentle breeze. She clapped her hand over her mouth before the squeal of joy escaped.

Antonia watched Carolina lean her bike against the front railing of the small porch and step up the two stairs. She unlocked the front door, opened it, and gestured Antonia to follow her inside.

"It's not much," she said. "Only two rooms. This is the living room."

Antonia entered a small square room with one overstuffed chair, a coffee table and a small platform bed against one wall and covered with lots of bright pillows.

"And here's the kitchen," Carolina said as she walked through the doorway into the next room.

"*La cocina,*" Antonia said.

The kitchen was nothing more than a double hot plate, a small refrigerator, and two cupboards. There was not even a toaster oven. There was no space for a table, only a small counter along one outer wall under a window that looked out on the yard.

"The bathroom is back here and up there is where I sleep." Carolina pointed to a small wooden ladder that led to a peaked space under the eaves above the kitchen and bathroom with barely enough headroom to sit upright.

"You can sleep on the platform bed in the living room. I built it myself with two-by-fours. I think it's comfortable. And here's the back door, see."

"*¿Una puerta? ¿Se puede abrir?* Open?"

When Carolina opened the door into the backyard, Antonia walked outside. The yard ended at a wall of forest, thick and dark. Tall hedges lined both sides. It was large, overgrown, and perfect.

"You have *jardín*?" she asked.

"*¿Jardín?*" Carolina asked.

"*Sí, jardín.* Garden, yes?"

"No, I don't have a garden. I don't have time for a garden. I go to school. And I work."

"You *estudiante*?"

"Yes, I am a student at the university, I have a part-time job at a health food store, and I teach an English class, too," Carolina said. Pointing to Antonia, she asked, "Are you a student?"

"*No, ya no.* Long time now."

For a moment they were silent, looking out over the yard, each lost in her own thoughts. Then Carolina turned and asked "*¿Quieres un baño,* Antonia?"

"*Sí,* bath good. *Pero no tengo ropa limpia.*" She looked down at her dirty blue jeans, tank top and torn sweatshirt.

"No problem. I've got something you can use," Carolina said. She took a pair of clean sweats and a towel from a tiny closet and passed them to Antonia. "*Para ti,*" she said.

When Antonia hesitated, Carolina shoved the clothes into her arms with a smile on her face and led her towards the bathroom.

"Carolina?"

"Yes?"

"You have Tampax?"

"Of course." She opened a cabinet in the bathroom and showed Antonia the supplies. "Help yourself, okay? Now, let me show you how to make these old faucets cooperate."

Later, alone in the bathroom, free of her dirty, bloody clothes, Antonia sank into the warm water and relaxed, truly relaxed for the first time in as long as she could remember.

Four

AS SOON AS I CLOSED the bathroom door, I went to the freezer and took out a packet of frozen ground beef. I put it in a large pot, added a bit of water and set it on the hot plate. Blood oozed from the meat as I chopped thawed bits from the frozen bulk. As it cooked, I found a potato, an onion, and some carrots in the refrigerator, and chopped everything into bits. I dumped it all together, added some broth, and set the soup to simmer.

In the living room, I used an oversized cotton dishcloth with "Los Arboles Sunday Market" stamped in the corner to cover the old coffee table and set it with napkins, water glasses, and spoons. What else? Bread. We need bread with the soup, I thought. I was digging for the bread in my backpack when my fingers landed on the teapot safe in a bundle of newspaper. Had it really been only that morning I met Mama Lucy? So much had happened in a single day.

I unwrapped the teapot and held it out in front of me to examine it. I couldn't believe she gave it to me. In the kitchen sink I washed it with the care of a new mother bathing her infant. I set it on the narrow counter beside the stove and rummaged through the cupboard above in search of tea. Finding none, I groaned in frustration.

The sound of water draining from the bathtub told me Antonia would appear soon so I picked up the newspaper wrappings and finished setting the table. As I gathered the paper in a ball, I felt something inside. I shook the paper. A small bag fell to the rough hardwood floor. I knew, before I bent to pick it up, Mama Lucy had wrapped a bag of her special tea blend into the package and I didn't even see her do it. For a moment I fingered the bag. Feeling a sense of contentment I hadn't felt in years, I set the tea next to the teapot. My new prized possession.

A few minutes later, the bathroom door opened and Antonia walked out the back of the cottage carrying her wet jeans, t-shirt, sweatshirt and underwear. She must have washed them in the bathtub. She spread her clothes over a few sturdy, low bushes to dry in the evening shadows.

"Are you ready to eat?" I asked. "*¿Comer?*"

"*¿Otra vez?*" Antonia asked, a look of surprise on her face.

"*¿Otra vez?* Again? Yes, again. It's dinner time. Past dinner time. *Cena.*"

"*Cena.* Okay," she said with a smile and followed me into the cottage. She stood in the kitchen and sniffed the air with exaggeration. "What is? Smell good."

I lifted the lid. "Soup."

"*Sopa.*"

"It's just hamburger soup. Meat and vegetables. Nothing special. I hope you like it." I filled two bowls and handed them to her, nodding toward the other room. "Here take these into the living room, okay?"

We settled onto the pillows on the floor in front of the coffee table. "Bon appétit," I said.

"*Buen provecho,*" Antonia said.

After dinner, I made tea in the new teapot as Antonia washed the dishes.

"*Muy bonita,*" she said, caressing the side of the plump yellow teapot with a wet index finger.

I struggled to tell her about the old woman in the market, but it was too much. I couldn't explain something I struggled to understand in my own language let alone in a mix of English and Spanish. In the end I settled on, "*Un regalo.* A gift today from an old woman in the market. A friend."

"*Un regalo de una amiga vieja. Muy bien,*" Antonia said.

I didn't know how to do it, but I knew I needed to ask some questions. Once we were settled in the living room with hot cups of Mama Lucy's tea, I plunged ahead. "Where are you parents, Antonia?"

"*No sé.*" Tears welled in her large, brown eyes.

"I'm sorry. I need to know. How old are you?"

"*Catorce. Casi quince.*"

Almost fifteen. The coming of age year in Mexican culture, in most Latin American cultures. The age when a young woman is dressed in a princess dress of lace and tulle with a jeweled tiara on her head and presented to society as a young woman, a *quinceañera*. I knew about this tradition, had studied about it in a comparative cultures class. I knew it was a tradition passed down from the time of the ancient Aztecs back in 500 B.C. So where was Antonia's family? Why weren't they preparing her *quinceañera* celebration? My god, I thought, how can she be homeless and alone and not even fifteen?

All these thoughts flashed through my mind in a nanosecond. What I said was, "*Catorce?*"

"*Sí. Casi quince.*"

My parents were a pain, true, but they were my parents, and I had a home where I could go if I needed a place to be, a place to collect myself. At least they cared, in their controlling, suffocating way. "Your parents? Where are your *padres*?" I asked again.

"I no know."

"I don't understand."

"*No sé. La migra* they come. They take *mis padres y todos los otros.*" Again her eyes filled and her tears ran down her cheeks.

I went for a box of tissue in the bathroom and offered it to her.

La migra. INS. The Immigration and Naturalization Service. That's what it was called back then. Later it became ICE, an acronym for Immigration and Customs Enforcement. Then, like now, it was the most feared of all enemies of Latin American workers in America, both legal and illegal.

La migra. I'd heard the words from my students, the mushroom pickers I taught in the overcrowded apartment on River Street. At least a dozen people crammed into a one-bedroom apartment intended for no more than two or three. Bed rolls in every corner. But neat. Always neat, clean, and organized. Always ready to run at a moment's notice.

An immigration raid was a nightmare. A very real, repeated nightmare I remembered from my childhood. Mound City, a fertile agricultural area, depended on migratory labor for economic survival. Rich in apples and cherries, hops and grapes—all labor-intensive produce requiring large numbers of farm workers for very short periods each year.

My parents were not large landowners, but they owned their home and an extensive apple orchard. Like others in their valley, they relied on migrant workers to pick the crop every autumn. I had fond memories of the laughter and food, the children and chaos that arrived once a year. I remembered working side-by-side in the orchard with girls like Antonia who I struggled to communicate with for days on end. I gathered Spanish words, just as I gathered apples. When I couldn't communicate with words, I learned to express my ideas in gesture.

I remembered the first time I saw an INS raid when I was still a child. I was on my ladder as the call spread through the orchard: "*La migra, la migra, la migra.*" A soft echo floating through the branches from tree to tree like some kind of whispering insect. I watched in confusion as dozens of workers jumped from their ladders, pulling the straps of the canvas picking bags over their heads and dropping the fruit to the ground as they took off through the orchard in a desperate attempt to outrun or outsmart the armed immigration officers.

"Where did they go?" I asked my father.

"Quiet girl." The answer was stern. "Keep picking. Say nothing."

And we picked. Mom, Dad, and a handful of migrants who had not run.

I wondered why all the workers suddenly ran as though their lives depended on it. When older, when I understood what happened in the orchard that day, I realized that for some, they did. For those from places like Honduras, Nicaragua and El Salvador, countries that the United States considered friendly allies despite their abusive military dictatorships, arrest and deportation was often a death sentence.

Shaking away the cobwebs of memory, I looked at the situation I was in now. I knew Antonia was in trouble. More than likely, she was an undocumented illegal immigrant. A fugitive from the American legal system. I sat for a long time considering my options. I knew the illegality of what I was doing, the risk.

I saw my tiny home through her eyes and understood. A hidden cottage, with both front and back doors, set in the middle of a large, overgrown yard with empty, equally overgrown lots on both sides, and a deep, forested ravine to the rear: it was the perfect hiding place.

"Antonia, you can stay here, okay? You can stay with me. You'll be safe here," I said.

We sipped our tea and sat on the homemade sofa/bed paging through old magazines and pointing at pictures, teaching each other the words we didn't know. I didn't own a television, but we listened to music as night fell and darkness blanketed the cottage.

"Antonia, tomorrow, *mañana* I need to go to school very early. Spring quarter begins. I have a class, *una clase*, at eight o'clock. *Una clase a las ocho*. Then I have to work. *Mi trabajo*. I won't come home until about four, *las cuatro de la tarde*, okay? You can stay here. No problem."

After I felt certain that Antonia understood, I headed for the bathroom to get ready for bed. When I came out in my pajamas, Antonia still sat in the same spot, and I realized I hadn't prepared the bed.

"Let's make your bed, *tu cama*, okay?" I carried a set of sheets into the living room and pulled the cover off the sofa/bed. When I shook out the clean sheets, Antonia grabbed the opposite end and together we smoothed them and tucked in the edges. After we added a comforter, I wished Antonia good night and started to leave the room.

"Carolina," she said. "Thank you. *Muchas gracias*." She wrapped her thin arms around me in a surprisingly strong embrace.

"*De nada*, Antonia," I said, these Spanish words slipping easily from my tongue. "*Buenas noches. Nos vemos mañana*."

Five

THE SUN WAS ALREADY HIGH when Antonia opened her eyes the next morning. She bolted upright with a start and stood in the middle of the small living room with the comforter wrapped tightly around her shivering body as she struggled to remember where she was. She pieced together the events of the previous day and a slow smile spread across her face. Then, she crawled back under the warm covers and lay without moving a muscle, like her parents had taught her years before. She stayed there for a long time but she couldn't get back to sleep. Her eyes were open wide, staring at the white ceiling. Memories washed over her and soon there was wetness on her cheeks. A sign of weakness. And weakness was not an option in Antonia's world. Weakness meant deportation, and deportation meant death.

She was only a child when it had begun. She hadn't understood the violence in the streets of her barrio. From one day to the next it seemed as though the city was on fire. Her parents no longer allowed her to play after school with her friends. Then, she could not even go to school. She argued and cried and begged, but her parents were firm. Stay out of sight. Speak to no one. Trust no one.

She remembered her father and mother coming and going from the house late at night when they thought she was asleep. She remembered other men and women sneaking silently in and out of the house. Then it was her own turn to depart under the cloak of darkness. Her family walked for days and days and days. Sometimes it seemed like they would never stop walking.

She remembered hiding silently amongst the cattle in a packed train car, fearing their huge hard feet. Fearing more the men with rifles who stood along the sides of the tracks at each stop.

She remembered a big station wagon with an American driver. Who was this man? She didn't know. Later, after endless nights on the road, when they had abandoned the station wagon, she remembered the sound of his gentle voice and the strength of his arms when she could no longer walk and her own father had become too weak to carry her.

She lost track of the months as they passed. At times it was only her and her parents. At other times they were with a small group of strangers. Sometimes they slept in the wilderness. Other times they hid in churches. On and on they traveled until finally they reached a river. El Rio Grande. She'd heard her parents talk about it in whispered voices at night as though it were an insurmountable barrier. She had imagined it to be a wide, flowing river of fury. It was nothing more than a trickle.

She remembered the happiness as well as the fear in her mother's eyes the day they planned to cross. They had received word of an offer of help. Members of an American church agreed to aid them across the trickle as well as to hide them, to help them on the other side. And so they crossed. At night and in silence. She felt the tightness of her father's arms wrapped around her, the warning of silence in his solemn eyes.

Then they were safe in a house of God, with food on the table and mats on the floor. They were safe. Her parents laughed and cried and laughed some more. Other families in the church basement watched them with tired eyes. Their joy had run out; reality had hit them and the adrenaline had stopped coursing through their veins. Now it was time to build a new life. A life under the constant threat of deportation.

Even as a young child, Antonia knew her parents had broken American law by entering the country under the darkness of night, leaving one station wagon in Mexico, running through the desert to another car on the other side of the trickle. She knew they were fugitives, and as fugitives they began their new life in America – grateful for the temporary reprieve from the constant threat of death.

As a child, Antonia understood in fragments. She knew fear. She felt her parents' fear. She could smell their fear, like a dog sensing danger. As she grew older, she understood more, slowly piecing together her history from her own memories and the stories she heard from others.

Their travel did not stop when they entered the United States, but their life changed again. They no longer moved in darkness and fear. Instead they followed the harvest from southern California to eastern Washington and back to California. A half dozen nomadic years slipped away. Here and there Antonia attended American schools, but she fell further and further behind with each passing year.

As Antonia lay in Carolina's living room, she sighed. She understood far more English than she could express and even more than she let on. She'd learned from experience that people say things, that she could learn things, if they thought she didn't understand what they were saying. Now she was in this little house, warm and comfortable, with food to eat, and a new friend who was helping her. Like the American many years before in the station wagon crossing the desert. But could she trust her? How much could she tell her? How much had she already guessed? Again tears flooded Antonia's eyes, droplets formed on her long, thick lashes. Again she was lost in memory.

They had only just arrived in this part of California where her father had found jobs for all three of them. At eleven, Antonia had begun to work side-by-side with her parents, one more pair of hands to put food on the table, to build a future together in America, the land of freedom for all. This was what her parents taught her.

Her family worked the late autumn vegetable fields. It was miserable, back-breaking labor but good money. Soon winter would come and money would be harder to get. So they struggled together, the three of them.

That's when she heard the call. It spread like wildfire in tall dry grass. *La migra.* They surrounded the field, maybe eight or ten of them, encircling the workers like cowboys at a round-up.

Her parents had warned her about this, about the possibility that one day *la migra* would arrive. They had made a plan. They would each look for the best possible escape route, and then they would run. They would head in different directions, running as fast as they could. They would stay low and hide, if possible.

Antonia had protested. She did not want to run without her parents.

"It's best to run alone," her father had told her.

"You are small and fast. You must run like the wind. Later we will find each other," her mother had told her.

So that day in the field, she knew what she had to do when her mother whispered, "Run." Still she hesitated.

"Run," her father insisted.

"*Te amamos, hijita,*" they both said. "We love you. Now run and keep running and don't look back. Stay low, out of sight. We all must run."

So she had run. She ran and ran and ran. She carried nothing but a small bilingual dictionary her parents had given her just after they'd entered the United States, the dictionary that never left her pocket. No bigger than a deck of cards, she felt the comfort of its weight against her thigh as she ran. She stayed low and when she heard the voices of the big white men with guns, *la migra*, she flattened her small body to the ground and held her breath. They walked right past her without seeing her in the row beside them. After a while, when the flat irrigated rows became dry weeds and a low hill rose before her, Antonia knew she was outside of the circle, beyond the line of *la migra*. Staying low to the ground, she crawled up the hillside.

As the INS agents tightened their circle, she heard the cries of men and women below her who were caught, forced to the ground, and dragged to the parked vehicles. Panic pushing her forward when mere strength was insufficient, Antonia kept scrambling until she reached the top of a knoll far beyond the edge of the field. There she collapsed.

From the distance, she could see the agents shoving a line of field workers into vehicles. Too far away, she couldn't identify her parents, didn't know if they'd been arrested or if they had escaped like herself. Maybe they were outside the line on the opposite hillside. Maybe they would find her. Maybe she would not be alone.

She would wait. That was their plan: wait until *la migra* left and then they would search until they found each other.

In the field below, *la migra* made a final sweep. From one end to the other they walked, checking the rows, making sure no one hid. She heard a scream at the far end of the field and watched two men haul a small person like herself to the nearest van. Then another. Then a third. Finally the agents returned to their vehicles, slapping each other on the back. Their boisterous congratulations carried on the wind to the top of the hill where Antonia watched in horror. As they drove away, she let out a sigh of relief followed by a scream of desperation.

On the knoll as night fell, she sat, her arms holding her knees tight to her chest. For the first time in her young life, she was alone. Completely, entirely alone. The world became dark around her, the sky full of stars, the only sounds the music of crickets and owls. She huddled in a ball, tired and terrified. Unaware of hunger and thirst, she cried herself to sleep fearing what may have become of her parents.

She woke to the sound of birds overhead, but there was only silence in the field below. No workers, no bosses, no immigration agents. She sat on the knoll for hours watching the sun rise, waiting for her parents to find her, hoping against all hope that they had gotten through the line as she had done. When the sun was high overhead, she stood. Slowly she made her way back down the hill and returned to the place she'd last seen her parents, but there was no sign of them. She gathered some tomatoes from the devastated plants and a few water bottles abandoned by workers as they fled in a desperate attempt to escape. She returned to the knoll. She stayed for two more nights, waiting for her parents. But they did not come for her.

No one came. The field remained empty, but Antonia knew it would not be abandoned forever. Soon a new group of migrants would be brought in to salvage as much of the crop as possible, and she did not want to be found there. She descended the hill one last time and crisscrossed the field collecting whatever she could find and carry. A scarf here, a jacket there, even a wallet with a few dollars in it.She found a small backpack and filled it with her collected items and as many tomatoes and water bottles as it would hold. Like *la migra*, she did one final sweep of the large field searching for some sign of her parents. She even circled the surrounding hill tops, but there was no trace of them. Finally she knew it was time to leave.

Not knowing where to go or even where she was, she headed to the small dirt road and began to retrace the route they had come. She remembered they had passed through a small beach town and headed in that direction. As she walked, she thought about the old car her parents had managed to buy the summer before. Looking over her shoulder, she saw the battered white sedan parked at the side of the road, one in a long line of old model sedans, station wagons and pickup trucks. Abandoned, like her. What would become of them? What would become of her? With no keys and no knowledge of cars or how to drive them, she walked away leaving everything she knew behind her.

As she lay in Carolina's cottage, Antonia allowed herself to remember the pain, to feel the loss, for the first time in the months that had passed since her parents disappeared. It took her breath away. She cried in agony and curled herself into a ball, the sheets and comforter wrapped tight around her body and over her head. She lay there as the hours ticked away, sobbing and remembering until the sun rose overhead, until its slow descent into the Pacific. She did not get up to eat, to dress, to use the bathroom. Antonia didn't move until she heard the sound of footsteps on the front porch.

Six

THE DOOR WAS CLOSED on a beautiful sunny day. I'd have had the front and back doors wide to the sun and breeze. Maybe she was out back. Maybe she didn't know it was safe to leave the doors open. Maybe she'd left.

I laid my bike against the porch and hurried to unlock the door. I swung it open and there she was. Wrapped in the comforter from her bed, she stood in the middle of the living room like a deer in headlights with red-rimmed eyes and tear-stained cheeks. Her hair was a tangle of long black curls and she was still wearing my baggy sweats.

"Hi, Antonia. Are you okay?"

"*Sí*. Okay." She rubbed her eyes with her fists like a young child, a pretense of waking up.

"But you're not dressed. Have you been sleeping all day?"

"Yes, sleeping. Very tired."

It was late afternoon. She'd been in bed all day and I was certain she hadn't been sleeping the whole time. "Did you sleep well?" I asked, determined to keep up the pretense.

"*Sí, bien. Gracias.*" She moved towards the back door. "Now I get dressed."

I watched as she went outside to gather her clean clothes from the bushes. She closed herself into the bathroom and the sound of running water soon filled the cottage.

"Okay, don't talk to me," I muttered to myself as I set down my backpack and went into the kitchen to see what to make for dinner.

When Antonia emerged from the bathroom with hair combed and a smile on her face, I was working on a vegetable omelet. With a wall of silence between us, we sat down on the living room floor and ate.

Finally I broke the silence. "I teach an English class tonight."

"You teacher?" Antonia asked in surprise. "No student at university?"

"I am a student and a teacher. I teach migrant workers. I go to their apartment to help them learn English." I spoke as clearly as I could keeping my vocabulary simple. "I'm going tonight. Do you want to come?"

"*Sí. Mi ingles* bad."

"Don't worry. It's not that bad. At least we can understand each other, right?"

"*Sí*, I understand you."

"My students are from Mexico. Are you from Mexico, Antonia?

"No. No from Mexico."

"Where you are from? Maybe I'll go there for a visit."

"Oh no!" Antonia jumped to her feet and almost shouted the words. "Very bad."

Her reaction was so violent, I stared in surprise. Then, in a voice little more than a whisper, I asked, "What's bad?"

"*El gobierno es muy malo.* Very bad. Kill many people."

"Where are you from?" I asked again.

Antonia said nothing.

"I read about the violence in Latin America. Is it still bad? When did you leave your homeland?"

"Long time now."

"How did you come to America?"

"We walk, take train, drive car, walk more." Antonia sat back down on the pillows.

I leaned forward, listening to every detail, wanting to understand. "We? You said 'we.' Who did you walk with?"

Antonia burst into tears and huddled in misery, her face cupped in her hands.

"My god, what did I say, Antonia? I'm sorry. I'm so sorry."

I slid around the coffee table to Antonia and wrapped an arm around her shoulders. I waited, holding her until her sobs relaxed into gentle tears.

"What is it? What did I say?"

"No problem. I say too much. *Mi papa* say no say nothing to nobody. I no say nothing."

But I heard doubt and confusion in her voice. "Okay. It's okay," I said. "You don't need to tell me anything. But I want to help you and I can't help if I don't know what you need. You're too young to be alone. Where are your parents?"

Again, Antonia burst into tears and I rocked her in a tight embrace until the sobs were nothing more than a trace of tears on her cheeks. I didn't understand and needed some answers, so I whispered the question again. "Where are your parents? *Donde están tus padres*?"

"*No sé.*"

"Come on, Antonia. Talk to me."

To my surprise, she did.

Seven

"**I GO TO SCHOOL** every day like all children. One day *mi mami* say I must to stay home. I watched from window as other children passed our house with their books, and I asked her why I no can go. She say be quiet and send me to my room with schoolwork to do."

"What did your parents do? Did they have jobs?" Carolina asked.

"*Mi papi* worked for government, old government. But he not like old government. He wanted to change the government. *Mi mami* was history teacher in *secondaria*. High school, no?"

"Yes, high school. So what happened? Why'd they pull you out of school?"

"It no was safe."

She struggled to find the words to explain the memories that haunted her dreams. For months gun shots had shattered the nights. For weeks the curtains were pulled tight day and night. Her parents told her to stay in her room, but that didn't stop her from peeking each time someone crept through the backdoor and across the courtyard to the tiny passage that led to the alley behind the house. For weeks men and women in dark clothes, faces covered, snuck in and out carrying large backpacks. They sat for hours whispering deep into the night, the cigarette smoke wisping into Antonia's bedroom, but they didn't frighten her. Only the gunshots, the screams, the terror frightened her.

"One day, before the day when school stopped for me, *mi mami* and I walked to school. We passed a white wall. It had holes in it and dark red marks. What is it? I asked *mi mami*, but she no answer me. She only walked faster."

"So was it ... was it dried blood?" Carolina asked.

Antonia nodded and held her new friend's wide-eyed stare. "One morning we passed *un cuerpo*, how you say?"

They paged through her tiny dictionary looking for the word neither could translate.

"Dead man," Antonia said. "No, boy only. Maybe fifteen. His mother sit beside him, crying and crying. *Mi mami* take me home and locked the door. She say stay there and she go back to help the other mother. Then no more school."

"How old were you?"

"Just little. Only six or seven. We stayed for maybe six months more and then we leave."

"Left? How?" Carolina asked.

"*Ey, no recuerdo todo*. Hard to remember everything. Long trip. Many, many weeks. Maybe months. We left in the night. First in car with friends of my parents. Then we take bus, then train. Always to north."

Carolina didn't ask where she began her journey, didn't push for details, and Antonia was grateful. She'd already told too much. She'd already trusted this *gringa* with too many details of her story. But she needed to tell, needed to get the pain out. She told Carolina how her parents paid money to get across the border into Mexico and how this person took all their money but abandoned them when the *federales* came too close.

"How long were you in Mexico?" Carolina asked.

"A long time. Months. Maybe a year. *Mis padres* no have more money to pay the *coyotes* to help us. We sleep on the streets. One day we go to a church. *Mi papi* talked a long time with the padre. The padre helped us. He tell us where to go and who to trust. We went from house to house, town to town all the way north."

"Like the underground railroad," Carolina whispered.

"Not always on railroad. Sometimes we walked. Sometimes people give us rides in their cars. Then we come to the Rio Grande." She shook her head in memory.

"What? What happened?" Carolina asked. She shifted in her big chair where she sat across from Antonia who was cross-legged on the homemade sofa bed.

"*No es nada.* For long time I heard of the Rio Grande like big river we must to cross to be free. When I see it, I surprise. It was only a little dirty water. No big river at all. I asked *mi papi* why we no walk across. I jumped up and down. I did not know what freedom mean, but I wanted it because he wanted it. '*¡Silencio hijita!*' he say. I no understand why he no want people hear me. Later *mi mami* explained we go to U.S.A. without papers. We will be undocumented illegal aliens. All bad words. If they catch us, they send us back. If they send us back ..."

Antonia's voice choked with tears. She couldn't continue. Her stare was direct, unflinching and full of sorrow when she met Carolina's eyes.

"If you were sent back, your parents would be arrested," Carolina said.

"*Sí.*"

"But you crossed and you were not caught."

"Yes. We go at night. *Mi papi* carried me across like a baby. The men take us to a house. Then to a church. Then to more houses."

Antonia told how they stayed in hiding for weeks, even months, until her father and mother felt safe enough to start looking for jobs. They tried to find restaurant or construction work, but after endless rejections, necessity forced them into migratory field work. It was the one area of the American economy that appreciated their willingness to do back-breaking work for almost nothing at all. The community of workers pulled her parents in, gave them a new start, a place to belong in this strange new world.

"Were you always moving, never in the same place more than one season?" Carolina asked.

"*Sí.* We go west from Texas to Nuevo Mexico, Arizona and California. Then one day *la migra* come."

"When was that?"

"Before winter."

"Before winter. You mean October or November. That was what, like five or six months ago?" she said.

Antonia watched as understanding crossed Carolina's face.

Eight

FOR A LONG TIME we worked at piecing the story together in a mixture of Spanish and English, consulting Antonia's tiny dictionary when communication broke down. Finally Antonia exclaimed, "You have *clase* tonight?"

"Oh lord, yes. I have to go or I'll be late. Do you want to come with me?" I asked as I scrambled to my feet and carried our dishes to the kitchen sink.

"Yes, I come."

"We'll have to take the bus. Are you ready?"

"*Sí*, but no money for bus."

"I've got a pass. Let's go." I grabbed my teaching bag and we were off.

When we got to the apartment on River Street, when I knocked on the door and introduced Antonia, when the women clustered around her like hens on a handful of tossed grain and ushered her into the kitchen, I knew I wouldn't see her all evening. A pang of jealousy got me, but I sighed and began class. It was always the men who studied while the women stayed in the kitchen, cooking, chattering, supervising the homework of those children who they managed to enroll in school. It took a brave mother to enroll her kid in a public school. Fear of deportation ran deep. I knew this, just as I knew Antonia had been ushered into an inner female circle that I was not part of.

I sat in the crowded living room with a half dozen men ranging in age from sixteen to fifty-six. As at every other class, I began by asking the men for examples of communication problems they'd experienced during the week. This time a young man whose pregnant wife had yet to be seen for a pre-natal appointment despite having progressed to the third trimester raised his hand. Like many immigrants, legal as well as undocumented, they were fearful of approaching the local free clinic. So together we role-played making an appointment with a doctor's receptionist and then another conversation with the doctor. The pregnancy grew, as these things tend to do, to a discussion of Raul's chronic backache and Jesus's lost finger and Eduardo's mother's diabetes. And so the vocabulary lesson expanded to body parts and illnesses and treatments.

I wasn't an experienced teacher and had zero training, but I knew I had a knack for it. At times I seemed to be able to read my students' minds, understand what they were trying to say despite their limited use of English and my own prohibition of Spanish.

But the night of Antonia's first visit, they ignored my no-Spanish rule in the apartment during class. As we sat in the living room with my large paper flipchart and a rough drawing of the human skeleton, I caught whispers of Spanish floating in from the small kitchen to the back of the apartment where Eduardo's mother, Guillermo's pregnant wife, and a few other women were making dinner. The meal preparations were slow, the women busy learning Antonia's story. The story I struggled to piece together.

Now I was frustrated. Maybe even a bit angry and hurt. I knew that in five minutes Antonia trusted these women more than she trusted me despite having opened my home to her. The bond they shared in the kitchen extended far beyond a common language. No, the bond they shared was neither linguistic nor cultural, though certainly both helped. Instead, what tied them were their stories of immigration, their migratory lifestyle in a land they didn't understand, and their constant fear of deportation.

After several minutes of trying unsuccessfully to focus on a story involving a fractured bone, I called for a break. I headed into the kitchen to join the women. Silence fell.

"Why do you stop talking when I enter?" I asked. The women dropped their eyes and busied themselves with cooking tasks. "I feel left out," I tried again. Still, they responded with silence. "Okay then," I said. "Let's try to speak English. This is our English lesson, right?"

"*Sí*, Maestra," said one of the women. "We talk only *inglés*."

"Come join the class, okay?"

"We finish cook first," another said.

I knew it was impossible. I was the outsider. I could teach them English and even learn their language, but I was not one of them. Antonia was. I was glad I'd brought her with me even though I felt left out. Antonia needed support, and she needed to find her parents.

Before I knew it, an hour had passed and the women were bringing food to the table where I sat with the men. The fragrance of green chilies, roasted garlic and corn tortillas filled the small apartment. I watched as Juan Luis, a young lanky *norteño*, stood and insisted Antonia take his chair and then brought another from the kitchen and squeezed in beside her. I saw her smile and heard her quick Spanish. I was familiar with Juan Luis's melodic Spanish of northern Mexico and could hear the difference in accent when Antonia spoke, but I already knew she wasn't Mexican. Where was she from? El Salvador, Nicaragua, Guatemala? If she wanted to tell me, she would. If she didn't trust me, I'd have to live with it. I watched and listened as we feasted on *frijoles refritos, enchiladas verdes de pollo* and *arrozo*. Because I was not the center of attention and because I wasn't trying to make them stick to English while we ate, the room was a clatter of conversation and laughter.

The plates were empty and the men exhausted. I knew they'd be back at work before sunrise. It was time to go.

"Maestra, no ride *bicicleta* today?" Juan Luis asked as I gathered my teaching materials.

"No," I said. "We're on the bus tonight."

"*Ey no*. Too late for bus. I give you ride home."

Though the words were directed to me, his eyes were on Antonia. I hesitated. I'd never shared my address with my students. Never shared anything of myself. Now, a ride home? Still it would be a whole lot quicker and easier than taking the bus. And it was late, much later than normal.

"Okay," I said.

We squeezed into the cab of an old truck, Antonia in the middle. The Mexican eagle and serpent adorned the wool blanket that covered the bench seat and bright red rickrack with tiny pom-poms trimmed the windshield. I gave the address, a few directions here and there, but mostly I remained quiet while Juan Luis and Antonia chatted like any two teenagers attracted to each other. I felt like an old chaperone at twenty-two. That's it, I thought. Time for me to learn Spanish. Really learn it. At least if I were fluent, I could eavesdrop.

When we got out of the truck and walked back towards the cottage, Antonia was subdued, but a bit of hope seemed to lighten her step. We walked through the large, dark yard in silence, picking our way along the path. When we reached the cottage, I told Antonia to take her turn in the bathroom while I prepared a pot of tea. My mind turned to the afternoon in the Sunday market. I remembered the loneliness I'd felt and the comfort of Mama Lucy's crowded pottery booth. I made a mental note to return to the market. Maybe I could convince Antonia to go with me, to venture out in the daylight without fear of arrest.

When she came out of the bathroom, fresh from her shower, I offered her a cup of tea.

"They know about *la migra* come."

"Do you mean the immigration raid that took your parents?"

"*Sí*, yes, *la migra*. They know. They hear *la migra* come and take many, many."

I knew who "they" meant. I knew Antonia was referring to the women in the kitchen and to Juan Luis, to the long conversations I had been unable to follow earlier that evening. "Do they know your parents? Do they know where they took them?"

"They say they take them all to *detención*. Then they send all back to own country."

With those words, Antonia cried. Once again her face dropped to her hands and her body crumpled into a ball.

For most Central Americans political asylum from the U.S. government was as impossible to get as a cheap flight to the moon. Despite the continued violence, the slaughter of parish priests, and the thousands of *desaparecidos*, the U.S. government maintained "friendly nation" status with a number of Latin American military dictatorships. The disappearances of so many seemed to make no difference in international politics. U.S. Immigration didn't offer political asylum to immigrants from ally nations.

I knew this not only from my studies, but also from my evenings in the apartment on River Street where I was learning as much as my students. Because our conversation classes covered whatever the students brought, U.S. immigration policies and practices were frequent topics. They controlled their lives. I never knew–and never would dream of asking–who was documented and who was not in that overcrowded apartment. There was always a core group of men, whose wives worked in the kitchen with an ear towards the living room, whose children slept on mats in the corners of the room. Others came and went, joining the class once or twice, disappearing, reappearing a week, even a month later.

As Antonia cried, I understood her parents had likely been detained and deported. And if political activism had fed their escape to the U.S., they would be taken into custody by military police as soon as they arrived in their homeland. They would be tortured to that point when death would be a release from misery. And then they would be killed when they were no longer conscious of the horrors being inflicted upon them. Was there room for hope?

"Maybe they sent your parents to Mexico. *Quizás la migra* thought they were Mexicans," I said.

"*Quizás*," Antonia said, but she did not sound any more convinced than I sounded convincing.

NINE

DETENCIÓN. DEPORTACIÓN. With each syllable Antonia jammed the shovel into the hard soil. *Detención. Deportación.* Protected by a thick layer of tall grass and weeds, the soil wouldn't give. She held the wooden handle with both hands and jumped on the metal foot rests. The ground fought back. The handle escaped her grasp and whacked the side of her head. She collapsed in the tall grass, hands to her head and rolled into a ball.

Detención. Deportación. Detención. Deportación. She wanted to believe *la migra* was too stupid to know her parents were not Mexican. She wanted to believe her parents were mistaken for undocumented Mexican migrants and sent back across the border, two among many. She wanted to believe, but her heart told her it didn't happen that way.

Her parents were known, part of the resistance, a plum for *la migra*. Brownie points for shipping them back.

Antonia saw the blood stained walls of the neighborhood of her early years. She smelled death's decay in the streets. She remembered the words her mother sang: *Yo no canto por cantar*. She overheard the stories of the Chilean resistance, of Victor Jara's broken fingers and chopped off hands. Let's see you play your guitar now, they said. His body was later thrown in the street riddled with forty-four bullet holes. This was before her time, even her parents' time, but it was the history of grassroots protest and underground resistance that led to her parents and all those who gathered in their darkened living room plotting into the night.

Antonia held herself tight in the tall grass behind Carolina's tiny cottage. She saw her parents. Her mother raped, bloody, in rags, rolled into a ball on a cold concrete floor hidden from light, from truth, from any knowledge of her existence. Death was her only escape. "Let go, Mami," Antonia whispered to the warm grass, the hint of lavender. "Let go. I will be okay."

She saw her father. How would they torture him? She didn't want to imagine it, didn't want to see it in her mind's eye, but there was no way to stop the images. Rape? Broken bones? Electrodes? Cattle prods? Cigarette burns? What would her father endure to guard the names of his friends and collaborators? Would he be forced to watch as they tortured and raped her *mami*? Would she be forced to watch what they did to him?

As she sobbed in the warm sun she prayed for their deaths. "Let go," she begged them. "Let go. I am safe. Do not worry for me."

Detención. Deportación. Death.

Her stomach no longer able to hold her breakfast, she stumbled to her feet and ran to the edge of the yard. She vomited until there was nothing left to vomit. Nothing left in her but agony and despair.

She kicked the shovel aside and tore at the tall grass until her palms and fingers bled. Once she'd cleared an area about ten-feet square, she found the shovel. She jabbed at the hard soil again and again until the earth relented. She dug through the hard crust and kept going, a foot deep, two feet deep. How deep for a garden? How deep for a grave?

A new wave of nausea washed over her. Now only dry heaves. She knew there would be no graves, no crosses, no stones, or markers. Only a mass dig. A hole packed full of tortured, mangled, bloody, decaying bodies. Bodies thrown on bodies. The Nazis burned their victims. But telltale smoke was nothing her government wanted. A genocide lesson learned.

Instead a new construction site would be bulldozed deep, shovels inadequate for this job. Bulldozers would dig the basement parking garage of another new downtown high rise. A hole filled with bodies and covered under the shadows of night. Where were the mangled bodies of her parents? This she would never know. She knew she had to accept this just as she had to accept the probable truth of their torture and death. Accept, because she knew they would expect this from her.

She remembered another song her mother once sang to her. She felt her mother's arms holding her, her words a lullaby: *Gracias a la vida que me ha dado tanto*. She looked at her bloody, blistered hands, at the new garden plot in the center of the overgrown backyard and she *was* grateful for what life had given her and also for what it had taken from her. She heard Isabel Parra's words in her mother's voice as she handpicked the turned soil, breaking apart the hard clumps, tugging out the roots and rocks, fingering the loose dirt with the love of a parent, her mother working a comb through her unruly curls, her father holding her in his tired arms, carrying her as they stumbled across the river that brought her freedom and their probable death.

Gracias a la vida. This life that took her parents gave her Carolina. She was safe, at least for now. For how long, she didn't know. She couldn't, wouldn't think about that. She had a garden space ready, a space that mirrored the garden in the backyard of her childhood home, the garden that hid the comings and goings of so many. She had a garden space ready for the baby plants Carolina promised to bring home from work. A garden to care for, to weed and water, to offer this new friend who took her in and gave her sanctuary. This much she could do.

She stood and brushed the dirt from her ragged jeans with the backs of her bloody hands. She jammed the shovel into the soft soil and headed to the shower. She would clean up, wash her clothes, bandage herself, and cook dinner before her new friend returned home. This too she could do.

Ten

SPRING SEEMED TO FLY BY. Antonia and I slid into an easy routine. I left for school at around seven-thirty every morning and stocked shelves every afternoon. The job demanded few brain cells. Just what I needed after hours of classes followed by research on my senior project. I wasn't paid much, but the owners were relaxed and the food expiration dates helped keep my kitchen stocked. It was sunny and warm when I road my bike home in the early evenings.

I usually found Antonia cooking dinner with the doors of the cottage open wide or working in the vegetable and flower garden she'd insisted on cultivating in a square of sunlight hidden between the backyard trees and the university green belt bordering the end of the property. She dug up the soil and planted her garden with discarded starts I scavenged from the co-op. By late spring the garden flourished. When she wasn't cooking or gardening, she read, and her English was improving a whole lot faster than my Spanish.

In the evenings when I wasn't too overwhelmed with homework and we didn't head down to River Street, we enjoyed long walks through the Los Arboles hills as the sun fell and the air filled with the scent of spring flowers and eucalyptus.

On class days, we took the bus to River Street. Each class was a repetition of the first. Antonia joined the women in the kitchen–women who could be her mother, but weren't–while I taught the men at the large table in the living room. We shared a simple meal of rice and beans or enchiladas or chilaquiles and then Juan Luis drove us home. Sometimes I wondered if he came by the cottage to see Antonia when I wasn't home, but I doubted it. He put in long hard hours. He didn't have time for Antonia no matter how smitten he might be.

As finals approached and graduation loomed, I began to worry. What would I do next? Work? Grad school? And what about Antonia? I was harboring an under-aged undocumented immigrant, but I preferred to think of it as sanctuary. I knew I should figure out who to contact, who might be able to help Antonia with her legal status as well as her search for her parents, but I did nothing at all except enjoy her company.

I knew if I were going to stay in Los Arboles, I needed a job, even a temporary job, so I got serious about looking. I also knew I had a knack for teaching. I knew I liked doing it. And I knew being bilingual would give me an edge. So I asked Antonia for help and she was more than willing to stick to Spanish-only a few nights each week and be my teacher. I brought home some Spanish books from the library, and we studied together. Before long the grammar and vocabulary I'd learned in all those high school and college classes resurfaced, and I watched my Spanish improve. When I saw the listing for a bilingual teacher's assistant for the Los Arboles high school summer program, I was ready. Antonia drilled me with practice interview questions we found in a library book. She made me respond in both languages. She tested my grammar and forced me to repeat and repeat and repeat until even my pronunciation improved.

On the day of my interview the sun was bright, the air fresh, the hills green. Thanks to Antonia, I aced the interview and they offered me the job on the spot. I rode home and dropped my bike on the front steps before I rushed around the cottage to the backyard where I knew I'd find her tending her garden.

"I did it, I did it, I got it!" I hollered. "You're looking at the new bilingual assistant for the Los Arboles high school summer school program. Thanks to you, I passed their silly Spanish test with flying colors."

Antonia stood, wiping her dirty hands on her jeans. "Flying colors? What is this? Colors no fly."

"You're right, colors no fly. Colors don't fly. But me, I can fly." I grabbed Antonia's hands and danced through the tall, unmown grass and wild flowers surrounding her garden and filling the uncultivated area of the large backyard. "It's a fulltime job, Antonia. Fulltime. That means I'll have enough money to pay my bills and save for grad school. If it goes well, they said they might consider keeping me on when school starts in the fall. I'm so happy."

"*Felicitaciones*, Carolina. I happy for you." Antonia slowed our dance and returned to calm. "You call your mama now? Invite your parents to come?"

"Oh, stop bugging me about that. I told you I'm not calling them. I'm not inviting them to graduation. I'm not even going to graduation. And they don't care about this job or any job I get. I can write them a letter and tell them I'm staying here. What's the big deal?"

But I knew what the big deal was. I had a mother. Antonia had lost hers. She wanted me to call and invite them both to graduation. I saw the disappointment in her eyes, but how could I explain they wouldn't accept her, they wouldn't even come if they knew she was my friend.

I remembered the day as though it were last summer. I must have been just a bit older than Antonia. As on so many other hot summer days, I'd snuck off to the river. It was a secret swimming hole, a place I met my friends–daughters and sons of the workers–at the end of a long day in the orchard. Somehow my father found me there. I never knew how. Did he follow me? Did he have someone follow me?

I was sunbathing in my new two-piece after a long, refreshing swim when my father stormed up, grabbed my arm, and dragged me to my feet. His face was red with fury as he spat his words. "Do you want to be as dark as them?" He threw my clothes at me. "Cover yourself up and come with me. Now."

"You can't make me," I yelled.

"The hell I can't."

He slapped me across the face so hard I fell back and hit the ground. My lip split and blood filled my mouth.

I watched as my friends gathered their clothes and disappeared into the woods as quickly and quietly as if my father himself were the dreaded *migra*. I knew they were safe. I knew my father couldn't fire them all, didn't even know which kids belonged to which parents.

He needed them, needed the labor to run his orchard and knew he couldn't chase them off his land, so he took out his anger, his frustration on me. And I hated him.

I hated the prissy white picket fence that separated me from the brown-skinned children, later teenagers, who spoke music instead of words. I hated the way the workers stood outside the gate, hats held in both hands in front of themselves, waiting for my father to go out and speak with them. I hated the attitudes of racial and social inequity that infiltrated our small town life–school, church, even sports.

The white kids were expected to succeed. The children of migrants were expected to fail, to disappear, and to return with each harvest, never able to maintain their studies or graduate. They were expected to bide their time in school only until they were old enough to work side by side with their parents in the fields. This injustice is what I knew, what my father and my grandparents before him knew. And my mother? She wiped my blood in silence and snuck food into my bedroom when my father wasn't looking. I never knew which ideas she shared with my father because she simply didn't say anything. At least not in my presence.

I studied my ass off in high school and left home right after graduation on a full scholarship to the university in Los Arboles. Hard work and perseverance paid off with a free educational ride that gave me economic independence from my father's control.

No, I didn't want my parents coming to California. But how to explain any of this to Antonia?

Eleven

"WHAT'S GOING ON?" I wondered aloud as we approached the River Street apartment. The lights were bright behind the front curtains, the rhythms of a Mexican *ranchero* and the smells of serious cooking wafted from behind the closed door. I paused thinking maybe I'd gotten the days confused. But then the door swung open before we even knocked, our arrival anticipated.

We stopped right inside the front door. The apartment had been transformed with white crepe paper streamers and bells hanging from the ceiling. The furniture was pushed to one side leaving an open area in the middle of the room. The table stood near the door to the kitchen heavy with steaming pots and platters still wrapped in aluminum foil and dish cloths for warmth. The distinctive fragrance of *mole* filled the room.

"What's going on?" I asked. "Did someone get married? A first communion?"

"*Una sorpresa*, Maestra," Juan Luis said.

At that moment, his mother came from the kitchen and took Antonia by the hand. "*Vete acá*," she said. She led her into the bedroom and closed the door, leaving me standing, surrounded by my students, as well as mothers, wives, and children, some of whom I'd never met. They were all in their Sunday best–the men in ironed dress shirts, the women in cotton dresses–making me uncomfortable in my khakis and tank top.

"What kind of surprise?" I asked.

"One moment, Maestra. You see," said another student, a middle-aged man named Javier.

"It looks like a party in here. Are you having a party? No class tonight?" I wondered why no one had bothered to tell me not to come.

"Maestra, this is *mi esposa*, Juanita," Javier said.

One by one my students presented their wives and children, even those I'd already met. Each stepped forward, the introductions polite, formal. Again I felt the distance between us as I had that first evening I'd brought Antonia to the apartment. I wasn't one of them. I'd always stuck to English when I entered the apartment. After all, this evening class was one of the few opportunities these students had to practice their English skills. I wasn't about to use their class to practice my Spanish. But this time I'd had it. There wasn't going to be a class tonight. Obviously a party had been planned and I was fed up with feeling like an outsider. Sometimes rules had to be broken, so I did something I'd never done before: I switched to Spanish.

"*Mucho gusto de conocerle. Qué bonita bebé,*" I said to the next woman introduced to me, one with a tiny baby in her arms.

There was a moment of stunned silence.

"*¡La maestra habla el español!*"

"*Solo un poco, nada más,*" I said.

"No, very good," the woman with the infant assured me.

They crowded around me, eager to share their stories, the stories they could not yet find the English words to express. For the first time, I felt more than their respect. I felt their warmth and acceptance.

Someone flashed the lights on and off. Silence fell over the room. When the bedroom door opened, I gasped and my hands flew to my mouth. We all broke into applause as Antonia entered in a floor-length fluffy white gown. A princess tiara crowned her head. Her smile was radiant.

Then, I understood. I'd made a chocolate birthday cake for Antonia, and we'd celebrated the week before. I'd even bought her a new pair of jeans. Antonia must have told the women about it.

Someone cranked up the music, no longer the *rancheros* and *corridos* of northern Mexico, but now a *cumbia* from lands to the south. One by one the men stepped forward and danced with Antonia. Before long, everyone was laughing and dancing, the room alive with energy.

I felt myself being guided to the middle of the makeshift dance floor. I had no idea how to dance, had never danced a single time in my conservative, sheltered life. My childhood flashed before me: late night *cumbias* filtering through my open bedroom window, the workers celebrating after the harvest. I was never allowed to join the fun.

"*No puedo bailar,*" I said.

"*Es* okay, Maestra," Juan Luis said. "*Todos pueden bailar. Yo te enseño.*"

Students became teachers. To my surprise, I could feel the rhythm and follow their leads, one after the other. The music was loud. The *cerveza* was cold. The *mole* and *enchiladas* and *calabacitas* were hot. And I loved it all.

"Can you believe this?" I whispered to Antonia when we stopped to eat.

"Did you know?" she asked.

"No."

"I tell them about the cake you bake me. I no think they make me a party. *Una sorpresa increíble.*"

For a brief moment I saw a trace of sadness in Antonia's eyes. "Your parents would be very happy for you, Antonia. They would want you to have fun and enjoy your *fiesta de quinceañera.*"

"*Es cierto,*" she said. The smile returned to her face as Juan Luis crossed the room and invited her back onto the makeshift dance floor. She glanced over her shoulder and grinned as he led her away. I gave her a wink and a thumbs up as someone put a *Negro Modelo* and a fresh plate of food in front of me.

Twelve

ANTONIA AWOKE THE NEXT MORNING, music humming in her ears, feet dancing between the sheets. She could feel Juan Luis's strong arms around her as they floated in the swirl of the white dress, the overhead decorations a blur. The smile on her face and joy in her heart lasted only a brief moment, that moment between slumber and wakefulness when the mind leaves the world of dreams just before reality shoves aside the ability to create fantasies and believe in them.

She opened her eyes to the white dress, like a fluffy white curtain, hanging from the doorframe between the living room and the kitchen. For the princess of last night had not slipped into bed still dressed, nor had she dropped the beautiful borrowed dress to the floor. Instead she had placed it with care on a hanger to greet her in the morning light, a reminder of the evening when she had been royalty.

She got out of bed, her heart heavy. She couldn't put on the new jeans Carolina had given her, a gift of generosity she knew her friend couldn't afford. Couldn't wear them because like the dress and the party and even Carolina's homemade chocolate cake, they were a lie. She pulled on her raggedy old jeans and pushed past the fluffy white dress on her way to the bathroom. Her princess-for-a-day tiara sparkled beside the sink. She washed her face, avoiding her eyes in the mirror, the eyes of a liar.

The backyard was sunshine-bright as she crawled between rows of young plants. Tomatoes, lettuce, herbs. Honest plants. She filled her fists with rich soil and asked her parents what to do. "*Soy una mentirosa,*" she whispered. "I lied and now I do not know what to do."

The lie was not an evil lie. But why had she done it? Why had she allowed it to get so out of control? Months before when Carolina had asked her age, Antonia had been afraid to tell the truth, afraid that if Carolina knew the truth, she'd send her away or, worse yet, call the police. So she added a year. Fourteen sounded better than thirteen. Later, that first night in the kitchen of the River Street apartment, surrounded by loving, inquisitive women, how could she tell the truth, a truth that would reveal the lie she'd already told her new friend? One lie leads to another and so it goes.

She watched the loose dirt filter between her fingers as she sat back on her haunches between the bean plants. Now she was a fourteen-year-old *quinceañera*. And a liar. To Carolina and her friends on River Street, even to Juan Luis, she was fifteen, but she knew the truth. She knew she was too young for the party last night and for the kiss Juan Luis gave her outside the front door when he brought them home, when he insisted on walking them to the door, when Carolina had disappeared into the back of the cottage.

"*Perdóname*, Papi," she whispered to her garden. "I know I am too young for his kiss."

But it was nice, she admitted with a giggle. She fingered the mouth Juan Luis had kissed. She felt his warm lips on hers. She felt his arms around her, strong and safe. She felt the rhythm of his footsteps. The entire evening played back to her from the moment outside the door when Carolina wondered what was going on, to her surprise in the bedroom as the women dressed her in white and adorned her curls, to the hours of dancing, first with Juan Luis, last with Juan Luis, but not only with Juan Luis, for a *quinceañera* must honor all with a dance.

She wanted to tell Carolina the truth, tell her it was only a little lie that grew from the fear of hunger and loneliness, but she knew she would not. She would hold this secret in her heart and be the *quinceañera* who was celebrated in the apartment on River Street because to tell the truth proved too difficult. What she wanted above all else was to be a little girl again, safe in her father's arms, with her mother at their side.

Thirteen

CREAK. CREAK. The chains groaned as the porch swing swayed to and fro. It was a warm summer evening, too warm to be cooped up in the small cottage. I heard the clatter of flatware in the sink, the running of water, the banging of a cabinet door.

"Antonia, get out here," I called. "You're missing the sunset."

"*En un momento.*"

"A minute will be too late," I muttered to myself. I knew it was pointless to argue with her. She had her ways, and her way in the kitchen meant leaving nothing unfinished, not an empty pot on the hotplate, a dirty spoon in the sink.

"You work hard every day. I cook and clean," Antonia insisted whenever I tried to do my share of the cooking or even wash up after dinner. She'd taken charge of the kitchen and I had to admit she was a whole lot better at it than I was. Her cooking was delicious and the tiny kitchen was always spotless.

Now she would finish the dishes and make tea before she came out. The sun would set and she would miss it. Again. It didn't seem to matter to her, but it did to me. Watching a sunset mattered even if it meant leaving dirty dishes in the sink. I'm not sure why. I rocked back and forth remembering another time, another place. A time when the sunset only brought trouble and pain.

My father sat in his rocking chair on the front porch, smoking his pipe, staring out at his land as the sun fell behind the hills that edged the orchard to the west. I'm not sure he noticed the sunset at all, only his land. But above him, from my second-floor bedroom, I watched the golds change to pinks and then to purples as the sun sank to the horizon, waiting as I always waited for the magical flicker of white light that flashed at the exact nanosecond when the sun disappeared.

"Norman, can you come in here?" I heard my mother call.

"In a minute," he said.

A few moments passed.

"I need some help here!" she called.

Silence. My father continued to rock and smoke, rock and smoke as the sun dropped and darkness fell.

"Norman?"

There was something in my mother's voice. Or maybe it was the repetition of my father's name. Or maybe it was the repeated requests. Whatever it was, I knew something wasn't right, something was off kilter. I bounced down the stairs and into the kitchen. I didn't feel I needed to protect my mother, but I knew she needed some attention and my father was so self-absorbed, he ignored her a lot more than I thought any man should ignore his wife.

"Don't worry about it, honey," Mom would say when I told her I thought Dad was being rude, unfair, selfish, or whatever the flavor of the day happened to be. "It's just what happens after so many years." But I disagreed. I didn't care how long two people were together, if they decided to stay together they should at least show each other a bit of respect, I thought.

I swung into the kitchen, gripping the doorframe. "What's up ...?" I started to say, but the words stuck in my throat.

My mother sat slumped at the kitchen table, her left hand wrapped in a blood-red dishcloth. I glanced to the kitchen counter. I saw the cutting board, the knife, the onions dribbled red, the trail of blood to the table. She didn't get any farther. There she dropped into a chair holding her hand in a blood-soaked cloth waiting for her husband, my father, to bother to put down his pipe and respond to her call for help.

I screamed. I screamed and screamed and screamed until my father lumbered into the kitchen.

"What the hell is all the god-damned fuss about?" he swore. Then he saw the blood and my mother's white face. "How bad is it?" he asked.

"Stitches," she said.

He scooped her into his arms and they were gone.

I stood on the front porch watching the taillights blurred by a heavy cloud of dust as my father broke every speed limit and law of common sense to get my mother to the emergency room.

I sighed. Now I was the one on the porch and Antonia was missing yet another sunset, the sunsets I still loved despite the memories they carried.

"You like tea, Carolina?" Antonia called from the kitchen.

"Sure, Antonia. But come out here now and watch the sunset. I'll make it in a bit."

"No problem," Antonia said.

But she didn't come out. Instead I heard the unmistakable sound of water filling a kettle, followed by the bang of the metal pot on the metal burner.

Another five, ten minutes passed. "Do you need any help in there?" Placing a toe on the ground, I stopped the rhythmic sway of the swing and stood as the first stars appeared overhead. Transfixed, I backed towards the door, unwilling to lose sight of the glory above me. As I pushed the door open with my hip, I heard a loud crash and a faint gasp.

It was the controlled gasp of someone who has learned from a very young age to hide all emotion, all noise in face of danger or disaster. I turned from the beauty of the night sky to see Antonia, hands still holding the old wooden tray, now empty, the teapot, cups, and plate of homemade cookies strewn across the living room floor.

"Are you okay? Are you cut?" I asked.

"No, I okay. But your teapot. Oh, Carolina, I so sorry." She picked up the scattered pieces of the sunflower yellow teapot. The round belly was still intact and the spout was only slightly chipped, but it no longer had a handle and the lid was in pieces.

"It was my fault. I wasn't watching where I was going. *Mi culpa.* I backed right into you," I told her.

"But your special teapot from Mama Lucy. I broke it."

"You didn't break it, Antonia. I broke it."

We went back and forth, each claiming responsibility as we cleaned up the mess of broken dishes, hot tea, and soggy cookies, but I couldn't convince her. Antonia continued to apologize, just as my mother had apologized for weeks after doctors stitched her sliced hand back together. She apologized to my dad for the expense, for the time he had to wait in the ER, for missing his god-damned sunset. Apologized so many times I finally lost it and yelled at her to stop. "It was an accident, Mom. Accidents happen. That's why they're called accidents."

And here again I told my friend, "It was an accident, Antonia. Accidents happen."

"But your beautiful teapot."

I tried to hide my sorrow, but tears betrayed me.

"Your beautiful teapot," she repeated, tears glistening in her own eyes.

"Yes," I said. "My beautiful teapot. But accidents happen."

Fourteen

ANTONIA DIDN'T HEAR Carolina leave the following morning. When the tap on the window interrupted her sleep, it seemed but a wisp of a dream she could not grasp.

"Come," a voice whispered. "We're leaving. Now. *La migra* is coming."

"*La migra?*" Still half lost in her dreams, the murmurs in her native language seemed nothing more than part of her sleep world. It wasn't her Spanish she heard, not her father's accent, but still it was her language, a man's voice that pulled her from her dreams.

"Antonia, wake up. Pack your things," the voice said.

"No," she said. "I can't leave Carolina."

"Carolina is in danger if you stay. You must leave with us. Now. My mother is waiting. The truck is out front. Get your things."

In that split second, Antonia was awake. She knew something was very wrong, knew Juan Luis had waited for Carolina to leave, knew he spoke the truth she had continued to push from her thoughts all summer: if she stayed, if she were caught, Carolina would be in trouble.

She scrambled from bed, stashed her few belongings into the tattered backpack she'd found the day her parents were taken, and followed Juan Luis out of the yard in absolute silence. The truck was parked a block away on a dead-end street out of sight. A heavy blue tarp covered the load in the back. Antonia imagined the boxes of clothing, kitchen supplies, and tools.

"Climb in," Juan Luis said. He took her small backpack and stuck it under the tarp as he circled to the driver's side of the cab.

The old truck crept northeast through the mountains that separated Los Arboles from California's central valley. Squeezed between Juan

Luis's mother and younger sister, Antonia wept in silence. Juan Luis's mother held her hand tight, and Antonia felt safe and protected. She was grateful, but her gratitude could not ease the grief in her heart.

As the truck inched through early morning traffic, she mourned not being able to say goodbye, to leave a note, to thank her friend for all she'd been given. She feared Carolina would think she'd left because of the broken teapot. If *la migra* came, as Juan Luis and his friends believed, the raids would be in the news, and Carolina would understand. That shred of hope gave her strength.

The hours folded one onto the next and the early morning departure replayed in her mind. The tap on the window, the quick packing. Who would tend her garden, she wondered? Who would water the tomatoes and pick the peas? Certainly not Carolina, she thought, a smile tickling at the corners of her mouth. Carolina loved the fresh vegetables and fragrant flowers. She loved sitting and chatting in the backyard after work. But she was not a gardener. Remembering their conversations, their odd mix of Spanish and English, Antonia fingered her pocket. It was empty. Her tiny dictionary, the only physical remembrance she had of her parents, wasn't there. With a shock, she knew she had forgotten it in the rush to leave. She could see it on the coffee table, could imagine Carolina discovering it there. Despite the pain of her loss, that thought, the thought of Carolina finding, holding, cherishing her dictionary, gave her comfort. It was as though she'd left her friend a gift. Her friend from Washington.

Washington. She played with the word, rolled the syllables across her tongue trying to make it a bit less foreign, less frightening. Washington. She hadn't left California since the raid that took her parents. But now, as the truck tires ate the miles towards the state's northern border, she was leaving behind all she had known, loved, and lost.

"We'll be back someday," Juan Luis's mother murmured to her in the soft Spanish of northern Mexico. "Maybe someday we go to Mexico together."

How lucky I am, Antonia thought. Accepted and protected. Maybe even loved a bit. She was another member of this odd caravan of friends and family, all heading to the promise of employment and safety in the orchards of Eastern Washington. Carolina's Eastern Washington.

"*Nos vamos* a Mound City?" she asked.

"*Sí*," Juan Luis said. "*Hasta al valle de* Mound City."

Fifteen

AS I RODE HOME, I thought about going back to the Sunday market and talking to Mama Lucy. I'd broken my promise, stayed home with Antonia on Sunday mornings. She was afraid of the crowds, of being in public places, of being caught. So I'd chosen to stay at home. We always slept late. When we finally got up, Antonia cooked a fine breakfast and we spent the day reading, studying, or just lounging in the backyard working on our tans. Or, I worked on my tan while she worked on her garden. Months slipped by and I never returned to visit Mama Lucy. I'd broken my promise and now I needed to ask the old potter if she could repair my broken teapot. Maybe she could fashion a new handle onto the side of the pot. Maybe she could shape a new lid to fit. Maybe she could calm the strange ache in the pit of my stomach.

Poor Antonia. She was so upset by the whole thing and it really wasn't her fault at all. I was the one who wasn't watching where I was going. Antonia couldn't be convinced or comforted. I wished I'd never told her about Mama Lucy and her gift. Maybe then Antonia wouldn't be so upset. Who knows, maybe I could convince her to visit Mama Lucy with me. Then my two new friends would know each other. Like Aladdin's magic lantern, Mama Lucy's teapot had brought Antonia into my life. That's all that mattered.

I walked my bike down the narrow path into the overgrown yard surrounding the cottage. Despite the warmth of the afternoon, the front door was closed. I leaned my bike against the porch and walked around to the back. I figured I'd find Antonia working in the garden–weeding, tying up the sweet peas, adjusting the sprinkler. There was always something to do in Antonia's garden. But the backyard was empty.

I circled the cottage and tried the front door. It was locked. I called out her name as I dug in my backpack for the key I hadn't used in ages. Antonia was always at home. Always in the garden or the kitchen.

I entered calling Antonia's name, knowing she was gone. But I searched the cottage from front door to back, even climbed the ladder to my sleeping loft to be sure. Antonia was gone and she'd taken what little she owned.

I collapsed on the homemade sofa–Antonia's bed–and buried my head in her pillow. Had it all been a dream? Had Antonia ever really been part of my life? Maybe she'd never been there at all. I turned on my side and scanned the room in search of evidence. My eyes dropped to the floor and there I saw it, half hidden by the coffee table: Antonia's tiny dictionary. I picked it up and fingered the pages, remembering the endless hours of conversation we'd shared, turning repeatedly to this little dictionary whenever we got stuck. Proof. I wasn't losing my mind. My secret friend was real, but why would she leave? Where would she go?

River Street. Without a second thought, I ran out the door, grabbed my bike, and headed back down the hill at breakneck speed. It was twilight when I reached the apartment, that melancholic hour when the sky is bruised purple and the world comes to an end.

I braked to a fast stop outside the first-floor apartment and pounded on the cheap wooden door. The noise echoed in the falling darkness, but there was no answer. I pounded again. Still no answer. I tried the door and it opened to my turn. As I pushed it, I heard a stern voice behind me.

"Hold it. You can't go in there."

I spun around to see an elderly white man. His tank top, tight across his bulging belly, showed remnants of what I could only imagine was his dinner.

"They're my students. I'm looking for a friend. Why is their door open?"

"They're gone. Just touching up the place."

"What? What do you mean gone?"

"Cleared out. *Adiós*. Gone. I have to say, though, they left the place clean. You have any idea where I can send the deposit?"

I slumped against the doorframe as though I'd been punched in the stomach. "Why?" I managed.

"Dunno. Didn't even give two weeks. Usually I wouldn't give 'em back the deposit without two weeks, but they left the place rentable and I already have a new tenant. Moving in tomorrow." He smiled the smug smile of a man pleased with life, with his own well-being.

"But when did they leave?"

"Dunno that either. I went out early this morning to get the paper. Came back and the place was empty. Dropped the keys through my mail slot. No forwarding address. Seems they left mighty fast, but I ain't one to ask no questions if ya know what I mean."

I knew. I figured this wasn't the first time this man had rented to undocumented farmworkers who disappeared unexpectedly.

"Did they have friends in the building? Anyone who might know where they're headed?" I knew the futility of the question even before the manager gave a slow shake of his head. Nobody knew anything when it came to the whereabouts of undocumented friends. With a deepening sadness, I knew I'd lost my students as well as my best friend.

"Would you mind if I walked through the place?"

"What for? Ain't nothing there."

"To say goodbye, I suppose. They were my students. Good people."

"Oh, all right. I suppose it ain't gonna hurt anything." He opened the door and switched on the light. The apartment glared from the bare bulb, the thin scrap of fabric that had been tacked to the ceiling to soften its harshness was gone. I looked around the living room. As the manager had said, the place was spotless and not a trace of the carefully stacked bedrolls or the fine Mexican cooking remained.

The apartment was a furnished rental. I hadn't known that, but it made sense now. The run-down sofa, coffee table, and large table were there and some of the pots and pans still hung from their hooks on the kitchen walls. I could feel the presence of my students, their wives, and children, hear the music of their voices, taste the richness of their food. Then they were gone.

I wanted to believe Antonia had come here, she was safe, she was not alone. It was too horrible to imagine her as homeless and hungry as she had been when we first met.

"Why do you think they left so quickly?" I asked the manager who stood outside the door tapping his foot, anxious to get back to his dinner.

"Dunno. But it happens all the time. Haven't seen the news yet. Maybe there was another raid down south or over the hills. Caught wind of it and split. You know how it goes. Word gets out that INS has come to town and panic spreads like wildfire. They'd be better off just lying low for a few days, but they always run. Too bad, too. They were good tenants. Always paid on time, always quiet, and respectful. Ah well," he sighed, a man resigned to the realities of his job.

Sixteen

I RODE HOME from River Street in the silent shadows and approached the dark cottage with dread. I spent that night and every night for the rest of the week sleeping on Antonia's bed waiting, hoping I'd wake up to see her looking down at me, her quizzical grin asking why I was in her bed. Every morning I showered, biked to work. The high school kids challenged me to alertness and allowed me to be swathed in Spanish in a way that kept my world with Antonia alive.

The day after Antonia's disappearance, the news was full of another crackdown on undocumented immigrants. There were raids in the fields, mushroom sheds, and tourist motels up and down the coast. I hoped Antonia and my students had left soon enough. Better that than arrest and deportation. But it bothered me to think of them on the run. They were good people doing work that needed to be done. Back-breaking work nobody else wanted–not for the miserable pay they received. Yet they were chased like criminals.

On Saturday I didn't get out of bed. What was the point? I couldn't find a single reason to get myself up. By mid-afternoon the wetness between my legs forced me out of bed. Damn. The sheets were stained red. I headed to the bathroom remembering Antonia's first day with me. After I cleaned myself up, stripped the bed, and started a load of laundry, I opened the back door to sunshine and Antonia's garden. I stumbled between the rows of peas and beans, tomatoes and chilies, all surrounded by a bright border of tall lacy flowers. I bent to tug a few weeds, then a few more. An hour later I was still working. It was late afternoon when I finally flopped onto my back and stared at the wispy white clouds floating above me. I was tired and hungry, and I knew what I had to do.

It was early when I climbed on my bike the next morning and headed to the Sunday Market, the broken teapot wrapped in newspaper on my back. It had been too long. I should've gone back. I had promised and I had broken my promise.

I made my way through the large, empty market as vendors set up their booths, arranged their fruits and vegetables in colorful piles, their flowers in white five-gallon buckets full of fresh water. I did not remember the exact location of Mama Lucy's stand or know if each vendor retained the same one every week, so I simply let my feet lead the way and wandered through the maze of stalls in various stages of preparation.

The sun rose and the crowd thickened. The aroma of fresh coffee and baked goods filled the air. Twice I saw pottery booths and thought I'd found Mama Lucy. Both times I was mistaken. The third time I asked the vendor for help.

"Do you know Mama Lucy?"

"Everybody knows Mama Lucy," the woman said. "She's been a mentor to all of us. Are you a potter too?"

"No. Just a ..."

"Friend?" she supplied. "She's straight down that way. Take the third left. Her booth is a block down on the right."

"Thank you," I muttered.

"Peace."

As I got close, my feet slowed. What if she'd forgotten all about me? What if she was pissed because I hadn't come back to visit like I promised I would? How would I explain Antonia's fear of crowds, our Sundays alone at the cottage? My feet got heavier with each step.

Sunday market was in full swing when I finally spotted Mama Lucy's white awning. I stood at a distance and watched shoppers enter, finger the colorful pottery, and leave, a few with carefully wrapped purchases, but most empty-handed. I couldn't do it. I couldn't waltz in and show her the broken teapot, her beautiful gift, and beg her to fix it. No way. I couldn't do it. I turned to leave.

"Hey, Biker Girl, I've been waiting all summer for that visit you promised. What's taken you so long?"

She stood with her hands on her narrow, bony hips, her braid hanging over her shoulder, a full-length apron covering her sweatshirt and skirt. Only her Birkenstocks poked out below the hem.

Trapped. No escaping now. I walked towards her. I tried to meet her eyes, but I couldn't. "Look me in the eye," my father would yell when he was angry about something. I never could do it. Even when I was innocent of whatever he thought I'd done wrong. Couldn't do it now either.

"I'm sorry," I told her Birkenstocks. "I totally messed up. I'm so sorry."

"I'm guessing there's a good explanation for this mess up of yours, Miss Carolyn Biker Girl. You have a story to share?"

"It's a long story."

"Good thing we have a long day ahead of us. Now come on in and have a cup of tea with a crazy old potter."

"Really?"

"Of course. What? You're afraid I'm going to be mad, maybe yell at you, call you some bad names, turn you away? No, dear Carolyn, that's not Mama Lucy's style."

My eyes filled with tears. I couldn't help it. All those tears I'd been holding in, a reservoir full of tears, began a steady flow down my cheeks.

"Come, Carolyn, it can't be so bad a good cup of tea won't make it better." She gave me a soft pat on my forearm.

What was Mama Lucy's magic, I wondered through my tears? But then I knew. I knew the moment after the old woman touched my arm. Mama Lucy listened. As simple as that.

"Settle yourself here, young lady." She set about making tea, ignoring the shoppers who milled in and out of her booth. She switched on the electric teakettle and scooped loose tea leaves into her old blue teapot. "So there's a story to tell and something to show me in that backpack of yours."

"How did you know?"

The kettle clicked off and she poured the boiling water over the tea leaves. "School's out, the pack's full, and you were about to scamper away like a frightened rabbit."

I unzipped my backpack and lifted out the wrapped bundle.

"Excuse me, young lady," said an older man with stooped shoulders. "Could you tell me the price of this platter? It's simply exquisite."

It took me a few seconds to realize he was speaking to me. I looked into the warm smile of a gray-haired man.

"Ummm, I don't ..." I turned to Mama Lucy for help, but she just gave me a nod and turned back to her teapot like it was open-heart surgery or something. I was on my own.

I remembered Mama Lucy didn't use the standard stick-on tags to price her pieces, so I looked at the man and responded as I thought she would have done if she weren't so busy making tea and ignoring her customers. I looked at the platter in his hands. I looked at the twinkle in his eyes. "Can you make an offer? What's it worth to you?"

"Let me see," the man said, thinking aloud.

I couldn't believe it. I thought for sure he'd walk away, but instead I could almost see him calculating.

"It's a house-warming gift for my daughter. She and her husband just moved into their first home. She painted one accent wall in the dining room this exact shade of red," he said, pointing to the deep sienna detail along the rim of the platter. "It would make a nice centerpiece for the table, don't you think?"

I smiled and said nothing at all.

"How about $150?" the man said.

I struggled to keep my composure, but to my dismay, the dam opened again. Tears filled my eyes and rolled down my cheeks before I could stop them. I tried to wipe them away, but it was too late.

"Oh my goodness." The man flustered. "I didn't mean to upset you. Perhaps $200 would be more appropriate."

I barely heard him, the image of my broken teapot blocking all thought. I knew then I could never afford to repair or to replace it. "It's okay. I'm sorry," I stuttered.

To my relief, as well as that of the confused customer, Mama Lucy emerged from the back of the large booth. "Thank you for your generous offer, but I think $150 will be fine. Would you like my assistant here to wrap it up for you?" She took the large platter from the man and placed it in my arms.

As the man got out his wallet and completed the transaction, I wrapped and taped the platter with newspaper as I had watched

Mama Lucy wrap my yellow teapot months before. When I finished, I offered it to the man, my eyes averted.

"Thank you very much, young lady," he said. "I hope I haven't disturbed you today."

Lifting my face to meet his eyes, I felt my confidence return. "Not at all," I said. "Have a good day. I'm sure your daughter will love your gift."

"I think so, too," he said. "It's a remarkable piece. Did you make it?"

"Oh no. Mama Lucy is the artist here. It is all her work."

"Amazing," he said, looking around for the elderly woman, but once again she seemed to have disappeared into the shadows. "Well, tell her that I'm very impressed with her talent. I'll be back for another visit soon."

As soon as he was out of earshot, I turned on Mama Lucy. "Why'd you do that? I don't know how much these things are worth. Why don't you put price tags on them or something?"

"I find it's a whole lot more interesting to let people offer what the piece is worth to them. It usually comes out fine that way."

The flood of customers was steady and heavy. It was as though word spread through the market that Mama Lucy's pottery booth was finally open for business. For hours I talked with customers. Although I couldn't answer their questions or even give them a price, I was like their conduit to Mama Lucy who rarely emerged from the shadows but who was always willing to answer my questions and approve or reject an offer. I asked each customer to name a price, and I was impressed by the fairness of the offers they made. Or, at least, the offers seemed fair to me. That first Sunday I ran each one past Mama Lucy. If an offer was too high, she lowered it. If it was too low, she gave another price–never negotiable. In most cases she simply gave a nod and the item was sold.

"My, my, my," Mama Lucy sighed as the day of shopping came to an end. "I haven't done this much business in years. If you keep selling all my pots, I'll have to go back to my pottery shed and make some more."

"I'm sorry. I thought you wanted to sell them. Why do you come here and set up every Sunday if you don't want to sell?"

"Oh, don't get all upset, now." Mama Lucy patted me on the arm. "Selling is fine. It's good. You're quite an asset. I'm just not sure this old body of mine can make many more of these things," she said, her arms spread to encompass the noticeably barren shelves.

"Oh, don't believe a word she says," boomed a deep voice, as a spry man hopped from the cab of a pickup that had stopped in front of the booth. He wore overalls and the hair under his dirty baseball cap was gray. "She's out in that shed of hers throwing a few pots every day. Her storage room is packed with stuff. Are you responsible for these empty shelves, young lady?"

"Well, I don't know. I guess I helped a bit."

"Nice job. Mom's quite the artist, but she sure isn't much of a saleswoman, is she?"

"Mom?"

"Yup, Henry Cabot. Lucy Cabot's son. Mama Lucy to you, I imagine," he said, extending a warm hand to her.

"Yes," Carolyn smiled. "My name is Carolyn Bauer."

"Nice to meet you, Carolyn. Has she hired you as a helper? I've been pestering her for years to get someone to help her out with sales, but she never listens."

As he spoke, Henry Cabot began to unload wooden crates from the back of his truck with the agility of a much younger man. Like a well-oiled machine, Mama Lucy wrapped each piece, passed it to Henry, and he packed it safely into a crate. It was as if it were one big puzzle and they already knew where each piece fit—only now a number of pieces were missing. I watched only minutes, then I was wrapping, as Mama Lucy sat on her stool and watched Henry and me.

All around us, vendors dismantled their booths. The Sunday Market disappeared into crates and boxes, trucks and vans. It saddened me in an unexpected way. It was the room after a party, the stadium after the big game. That old loneliness crept back and I began to dread the steep ride home in the coming darkness, the empty cottage I'd find when I got there, the long lonely week ahead.

"I really should go."

I turned to find Mama Lucy holding the broken sunflower teapot, a bemused look in her eyes. I watched her roll the teapot back into the crumpled newspaper and return it to my backpack.

"I'm afraid we never had time for that long story you were going to tell me," she said. "Something about what kept you away so long. Henry can finish the packing alone. Come walk with me for a few minutes and share your story."

We began a slow walk along the river behind the market. "On my way home last time, I met a girl under a eucalyptus tree." I told her all I knew about Antonia, about taking her to meet my students on River Street, and about the *quinceañera* party.

"We had such a great time together and then it ended so fast. Antonia made tea for us. She was carrying the tray and we knocked into each other. It crashed to the floor. Then the next morning she was gone. At first I thought she left because of the teapot, but my students disappeared too, and then I read about the big immigration raid. Now Antonia's gone and my teapot is ruined. Can you fix it? Can you make a new handle and a new lid?"

"My dear Carolyn, there are no coincidences and things change. They take on new forms and can't be returned to what they were before. This teapot is one of those things. But it's done its job, don't you think?"

In the fading light, I searched her wrinkled face. "I don't know what you mean."

Mama Lucy ignored my confusion. "Where did you say this girl is from?" she asked, her voice little more than a whisper.

"I don't know. She would never tell me. Only that she was Central American."

"And she was alone?"

"Totally. Living on the streets. I didn't know what to do, so I introduced her to my students."

"And now they're gone as well?" Mama Lucy asked, verifying the details of the story I'd laid in her gnarled hands.

"Yes. The apartment's empty. The manager said they left the same morning Antonia disappeared from my place."

We walked in silence for a while, a slow walk, an old woman's walk. When Mama Lucy spoke again, her voice was gentle. "The teapot is broken. It cannot be repaired. But the girl is strong. She's a survivor. She'll be fine." She touched my arm to stop me. "What about you, Biker Girl? What are your plans?"

"I'm not sure," I said. "My contract with the high school summer program ends soon. I don't know if they'll extend it. I'm not sure I want to stay there. I don't know what I want." I threw my arms up in frustration. "Nothing seems to make much sense anymore."

"Maybe it's time for a change."

"What do you mean?"

"I mean leave town, get a real education, go to Central America, see where Antonia comes from."

"Central America? But isn't there all sorts of violence there? Antonia told me it's a horrible, dangerous place. Isn't there a civil war going on down there somewhere?"

"The 1980s of her childhood were a mess throughout Central America. Times change, governments change, policies change quickly in Central America. Or perhaps nothing changes at all. Either way, it's a good time for you to go."

"You're serious, aren't you?"

"Absolutely. You're young and healthy. It's time you learned something about the real world instead of what you read in those books of yours up at that fancy university on the hill. Besides you graduated last spring, didn't you?"

"Yeah. But how am I supposed to go to Central America," I said, playing along with the idea. "Just buy a ticket and fly there? I couldn't afford it even if I wanted to go alone–which, by the way, I don't."

"Then find somebody to go with or an organization where you can make a difference."

"So you want me to be a missionary or something?"

"Heavens, no! What do you take me for?" Mama Lucy laughed a loud, hearty laugh. "No missionaries. But I did read Peace Corps has resumed operations throughout Latin America. Not sure that's a good idea either. Never know what our government's up to down there. If that's not your cup of tea, you could look for a teaching position in Managua or San Salvador or any of the larger cities. Or, you could strap on that backpack of yours and wander a bit."

We walked in silence. The thought of traveling alone terrified me. But teaching, yes. Teaching I could do, that I loved to do.

"I could talk to Professor Orozco. He's the guy who set up the class on River Street for me. Maybe he'll have some suggestions or connections or something."

"Sounds like a good place to start." Mama Lucy looped her arm through mine and we reversed direction. By the time we got back to the market, the awning and poles of the booth were collapsed in pieces on the ground. Henry Cabot rolled them with the ease of an experienced camper packing a tent.

"Ma, did you pay this young lady for her help today? You don't expect her to come back for free next Sunday, do you?" Henry asked, as he stood to put the rolled awning and poles into the truck.

"No," I said, a bit louder and with far more force than I intended. "I mean, it's not necessary. I'll be back. I promise. I mean, I'd like to come back next Sunday, if that's all right."

With the measured movements of age, Mama Lucy turned to look at me. Her lively eyes glanced at her son and back to me. "You'll be back, of course, and we'll have tea and talk some more about Central America."

"Thank you. And I'll help in any way I can, if it's okay. But now I've really got to go." I clutched my backpack and turned to leave.

"Where are you headed?" Henry asked.

"To get my bike. I left it at the entrance to the market."

"It's too late to be riding home, young lady. Come on now. You get that bike of yours and we'll throw it on top here. You can't be too far out of our way if you rode a bike to get here."

I wanted to refuse, but it was late and I was tired.

Henry drove us to the spot where I'd left my bike that morning. I unchained it and he lifted it into the back of his truck. I gave him directions up the steep hill towards the university and my lonely cottage. As we drove, I searched for the spot under the eucalyptus tree where I'd first met Antonia. When we passed the huge tree, I realized what a perfect hiding place Antonia had found.

As Henry pulled to a stop in front of the storybook Victorian graced with tiny white lights and climbing pink roses, Mama Lucy emitted a low, teasing whistle of admiration.

"That's not where I live. I rent a cottage—which used to be a gardening shed—in the backyard." I paused. "Or maybe it was once a potter's shed. It could have been, right?" I looked into Mama Lucy's all-knowing eyes.

"It could've been anything at all," Mama Lucy said. "Now it's your home."

"Right."

"You're a student then," Henry said.

"Not anymore. I graduated last June."

"Congratulations. My son, Jason, has one more year at Lewis and Clark in Oregon. All these great universities close to home and he had to choose one up north."

I smiled in the darkness as I climbed from the cab. "Don't worry, Henry," I said as he opened the driver's door. "I can get it." With an easy reach, I lifted my bike from the back of the truck and headed down the path to my cottage with a little wave over my shoulder.

Seventeen

WHEN I WALKED into Professor Orozco's office for my appointment, I was surprised to see another student there, a girl I recognized from a few classes but did not know at all.

"Jennifer's leaving next week for San Salvador," Professor Orozco explained by way of introduction. "I thought you two should meet. She'll be teaching at a new international language school there and they need more teachers. You've both been offering classes to migrant workers, but this will be different. They'll have an established curriculum and so forth. You'll need to go through some training. They're opening schools all over Central and South America, so you'd have the opportunity to move around. Are you interested, Carolyn?"

I looked at Jennifer and saw the invitation and the fear in her bright green eyes. She was as scared and eager and unprepared as I was. "Yes," I said. "What do I need to do?"

We spent the hour planning, filling out paperwork, and getting to know each other. "*Nos vemos* when you get there," she told me as we were leaving.

"If they give me the job," I said.

"Of course they will," Jennifer and Professor Orozco said in unison, both certain I would be accepted as easily as she had been. I wasn't so positive.

"They need good teachers, Carolyn," Professor Orozco said. "Teachers who care. You're college-educated and you have some experience. They'll be pleased to have you. And if by chance they've received too many applications for San Salvador, they're opening branches in Managua, Bogota, Caracas, and I don't know where else."

I left the university, my head spinning. San Salvador, El Salvador. Managua, Nicaragua. Caracas, Venezuela. I loved the way the words rolled from my tongue. If the Peace Corps had resumed sending volunteers, it had to be okay, I reasoned as I unchained my bike, but if I could get a teaching position with Professor Orozco's help, that would be so much better.

I continued working at Los Arboles High School during the weeks following our meeting and I spent Sundays with Mama Lucy at the market.

The letter arrived from San Salvador the day before the principal called me into his office. It was the last Friday afternoon of summer school when he offered me the job. A dream job. The first, full-time, bilingual aid the high school had ever funded.

"Your efforts here have made a difference in the lives of these students," he told me.

"Can I give you my answer on Monday?" I asked.

"Sure," he said. "Lots to think about, I suppose."

The letter from San Salvador was still in my backpack. Unopened.

The unopened letter lay heavy on my mind, the weight of the decision more than I wanted to deal with. I awoke Saturday morning to find myself in Antonia's bed. Once again I'd fallen asleep in the living room. I hadn't been back to my loft since Antonia had disappeared.

The letter on the coffee table made me groan. Turning over, I closed my eyes and tried to will myself back to sleep. No good. I had to deal with this. Either I got the job or I didn't. No, that wasn't it. If they wanted me in San Salvador, it would mean leaving Los Arboles, giving up this little cottage, losing my Sundays with Mama Lucy, turning down the job offer at the high school. All important decisions, but not the real decision, not the real loss, not the real reason I hesitated to open the letter from San Salvador.

If I left Los Arboles, I was giving up any chance of ever seeing Antonia again. If she returned to Los Arboles and came to find me, I'd be gone. I wasn't sure I could give that up even though I knew the chances of her coming back were slim. If she hadn't come back in over a month, it wasn't likely she'd come back. For all I knew, she was in Texas or Washington or deported. I shuddered. Would they deport a minor? Lord knows what would happen to her. I was helpless to do a damn thing about it and it broke my heart.

I might as well move on.

I pulled myself to a sitting position and picked up the letter. Light in my hands, the envelope onion-skin thin, it seemed impossible something so insignificant—all colorful stamps and smeared postal marks—could hold the power to change the direction of my life. That's not right either, I thought. I change the direction of my life regardless of the words written on this thin paper. "I decide," I told the empty room.

I slit the envelope and took out the folded letter. They wanted me. As soon as I could make it to San Salvador, the teaching position was mine. They'd arrange for optional housing as soon as I signed and returned the enclosed acceptance.

I set the papers on the coffee table and headed out the back door like some kind of sleepwalker. At the edge of Antonia's garden, I sat in the grass in my pajamas and cried. "I'm sorry," I sobbed. "I'm so sorry I couldn't help you. I'm sorry you had to leave. I'm sorry I have to leave."

My decision was made.

The sun was bright and the hills were autumn yellow as I fumbled with my bike lock. With quick steps I walked the long street, still empty of the hordes of Sunday shoppers that would be milling around in less than an hour, slowly growing in numbers from a few random individuals to a mass of humanity so tight you couldn't safely push a stroller through.

As I rushed through the still-empty market, vendors called out their morning greetings. I was now one of them. A regular. I'll miss this, I thought. I stopped in the middle of the street and turned a slow circle taking in the sights and smells of the market coming to life.

Yes, I would miss the brilliance of the flowers in their large white buckets and heady scent of fresh cinnamon rolls that filled my Sunday mornings. Still, I was excited. Mama Lucy was right. I held a university degree but was ignorant of the world.

Although, in the comfort of Mama Lucy's booth, I'd begun my true education. In the quiet of my own cottage I'd read the magazines, newspaper clippings and books Mama Lucy brought to me. I could now identify every country in Central and South America, rattle off a historical timeline for each, and explain the complexities of political issues and factions. I was ready to accept the offer that arrived from San Salvador. I felt it in my bones.

"Hey, Mama Lucy," I called as I approached the old potter's colorful booth. "I got the job."

The old woman stood in silence and absorbed my very being, my atoms, my soul, my life itself. She was fully there in the present and I could feel her support as I'd felt none other.

"Come, let's have our tea," she said.

We sat together for our morning tea, as we did each Sunday, and enjoyed those wonderful moments between the time Henry finished the set up and the arrival of the first customers. I plucked the letter from my backpack and gave it to her. She read slowly, carefully, a smile warming her face.

"Of course they want you."

"And the high school offered me a job too."

"Look at you. Your stars must be in alignment or some such thing. When do you leave?" she asked as she returned the letter.

"So you think I should go?"

"Of course you should go."

"And not take the high school job?"

"There will be plenty of high school jobs when you come back, if that's still what you want. Come back when you've worn holes in your traveling shoes."

"But I'll miss you."

"I'll be here when you come back. Send me a letter now and then."

"But what if Antonia comes back?"

"Do you think that will happen?"

"No," I admitted.

She handed me a cup of steaming tea. "I noticed you already signed the acceptance. You'll be mailing it tomorrow?"

"Yes." I couldn't hide my sheepish smile.

"Testing me, were you?"

"Or myself."

"Have you called your mother yet?"

"Oh, man, you sound like Antonia. You both sure know how to spoil a good moment."

"Have you?"

"No."

She dug into the pocket of her apron for her money pouch and dropped it in my lap. "There's no time like the present. Should be enough coins in there."

"Now?"

"Now. They're farmers. They'll be sipping their second cup of coffee by now."

I stopped at the front of the booth.

"That way." She pointed in the direction of the nearest public phone booth.

"So how'd it go?" she asked as soon as I returned her money pouch.

"Pretty much what I expected. Dad told me to come home and take care of my mother like any decent daughter would and when I told him that wasn't going to happen, he hung up on me. I had to call back to talk with my mom. At first I didn't think she was going to answer, but she finally picked up."

"Any better?"

"Different, not better. She cried, begged me to come home. For a visit, she said."

"What about it? You could go for a few days and fly out of Seattle, couldn't you?"

"Not a chance."

"Why not?"

"I'm not ready."

"What are you afraid of, Carolyn?"

"Why are you pressing so hard?"

"Because you are avoiding them, avoiding something. It doesn't help to run away from our fears. We need to face them, to conquer them, and until we do that, we carry them around with us like so much weight in a pack."

"If I go home, I'm afraid I'll get stuck there again. It was a fight to get away. I worked so hard to get the scholarships, to save money, to get the grades. I did all that to get away. I don't want to go back. Besides I can't afford the extra expense."

"I owe you for a month or two of Sundays. I've made more money in these last few months than I did in the past few years. You're golden, Biker Girl. I hate to see you go. But go you will, and I'm buying you a ticket to go home first."

"You don't give up, do you?"

"Not when I think it's important. Seeing your folks before you leave is important. I bet you haven't seen them in four years, have you? Never went back since you graduated from high school. Your poor mother. You should be ashamed."

"Me? What has she done? When has she come to see me? She's my mother, damn it."

"And you're not a kid anymore."

We were quiet for most of the day. Didn't bring it up. Didn't talk anymore about it. But I knew she was right. I knew I couldn't leave the country without saying goodbye. I'd go home for a quick visit and let them brag about their college-graduate daughter. I didn't think they'd do much bragging about my teaching position in San Salvador. And I certainly wouldn't tell them about turning down the job offer in Los Arboles, or about my dreams and motives. I wouldn't tell them that I was going to teach English, to offer the knowledge and skills needed to navigate immigration–both legal and illegal. I wouldn't talk to them about my desire to help immigrants adjust to the shock of living in a culture so different from their own. They wouldn't understand. When had they ever understood a thing about me? What I didn't yet realize, what I was too young, too sheltered, too naive to realize, was that I'd learn far more in the coming years than I could ever teach.

At the end of the day, after we loaded the last crate of pots into Henry's truck, after the booth was nothing more than a bundle of canvas and poles, I gave Mama Lucy a hug.

"Thank you," I said. "I know you're right. I'll face my demons before I leave."

Henry offered me a ride home, as he did every Sunday evening, but this time I refused. The evening was cool and beautiful. I needed the ride, the time to clear my mind, to think. Could I do it? Could I go back to the Mound City? Could I go to San Salvador? Each choice was as daunting as the other.

Before heading up the hill, I followed the river down to the flats south of town. I'd ridden past the River Street apartment building at least once a week since Antonia left, hoping, beyond reason, that I'd see one of my former students, that somebody I knew might have returned. But I knew I was only torturing myself. Mama Lucy's words echoed in my head as I turned my bike towards home: "Let it go, Carolyn. The teapot is broken, but the girl is strong. She's a survivor. She'll be okay."

I knew Mama Lucy was right. Besides what option did I have? Antonia was gone. I pedaled hard as I crested the steep hill to my cottage. What would Central America be like? Was it as bad as Antonia remembered or had it changed? I reached the narrow path to my cottage and dismounted, pushing my bike to the front door, and leaning it against the porch railing as I'd done so many times. Soon this special place would no longer be mine.

After I'd made the call home and mailed the acceptance letter, I sold or gave away most of my stuff. I didn't have much. What I didn't want to part with–my bike and books–Mama Lucy agreed to store for me.

Then the day finally came to leave my cottage. I'd spend the last few days with Mama Lucy before Henry drove me to the airport. The cottage was spotless. The landlord agreed to inspect and, if all was in order, she'd return my deposit immediately. As she walked through the cottage and out the back door, she saw Antonia's garden for the first time.

"Oh, my," she said. "It's beautiful."

Seattle, Washington
2011

Eighteen

I CHAINED MY BIKE to a rack, removed the clips from my trouser legs, and tossed my hair free of my helmet. I crammed the clips and helmet into my backpack, took a long drink from my water bottle, and stood for another full minute before heading across the large urban campus to the auditorium.

The heavy double doors were closed. As I opened one and peered into the darkened room, I congratulated myself on my timing. The continental breakfast was over. The convocation program was in full swing. Perfect. I gave myself a smug smile as I crept into the room. No mindless small talk. No trying to remember names of people I see on campus year after year but still can't recall. If they really cared how I spent my summer, wouldn't we spend some time together? If I really cared, wouldn't I remember their names?

I silently wished we were all required to wear name tags. It would take away the pressure of remembering. Maybe the name tags could indicate "faculty," "staff," or "administration." That way I'd avoid the awkwardness of convocation a few years back, the conversation still as clear as if it were only yesterday.

I'd approached the coffee urn at the same moment as another woman, a face I'd seen so many times I felt guilty being unable to attach a name. In a feeble attempt at small talk, I asked, "So how'd you spend your summer?"

"Working," the woman said before walking away, stone-faced.

Crap! Once again I'd mistaken a staff member for faculty. Staff worked all summer. Faculty enjoyed summers of leisure–or so the staff saw it. In reality most faculty struggled to find part-time jobs to augment the dismal salaries that barely got them through the summer with rent or mortgage paid and food on the table. And that was tenured faculty. For part-time adjuncts the situation was even worse. Still staff salaries were also horrible and they got even less flex time.

Convocation–the same silliness every September. A lame attempt to rally the campus community into a new academic year. I'd been with the college far too many years to be impressed and I hated the small talk so much I perfected the practice of arriving right as the speeches began.

As I made my way into the darkened room, I scanned the long rows of chairs lined up in perfect formation. Where to sit? Then I caught sight of Elsie sitting to the far right of the room towards the back. Staying in the shadows along the outer wall, determined to attract as little attention as possible, I slipped into the empty seat next to her just as a group of half a dozen or so of our colleagues ran onto the stage, a few in football uniforms, the rest in full, cheerleader regalia complete with pom-poms.

"Didn't think you were coming," Elsie whispered.

"Me? Wouldn't dream of missing the fun," I whispered. "I didn't know we had a football team."

"Rah, rah, rah!" She pumped her arm in the air.

We covered our mouths to muffle our laughter and settled in to endure the painfully embarrassing skit and a heartbreaking slide show intent on encouraging us all to dig deep into our miserable paychecks to give to those less fortunate than ourselves.

"God, it's the same every year, isn't it?" Elsie moaned.

"Just let us teach, right?"

The speeches dragged on, boring endless speeches intended to inspire us to greater service, a new academic year about to begin. I'm getting old, I thought. Old and cynical. When did that happen? When did I stop caring?

I scanned the faces to my left and right, some eager and intent, others as blank and bored as my own. When did the passion die? When did I lose the spark? And then my mind traveled. I was no longer in the half-empty auditorium zoning out the attempts at inspiration.

The sun was midday hot, cooking the stew of human and animal waste that filled the makeshift sewers lining the crooked stairs of uneven, irregular slabs of concrete. Stairs snaking up sharp ravines cut between the hills encircling the city. Here the city's throwaways lived in *casas de carton* that slid down the hillsides as quickly as the excrement in the ditches with each heavy storm.

"We go mid-morning. We leave by early afternoon. No more than an hour or two," Ernesto told me.

"Why?" I asked.

My innocence, or perhaps my ignorance, made him smile. "Safer that way." His dark eyes bored into me. "You sure you want to do this?"

"Yes," I said. "I want to go." And I did. I wanted to see the barrios, the living conditions I'd only read about in college textbooks and news articles.

I'd met Ernesto weeks earlier in a coffee shop. Not a coffee shop like we think of today. Not a Starbucks. This place seemed akin to how I imagined the speakeasies of the beat poets long before my time. A place with strong coffee, red wine, poetry, music and political activism. My friends had gone home early, but I had stayed, enthralled by the music, the conversations at the shared tables, the scene. It wasn't late. I felt safe.

"Your friends left," Ernesto said. It was a statement of fact not a question. "May I sit?"

I nodded.

"Why'd you stay?" His English was excellent, an educated man, the class of young wealthy men whose names filled my roster each term, men from upper-crust families who could afford the outrageous tuition fees of the international language school. I looked at him. He had wavy hair, brown-black eyes, a medium build. There was nothing unique about him but the kindness in his eyes and the grin at the corners of his sensuous, serious mouth.

"I like the music," I said.

He laughed, ordered two glasses of wine, and we talked, and later, walked through the night.

As I sat in the campus auditorium listening to a speaker intoning the virtues of some new educational research data, I remembered the passion of those all-night conversations and the slow realization that Ernesto was more than what he appeared. Grad student, yes. Sociologist, yes. But also, community organizer in a place where community organizing was neither supported nor appreciated by the controlling military regime, where it meant working with the disenfranchised living in barrios tucked away in gullies hidden from the wealth of the city. I looked up at the podium as a new speaker droned on about funding cuts and doing more with less. Less? We don't even know what less means, I thought.

I shifted my backpack between my feet on the floor wondering if I could get anything done, a bit of planning, or maybe read some of the hundreds of emails that accumulated during every quarter break, especially during the summer. Odd how fresh initiatives, exciting projects, important taskforces to address new needs always seemed to develop when faculty were neither available nor compensated to voice input. I seethed with bitterness, no not seethed, I no longer had the passion to seethe. I'd lost my passion over the past decade of security, of golden handcuffs. Now edging forty, the passion of that young teacher who climbed the broken steps of salvaged concrete slab and stone rising between narrow terraced rows of *casas de carton* was gone.

Again, I zoned out the droning at the front of the room, the periodic applause between speakers, and remembered the clusters of brown-skinned, dark-eyed children in dirty rags who trailed Ernesto and me through the barrio. Children holding hands, children laughing, children clowning for my camera like children everywhere.

The camera. What happened to that camera Mama Lucy gave me? When had I stopped taking photographs?

I remembered my final day in Los Arboles, the morning in Mama Lucy's kitchen. We had one last cup of tea as we waited for Henry, who would drive me to the airport.

"I'll send you postcards," I told her.

"Send me photos," she said. "I like them better. They're real. Don't send me pretty pictures. Send me real pictures."

"But ..."

"I know," she said, and she gave me a small package. "Send me a few of that orchard you grew up in too. You can figure out the bells and whistles on your flight home. Here's a few rolls of film to get you started."

Applause filled the auditorium. Elsie gave me a nudge and a grin. "Sleeping?" she said.

"If only," I said, still faraway. Where had all that passion gone? Where were the all-night political discussions? I'd become the establishment, a cog in the wheel, replaceable as a screw in a hardware store. A bore. I pretended to be working for a cause, to be helping those with the greatest need, but was I really doing anything more than pulling in a convenient, guaranteed paycheck? The golden handcuffs of tenure gave me a level of security I took for granted.

"How about we get out of this place?" Elsie said.

"Sounds good," I said.

Nineteen

IT WAS LATE AFTERNOON when I got off my bike in front of the house, a two-story craftsman home I'd bought years before when prices were reasonable, loans were readily available, and I felt flush with a new teaching position. The house was subdivided when I bought it: two apartments on the second floor and a larger one on the main floor. The idea of being a landlord was a bit daunting, but only until the day Gemila Kemmal responded to my listing. Over the years we'd become fast friends. I'd watched with pleasure as Gemi's home healthcare business flourished and Gemi herself transformed from a refugee, clinging to traditions of her Islamic ancestors, into a confident woman, certain of herself and her beliefs.

A few years after Gemi moved in, we decided to remove the wall that had divided the second floor into two rather awkward units. Now she enjoyed having a larger apartment for both living space and home office. At times I had to remind myself I was still a landlord, the house wasn't co-owned, and the deposit each month in my account came from this dear friend.

I walked my bike up the front walk where Gemi was deadheading the hydrangeas, bags of mulch piled at the edge of the sidewalk. I smiled at the baggy clothes, now her gardening clothes, once her daily work clothes. How she'd changed! She'd opened her heart to the world, while I'd shut down.

"How was it?" Gemi asked.

"Same old thing every year."

"That bad, was it?"

"This year they actually did a skit complete with cheerleaders and pom-poms."

Gemi laughed. A hearty, happy laugh.

"What really gets me isn't the silly skits or even all these so-called experts rattling off statistics and research results. What gets me is all the new TESOL graduates–Teachers of English to Speakers of Other Languages–coming out with master's degrees, full of new ideas about the latest and greatest ways to do this and that. Kids with no real-world experience. I mean, we work with immigrants and refugees who come from places some of these teachers can't even find on a map. They've never taught outside the U.S. How can they understand what our students have been through without seeing it, at least a glimpse of it, with their own eyes?"

"The violence, the poverty, the children?" Gemi asked.

"Yeah. How can they go to their fancy schools and get their fancy degrees and think they know what they're doing?" I slumped onto the front steps. I watched as Gemi cut open a bag of mulch and began to spread it with a mother's touch.

"My dear friend," she said. "It seems to me that you are sounding much like your old friend, Mama Lucy."

I laughed. "I suppose you're right. But she knew what she was talking about. Going south was the best thing I ever did."

"And now, my friend?"

"Now, I don't know. Sometimes it feels so meaningless."

"Until you close the classroom door."

I nodded in agreement.

"Don't lose sight of that. You serve students who need you, who appreciate your efforts. It still has meaning, my dear friend."

The sun warmed my back as Gemi turned the mulch into the soil.

I remembered the children. It was my last visit to the barrio. I'd promised and I didn't want to break my promise. Not to the children. Not to their mothers. I hadn't seen or heard from Ernesto in over two weeks. Either he had been arrested, killed, or gone underground, and there was no way I could find out without putting myself and others in danger. We'd talked about this possibility. I knew all I could do was wait. But I'd promised the children, so a month after Ernesto's disappearance I decided to keep that promise. I loaded my backpack with food, water, my camera, and a thick envelope. I knew the route, knew how long it would take, headed out early.

As I climbed the crooked steps, the children swarmed to greet me. "¿*Dónde vives?*" I asked each one. "¿*Dónde está tu mama?*" They only giggled and hid one behind the next, a chain of hiding, giggling kids. My accented Spanish, white skin, short blond hair, green eyes, and jeans were oddities in their sheltered barrio on the fringes of the modern world.

"¿*Dónde está tu mama?*" I repeated again and again until one tiny girl stepped forward and grasped my hand. She led me through a maze of cardboard and corrugated metal shacks with dirt floors and rag doors.

"Mami, Mami," she called as we approached one shack, indecipherable from the others by the untrained eye.

A haggard woman stepped in front of me, possibly no older than myself, stripped of her youth and beauty by the weight of poverty.

"*Buenos días, señora,*" I said.

"¿*Qué quiere usted?*" she demanded.

I drew the envelope from my backpack.

"¿*Donde está* Ernesto?"

"*No sé.*"

"¿*Donde está* Ernesto?" she repeated. "*Usted no debe estar aquí sola.*"

I knew I shouldn't be there alone, shouldn't be there without Ernesto. I tried to explain that Ernesto was gone, that I had made a promise, but the hardness in her face, the mask covering her eyes and concealing her soul, did not lift. I saw the fear behind that mask, but still I didn't leave.

Instead, I opened the envelope and removed the stack of photographs. I shuffled through them to find a few of her daughter. From the corner of my eye, I saw her shift towards me, lean in to see what I was looking at. "*Para usted.*" I handed her two photographs of her young daughter.

She hesitated.

"*Para usted,*" I repeated and pushed the photographs towards her.

"¿*Por qué, señorita?*"

"Because I promised."

"So many."

"Can you help me? Can you find the other mothers?"

With a nod, she led me into her tiny shack. There on a makeshift table, we spread out the photographs. In Spanish I struggled to follow, she told her daughter to run find *doña* this and *doña* that until the small shack was crowded with women, tears in their eyes, exclamations of joy in their voices, a timid *"Gracias"* from each as she claimed a photograph of her children. Ernesto had told me photographs would be special gifts, but I didn't understand the truth of his words until that moment. For many of these women, this was the first, perhaps the only, photograph they would ever have of their children.

It happened quickly, or so it seemed, the sorting of photos, the coming of the mothers, the exclamations of surprise and joy. Then they were gone: the mothers and the children and the photographs. I was alone with the tiny *niñita* and her mother.

"¿Donde está Ernesto?" she asked again, the mask gone, the urgency clear in her voice.

"No sé," I repeated. *"Desaparecido."*

I said the dreaded word and her face crumbled. The horror was that I truly did not know what had happened to Ernesto or his *compañeros*, young radicals, red-wine-drinking leftists plotting for schools and running water, electricity and public restrooms for these people living on the hillsides in *casas de carton*. He gave me books to read, taught me his history and politics, music and dance, he made love to me, and then he disappeared. He was there and then he was not.

She took my arm and led me to the door. *"Venga usted conmigo."* She walked me all the way to the bus stop at the bottom edge of the barrio, her daughter tagging along behind us. *"No regrese usted sola,"* she told me.

I saw the warning in her eyes. I saw her concern and feared my presence may have put her in danger. She stood at my side holding her daughter's hand for what seemed like an eternity, refusing to leave until a bus arrived. There were no taxis in this part of town or I would have taken one despite the cost. My stomach growled. The weight of my backpack reminded me I hadn't eaten since early morning. In the time we'd spent together, they had eaten nothing either. I dug out an apple, a mango, a packet of coated peanuts, and offered them to the woman. She shook her head no. I motioned to her daughter. She gave a slight nod of consent. I knelt in front of the girl to offer her the fruit. Delight in her eyes, she received the mango and began to peel it with her teeth, juice dripping from her chin. I laughed as I stuffed the nuts into her pocket.

When the bus finally arrived, I pushed the bright, red apple into the woman's hands and jumped aboard. "*Que vaya con dios,*" she called to me as the doors closed between us.

I opened my eyes to see Gemi gazing at me. "You were far, far away, my friend."

"Memories." I gave myself a shake. "What about you? Aren't you home a bit earlier than normal?"

"Indeed. I lost my afternoon client. Mrs. Anderson passed in her sleep last night."

"I'm sorry. Was she the one who said you dressed worse than her maid?"

"No, that would be Mrs. Newbury. Fortunately, she is still quite well." Gemi paused. "She told me she was unable to recommend me or even retain my services if I didn't make some changes."

"That's right. What a character!" I laughed remembering Gemi's indignation. "She gave you the name of her personal shopper, right?"

"I must admit, the old dear forced me to take a good look in the mirror."

"And look at you now," I said.

With a smile, Gemi turned the conversation. "It's good to have you back, my friend. Tell me, how was your visit to California this time? We have had no opportunity to catch up, have we?"

"I haven't even unpacked or done laundry yet, just got back, and had to rush off to convocation this morning. But the visit was great. Mama Lucy's getting up there now."

"Eighty-eight this year, is it?"

"You've got a great memory, Gemi. She still gets around and Jason spends as much time as he can with her during the summer and quarter breaks."

"Good boy."

"Not such a boy." I felt the color warm my cheeks. I couldn't stop it.

"So that's how it is?" Gemi asked.

"He's married." I said it with more force than I'd intended.

"And does his wife come to Los Arboles with him on all these long visits?"

"No. She's not a teacher. Doesn't have the same vacation time."

"Mama Lucy is fortunate to have both you and Jason keeping an eye on her."

"We're almost never there at the same time. I think Mama Lucy tries to spread out our visits so she has less alone time. But this summer she got her dates confused and our visits overlapped by almost a week." I saw the quizzical arch in Gemi's right eyebrow, the smile in her eyes. "Okay, it was nice. I got to know him better. You know, I've heard about him for years, seen him off and on, a day here and there, but I didn't really know him. Seven days in the same house was new."

"And nice?"

"Yeah, but he's married."

"Perhaps Mama Lucy knows something you do not know."

"Are you suggesting she scheduled our visits at the same time on purpose?"

"Perhaps," she said.

As I stretched my legs out in front of me on the warm steps, soaking up the last of Seattle's late summer sun, I saw Jason's auburn hair and his long, lean body. With a desire so strong it took my breath away, I wanted to be with him in the rolling yellow hills of Los Arboles. I gave myself a hard shake.

"I suppose I better go figure out what I'm doing in my classes tomorrow," I said as I got to my feet and swung my backpack over my shoulder. "Later alligator."

Twenty

ANTONIA MADE HER WAY through the endless building. It was as though a whole city block, or maybe two, were connected by one, long hallway. Makes sense in the winter rains, she thought, but hard to be trapped inside on a sunny autumn day.

She walked the hallway until she found room 362 in a maze of passages to one side of the central hall. She glanced at her watch: 8:51 a.m. Nine minutes early. But already a half dozen students stood outside the door talking in small groups, students who knew each other, maybe from a previous quarter, maybe from an earlier class. The advisor had offered her the eight o'clock class as well, but she explained she needed to take her son to elementary school before catching a bus to the college.

She saw a paper taped to the door: 9:00 – 9:50 a.m. ESL 098 Carolyn Bauer, Instructor. "Carolyn Bauer?" It was a whisper in a voice Antonia hardly recognized as her own. *"No puede ser."*

Suddenly the door opened and the hall filled with students, laughing, talking, hoisting heavy backpacks over bulky jackets. Winter clothes weren't necessary yet, but new school clothes were meant to be worn on the first day of school. Antonia knew this. Her young son was teaching her how to be a student in America. She smiled watching these young students–definitely not an ESL class. From experience, Antonia knew ESL classes in Seattle were a mixed bag of multi-aged students of varying educational levels from every country on the face of the earth.

Although she'd never gone beyond primary school in her homeland, Antonia had learned geography and history and culture in ESL classes through the years, both from teachers and fellow classmates. She had also discovered public libraries and read voraciously in both English and Spanish. Still her writing wasn't at college-level yet.

As the room emptied, she entered, taking in the arrangement of individual desks in the large room, the white board and the computer station at the front, and the bank of windows to the side, opposite the door. She headed towards the windows, drawn by the light and the gardens below. Seated, she tried to steady her nerves. Carolyn Bauer. It's not such an unusual name. How long had it been since that cottage in Los Arboles? Ten years? No, fifteen now.

She watched the seats around her fill with students speaking words she couldn't understand, words she knew were not English. She watched as these others opened large backpacks and got out notebooks, pens, dictionaries. She remembered a small tattered dictionary she'd had long ago which she'd forgotten when she had fled Los Arboles. Taking a spiral notebook from her worn backpack, she made a mental note of the items she needed to buy, and tried to think of where she could find the money, what she could skip in order to get what she needed to be a student again.

Deep in thought, Antonia was startled by a voice at the front of the room. "Good morning. I'm Carolyn Bauer and this is ESL 098. A big group! Are you all in the correct class?" Murmurs spread through the room. One student stood and showed a paper to the teacher before walking sheepishly to the door. "Let me read through the roster and while I'm doing that, could you each fill out this questionnaire? I'm particularly interested in your contact information and your answer to question number seven about your career goals."

Antonia watched in stunned silence. Carolyn Bauer. Carolina. Sure, there was a bit of gray in her sandy blonde curls, and the creases of age, experience, and weather showed on her face, but it was the same woman. The same tall, slender, athletic body. The same casual style and precise intonation.

Antonia watched as this older Carolina in khakis, a lightweight blue pullover, and loafers circled the room with the fluid movements of a dancer, handing out papers while she spoke. She knew this was the woman who took her in, fed her, gave her a home, and possibly saved her life a decade and a half earlier. Where had all those years gone?

Antonia wanted to know what Carolina's life had been like. She wanted to tell Carolina about her own life, about her time in the fields, and now as a certified nursing assistant, about her adorable son, about her dreadful husband. No, not that, she did not want to talk of that.

Most of all she wanted to apologize to Carolina for disappearing from her life so long ago. These thoughts played against each other as she listened to Carolina's voice read the long list of impossible-to-pronounce names, names that seemed to stem from every language in the universe.

"Carmen Meléndez."

She heard her name and responded as had the students before her. A slight wave of the hand, a smile, and a name Carolina would not recognize.

Later that day, Antonia entered the break room of the dementia care facility, poured herself a cup of coffee, and settled in a chair across the table from Mehret. "*Dios mío*, this stuff is horrible," she said.

"That's why I bring my tea from home." Mehret pointed to the thermos on the table between them. "How are you today, my friend? How was your first day of class?"

"You remember!" Antonia said, surprised that this colleague had remembered her decision to return to school, remembered that classes had begun this week.

"My sister also attends college. She too began today," Mehret explained as though reading her mind.

Antonia smiled at their shared struggle to communicate in a language still foreign to both of them, as foreign as the culture of the elderly souls they were paid a pittance to care for despite the years each had lived in America. "I am taking English class," she said.

"But you speak good."

"Not good enough. And I cannot write good enough for college classes," Antonia said.

"You will get a degree then?"

"Yes. I want to be a nurse someday. Or maybe a teacher."

"You will."

"Something strange happened today, Mehret."

"Yes? Tell me."

"I went to my class for the first time. I saw my teacher, and I know her from before."

"Before?"

"Yes. Long ago I know her, knew her." Antonia corrected her grammar and took a sip of coffee, remembering the young *gringa* woman who stopped to sit with her under a large eucalyptus tree and shared her food, of a tiny cottage in an overgrown lot, of a large garden, and a homemade bed.

"Tell me," Mehret said.

"I knew her long ago," Antonia repeated. "She helped me when I had nothing. But then I left her. I did not see her or talk with her in fifteen years."

"A lifetime," Mehret said. "Are you certain this woman and the other, they are the same?"

"Yes," Antonia said. "*Sin duda*. I have no doubt."

"And she recognized you? You gave her a big hug?"

"I was Antonia then. Now I use my other name. She does not know Carmen Meléndez." Antonia lowered her eyes in shame.

Mehret sat in silence waiting for Antonia to continue. Like most immigrants and refugees, Mehret knew the story would come only when the teller was ready.

"I did wrong," Antonia said. "And I left my friend *sin palabra*. Without talk."

"Wrong?" Mehret said. "I cannot believe you. You could not do wrong."

"I broke something, a teapot, a very special teapot of teacher Carolina. Now if she knows I am me, what will she do? She will hate me? She is *enojada*?"

"¿*Enojada*?" Mehret stumbled over the Spanish pronunciation, but Antonia didn't smile this time, didn't even notice.

"*Sí*. Angry. Is she still angry with me, you think?"

"After so many years? No, I think she will not be angry. I think she will be happy to see her good friend again. Will you tell her?"

"No," Antonia said with a sad shake of her head. "Not yet. Maybe later. Maybe at the end of class. If she is angry, maybe I will not pass the class."

"I do not think she will still be angry, Carmen. This is only fear that speaks."

"Maybe you are right, but I take no chance."

Twenty-One

"WELCOME HOME, Carolyn. I see you are still riding that pathetic bicycle of yours."

"Yup, first day of classes. And don't badmouth this bike. It's served me well for almost thirty years. Why would I replace it? It gets me to class and home again and the parking rates are perfect."

We laughed. Always the same Gemi, always teasing me about my rusty, old bike, always trying to convince me to upgrade. Using the cable from my backpack, I locked the bike to a railing on the front porch.

"Do you really think the lock is necessary? Who would steal such a thing?"

"Give me a sec to change my shoes," I said.

A few minutes later we headed out for our walk. Ever since Gemi started walking to help rehab one of her clients, she'd become a regular and it was a routine we both cherished. A chance to catch up and get some fresh air and exercise at the same time. We headed north along the tree-lined streets of our Capitol Hill neighborhood, the houses growing grander by the block as we approached Volunteer Park.

"So tell me more about your time in California? Is Mama Lucy well?" Gemi asked.

"She's doing great. Slowing down a bit, but then who doesn't at eighty-eight, right? She isn't throwing pots anymore, but Henry still sets up her booth each Sunday to sell the stockpile she's accumulated through the years—and some of Jason's and her apprentices' pieces. She's still teaching, so her pottery shed is open and productive."

"Jason?" Gemi said. "I wasn't aware he was a potter as well."

"I guess he's been doing more and more through the years. Mama Lucy says he's a natural, but he only does it when he's visiting her. I guess his wife isn't very supportive. "

"How unfortunate."

We entered Volunteer Park, the large, peaceful sanctuary crowning the north end of the hill with intense beauty, both natural and manmade. On rainy days, we'd slip into the Asian Art Museum or the Conservatory, but on days of brilliant autumn sunshine like today, we shuffled through the crisp, fallen leaves, enjoying the musty, earthy smell that filled the air with each footstep.

As we walked along, I sang the line about the bluest skies from the old television show. "I don't know if they're really the bluest in Seattle, but they're sure magnificent today."

"True enough," Gemi agreed.

"You know, it gets harder to leave Mama Lucy each time. She still gets around and is as sharp as she's always been, but I know she won't last forever."

"You've been good to her, going to visit every chance you have."

"She's been good to me. I think we all need a surrogate mom or aunt or somebody to make up for what we don't get from our birth moms. Oh crap, I'm sorry, Gemi. That was so rude of me."

"Do not worry, my friend. I lost my mother long ago, but before the bombing took her from me, she was everything a mother could be. I had a blessed childhood and I am grateful for that. I'm glad you met Mama Lucy at a time in your life when you felt alone and so terribly misunderstood."

"Yeah, my folks are okay, but we've never been able to talk to each other the way Mama Lucy and I can. That's the way it goes, I guess. Too much baggage."

We walked in companionable silence for a while.

"How was your first day of classes?" Gemi asked.

"Off to a good start, I suppose."

"You sound pensive, my friend. What's on your mind?"

"The weirdest thing happened today."

Gemi waited for me to continue.

"It's nothing. It's just that as I was taking attendance this morning, you know, making sure everybody was in the right class, there was this one student, Latina, in her late twenties or early thirties, beautiful woman, with long dark curls and almond eyes. I could swear I know her from somewhere. "

"Maybe a returning student? You have told me of students who study until they have enough English to get entry-level jobs and then return, perhaps years later, for the skills they need to climb the socio-economic ladder. Could this young woman not be a former student?"

"I suppose," I said. "But I don't know. You're going to think I'm nuts, but she reminds me of a girl I knew a long time ago."

"Antonia? The girl you sheltered in Los Arboles back when you were a student?"

"You remember everything!"

"My memory serves me well at times," Gemi said with a laugh. "Besides, I believe we have perhaps told each other all our stories and secrets through the years, don't you think?"

"True, but you remember them. Anyway it's not her. Different name. Besides she was probably deported years ago."

"Names can change. Perhaps she has married."

"Even her first name is different. I don't know what to think. It's weird, I guess."

Gemi only nodded.

We passed the glimmering glass structure of the conservatory and completed our loop of the park.

"And your mother? What have you heard from Mound City of late?" Gemi asked, pulling me from my thoughts. "Is she adapting to her new challenges?"

"Seems so. I called her as soon as I got back from Los Arboles. As always, she says she's fine. Dad says one hundred percent of her vision is gone now and she can't manage a thing. Her doctor doesn't seem to think anything can be done to help her. I wish I could be sure she's getting the best medical attention, but I can't convince her to let me bring her to Seattle for a second opinion."

"Might your father be the problem?"

"Yeah. I'm sure she doesn't want to make waves. She says she can get along fine at home. Shopping is a challenge, so she has to depend on Dad for that."

"He still hasn't agreed to home healthcare then?"

"No. He says he can take care of everything and if I'm not willing to go back and help out like any decent daughter worth her salt, he sure as hell isn't going to have some stranger come into his house and stick her nose into their business."

"So nothing has changed at all," Gemi said.

"Exactly. But sometimes I wonder, you know. Maybe I should move back and help out. Neither of them is getting any younger."

"There are other options, my friend. You've done the research and offered your father the names of several good home healthcare services. I believe you even offered to cover the cost. If he refuses to make the call, I do not believe you should feel responsible."

"Yeah I know. But still they're my folks." I shuffled my feet through the dried leaves, brilliant fall colors still adorning the tree limbs overhead. "I have a new secret," I said.

"Indeed?"

I nodded my head. Gemi said nothing.

"It's no fun if you don't beg."

"Oh, please, please, tell me your secret, my dear friend. I will die if you refuse to tell me. Please, please, tell me." She held her hands together, palms touching, the perfect supplicant.

We laughed until tears filled our eyes.

"Mama Lucy called last night," I said as I dried my tears on my sleeve.

"Already? You just left her."

"It turns out Jason's wife has been having an affair for some time now. He found out late last spring. They tried counseling, but I guess she decided she wanted a divorce."

"Poor Jason," Gemi said.

"Yeah. Apparently the other guy is loaded. She claims she's tired of counting pennies and doesn't want to raise any kids in poverty."

"Poverty? I didn't know Jason or Mama Lucy were struggling."

"They aren't. That's the point. It's ridiculous. Anyway, I guess the divorce is final. Good thing they never had kids."

"Interesting news, isn't it? One can't but wonder how long Mama Lucy has known of this problem."

"You mean the overlapping visits this summer? I asked her about that, but she just laughed. I called her a busybody and a match-maker and told her to cut it out or I'd cancel my next visit."

"I imagine she laughed all the more."

"Yup. She told me I'd never have the heart to deprive a crazy old potter of a visit."

"A very interesting turn of events, my dear friend. Do you suppose Jason will be visiting his grandmother this Christmas when you're there?"

I turned away, unwilling to let her see me blush again, and determined to change the direction of our conversation. "By the way, how's it going with that man of yours these days? Where will you and Antonio be spending the holidays this year?" I watched the wide smile light up Gemi's dark face and the twinkle brighten in her black eyes. "That good, huh?"

"Indeed. Antonio is a very special person."

"Am I hearing wedding bells?"

"Let us not jump to conclusions, my dear friend. I was once married, remember? I'm not quite certain I wish to marry again."

"Well, I'm all for whatever brings you the greatest possible joy. You deserve some romance and happiness in your life again."

Twenty-Two

ANTONIA GLANCED AT the scattered newspapers on the break-room table. Her eyes stopped on a photo of her man. He was an *abogado*, a man who practiced law and worked for the government. She was proud of her educated man, proud she shared her life with a big man, proud her son's father was an important man. But never, never had she seen her man's face in the newspaper. They didn't get the paper at home. No reason for it, her man said. He read it at his office and she wouldn't understand it in English anyway. Antonia had been annoyed. She remembered thinking that reading the newspaper could help her improve her English, but she had said nothing.

Now she sat at the break-room table and held her man's face in her hands. That's how she thought of him, her *hombre*. To others she called him her husband, her *esposo*. But never to herself. She knew the truth.

Her eyes scanned the article. Fear crawled her spine as she struggled to understand: immigration services, deportations, honored. Slow down, she told herself. Slow down, read carefully, make sure you understand. She took out her dictionary, a small one she could always carry with her, tiny enough to slip into any pocket. She struggled through the article, translating to make sense of the impossible.

At the sound of the door, Antonia glanced up. "Mehret," she said. "This man, why is he in the newspaper?"

"Let's see," her friend said. "Looks like he got an award of some kind."

"For helping immigrants?" Antonia asked, her voice laced with fading hope.

"Oh no, the opposite," Mehret said. "He's in charge of deportations. Why? Do you know this man?"

Antonia froze, unable to respond. She knew Mehret's read was accurate. It confirmed her own.

"Do you know him?" Mehret asked again.

"*Es mi esposo*," Antonia said. "My husband."

"You did not know?"

Antonia only shook her head, unable to speak, to think, to make sense of any of it.

"Listen, I have to go. I only came in to get a clean glass for Mrs. Franklin's Boost, but I'll be back soon. We'll talk after the shift ends, okay? Don't leave before me today. Wait for me, okay?"

Antonia nodded without listening, without understanding her friend's words. She remembered the day, over six years before, when she met her man. She remembered how the air had shifted between them.

Kline had come to visit his mother. It was her first job as a certified nursing assistant, a CNA. She was proud, happy, and always afraid of being discovered.

She'd made it for more than a decade without an identity, but she'd grown tired of migratory field work. For the kind of job she wanted, she needed training and she needed a green card. It wasn't until she started asking questions that she learned an identity was as easy to buy as a carton of milk. You only had to ask the right person the right question, and be ready to pay the right quantity of cash to buy an identity. Using her mother's name–Carmen Meléndez–she enrolled in a CNA program, passed the state licensing exam, and got her first job as a nursing assistant.

She remembered how he said hello when she entered his mother's room. She remembered the intensity of his blue eyes and how he thanked her for the care she gave his mother, a woman far younger than her fellow patients. And she remembered their conversations each time he visited his mother, a woman so lost in early-onset dementia, she recognized neither of them, but seemed pleased by their smiles, their touch, the sound of their voices.

One day he asked her for help with his Spanish homework. He was finishing a law degree and thought some knowledge of Spanish was important. The Spanish lessons became long walks, then Sunday drives. He took her to areas in and around the city she had never known. He passed the Washington State Bar exam and he asked her out to dinner to celebrate. The day he was sworn in there was no one celebrating, no family, no friends. When she asked about it, he tensed. They were busy. Nothing more.

He asked her to marry him, and she told him her truth. He listened in silence, his face turning to stone. She thought it was sympathy her man felt. A few days later, he explained common law marriage, told her he needed her in his life, begged her to be his wife in truth if not in law. She argued for legalization, for citizenship. He got angry. She let it go and moved in with him, suspecting already that she was pregnant, telling him, keeping no secrets from him.

Only after Carlitos was born did she realize the error of her honesty. She'd never told a soul her story. Now this man, who said he loved her, this man who fathered her son, this man who beat her in drunken rages, knew her secrets.

Carlitos was still nursing when the violence began. She remembered the first beating as though it were yesterday. She didn't know whether it was Carlitos's cry or the slam of the front door that woke her. She was on her feet and at the side of the bassinette before she was fully awake. Cuddling Carlitos to her swollen breasts, she sat to nurse him as Kline banged his way into the bedroom.

She'd seen him drunk before but never like this. He hadn't been home for almost a week, hadn't bothered even to call this time. He stumbled into the bedroom so drunk he couldn't hold himself straight. Her eyes were daggers.

"Get out," she hissed.

"Don't tell me what to do, bitch," he slurred, loud and mean.

"Don't use that word. I do not deserve that word."

Carlitos released her breast with an inconsolable scream.

"Now look what you do," she said. She stood to pace back and forth, trying to calm the crying baby.

Kline stumbled towards her, but she gave him her back. He swung her around and slapped her across the face so hard she spun like a top. She fell on her side on the hardwood floor, Carlitos still tight to her chest, and rolled into a fetal position. Kline kicked her again and again — her back, her buttock, her thighs, but not her baby. Oh, god, not her baby. She shielded him with her arms, her breasts, her belly, giving Kline her back, listening to his grunts, each kick a grunt. She held her breath, held in her groans, her screams, her pleas for help.

He grabbed her long black curls, the curls he claimed to cherish, and dragged her from the bedroom, down the hall to the kitchen. She couldn't resist without dropping her baby, so she did not resist. "Where's my dinner, bitch? Can't a man come home to the apartment he's paying for and get a decent meal?"

She said nothing.

"I'm talking to you, you ungrateful wetback," he hollered, giving her another kick. "You want to get sent back when I'm done with you?" With a fist full of her hair, he yanked her to her feet. Her face was red, imprinted with the shape of his hand. Blood flowed from a split in her lip and from her nose.

She heard his gasp, felt him release her, saw him stagger to the living room. "What have I done? Oh, shit, what have I done?"

With one arm still tight around Carlitos, Antonia collapsed into a chair, catching her breath, soothing Carlitos quiet. "*No te preocupes, amorcito. Estamos bien. Todo esta bien.*" But even then, even that first time, she knew it would never be okay. They would never be safe.

She laid Carlitos on the kitchen table ignoring the drunken snores from the living room and her own suffering. She unwrapped his blanket and diaper, removed his one-piece fleece pajamas. She examined his naked body inch by inch. Carlitos gurgled, smiled, and fell asleep, exhausted, perhaps, by this middle-of-the-night game his *mami* was playing. Antonia affixed her son's diaper, tucked him back into his pajamas, and carried him to the bedroom. She kissed him on the forehead and put him to bed.

She snuck into the bathroom and washed the blood from her face, to the kitchen for frozen bags of vegetables, then back to the bedroom. She locked the bedroom door and climbed into bed, one makeshift ice pack on her face, two more under her back, and lay for hours unable to sleep. She had nowhere to go, no one to turn to, no way to escape. Her man knew her secrets. His threats of deportation meant nothing to her. She knew she could survive anywhere. What she wouldn't survive would be the loss of her son and, this too, her man knew.

She lay in bed and began to make the excuses she later learned to be common in situations like hers: he'd had a bad day at work, it won't happen again, he loves me, really he does. She fell asleep wondering if the melted vegetables would still be edible.

It was still dark when Carlitos woke for his next feeding. She rolled to her side to get up and fire shot through her back, but Carlitos insisted so she found the strength to force herself up, to bring him to bed with her, to nurse him, and together they returned to the mercy of sleep.

When again they awoke, sunshine poked around the curtains, and once more she nursed him in bed. But she knew she had to get up, change his diaper, find something to control the pain that held her.

She pulled herself to her feet, carried Carlitos to the safety of his bassinette in the corner, and made her way to the door. There she listened, her ear to the wood. No snoring, no water running in the bathroom or kitchen, no rustle of papers from his briefcase. She unlocked the door without a sound and hobbled down the short hall past the open bathroom to peek into the living room and kitchen. Empty. A wave of relief washed over her.

His note was on the kitchen table, an apology. From a man who didn't have the *cojones* to stay and face the reality of what he had done. She wadded the paper into a ball and burned it on the gas range.

Once again, Antonia didn't hear the door as Mehret entered the break room. It had been another long, violent night. In the six years since that first beating, Antonia had learned to manage her man, calm his drunken rages, avoid his violence, for the most part. But last night he had been out of control. It seemed the newspaper article was not something he had wanted, and he took his anger out on Antonia. She sat with her head in her hands, her untouched dinner before her atop the newspaper.

"Hey there, " Mehret said.

Antonia winced at her friend's gentle pat on her back.

"What's wrong? I hurt you." A statement, not a question.

"Nothing. It's nothing," Antonia said.

"It's something, Carmen. What's wrong? What are you hiding from your friend?"

Mehret was a friend, or the closest thing to a friend Antonia had known in years. Hers was a life of secrets and violence. Her man had shown her the danger of opening up to others. She kept to herself, didn't share her stories or even take part in light conversation with her co-workers. Although she and Mehret had worked together and taken breaks together for several years, they rarely met outside of work. Antonia simply couldn't allow herself the comfort of a confidant.

Mehret didn't know much about Antonia's past or her present beyond the basic facts: Central American, living with an American, one son in first grade, studying ESL at a local college. Though similar in age and job experience, the two young women shared little of themselves or their immigrant experiences. But Mehret had seen Antonia's husband's face in the newspaper, and now, when Antonia winced and dropped her guard, tears filled her eyes and overflowed.

"What is it, my friend?" Mehret asked.

Antonia cried in silence.

"Come. Show me," Mehret led Antonia like a young child into the restroom. "May I?" she asked as she lifted Antonia's tunic.

Antonia winced again at the gasp that escaped her friend's lips.

"Your husband?"

Antonia nodded.

With the same soft touch Antonia had seen Mehret use with their elderly patients, some with skin as thin as delicate parchment, she felt her friend's fingers spread ointment, felt the ointment calm the angry welts across her narrow back.

"Why do you let him do this to you?" Mehret asked. Her voice was calm, without a trace of judgment.

"What can I do?" Antonia said.

"Leave him."

"It is not so easy. I am illegal. He knows my story. He says he will get me deported and keep my son."

"There must be a way," Mehret said. "Can you talk to your teacher, the old friend you told me about?"

Antonia only shook her head.

Twenty-Three

I HEADED INTO the campus restaurant, my backpack heavy on my right shoulder. It was a small room holding a half dozen tables with windows along two sides that opened to the rain-soaked flower gardens. I preferred the corner table with its view of the walkways, of students—entering and leaving the adjacent cafeteria, heading across campus to my building. That's how I saw it: my college, my building, my office. After more than a decade of teaching here, it was my home, a place where I felt appreciated, if not always by my co-workers or the administration, always by the students. Not a day went by when a student, present or past, didn't stop me for a chat, to tell me of his or her progress or to thank me for the guidance I'd provided. I'd smile and offer my congratulations, often unable to attach a name to the face before me. The faces I never forgot, but the names were erased the day each quarter ended. A clean slate waited for the next quarter to begin. The only names I could ever remember were those of the students sitting before me in the classroom.

I approached the hostess of the campus restaurant, a Somali student I'd helped navigate into the Culinary Arts program a few years prior, I struggled to find her name in the recesses of memory. Aliya? Amina? Aziza?

"Hello, Teacher. Can I help you today?" she asked.

"Can I have the corner table, please?"

"Of course. Will you be dining alone?"

"No, a friend will be joining me. I'll wait a few minutes until she arrives. How are you? How's the program?" I asked as she led me to the table. I listened as she told me about her progress and recent job interviews. "Have you had the opportunity to do a job shadow?" I asked.

"Job shadow? What's that?"

"You spend time on the job with someone in your field so you can get a good idea of what the work is like. In your case, you'd spend a few hours a week following a chef in one of the fancy restaurants downtown or in the kind of environment where you'd like to find employment when you graduate. Have you done anything like that?"

"No. I've never heard of such a thing. It sounds like a great idea. Oh, excuse me," the student said, looking over her shoulder towards the entrance where a small group had formed. "I must get back to work."

"Okay then, good luck to you." I sat alone going over the ideas I wanted to discuss with Gemi.

"Some serious planning going on, I see."

"Hey, Gemi. Thanks for meeting me here on campus."

"I've heard wonderful things about the Culinary Arts program here, so the pleasure is all mine, I assure you," Gemi said.

"They do pretty well. Everything from preparation to service is done by students. It's all part of the curriculum."

"What a wonderful idea, isn't it now?" Gemi said. "On-the-job training. A bit like the job shadowing you mentioned on the phone."

At that moment a waitress approached, another former student whose name escaped me. To my surprise, Gemi and the young woman began speaking like old friends in a language I didn't understand. A few moments passed before the former student said, "I'm sorry, Teacher, we'll speak English now. Can I get you something to drink?"

"It's quite all right. That was Amharic, wasn't it?"

"Yes, now what would you both like?"

"Tea for me, please," Gemi said with a smile.

"For me as well. Thank you. We need a minute or two to look at the lunch menu." After the student had left, I asked Gemi, "How did you know?"

"That the young woman is Ethiopian?"

"Yes."

"The features, the smile, the way she carried herself perhaps. I simply knew. It's like recognizing what you learn first. I left Ethiopia many years ago, but still I remember. And as you know, I visit now and again."

"I imagine you learned in a few minutes what I wouldn't know after a quarter or two as her instructor."

"Perhaps," Gemi said with a laugh. "But if it makes you feel a bit better, according to your former student, you are an excellent teacher. Demanding, but fair, honest and supportive, just as I always thought!"

"Spying on me? How unfair."

Gemi only laughed at my mock shock as the student/waitress returned and placed a small brightly colored teapot–pink for Gemi, yellow for me–in front of each of us. I fingered the lid of my pot, tracing the edges and remembering another sunflower yellow teapot.

"So tell me about this idea of yours," Gemi said after the waitress jotted down our order.

"Okay, so here's the deal. I'd like to set up a job shadowing program for the upper level ESL students. And it looks like I might have some administrative support."

"Tell me more."

"We're always asking students to identify their goals, but many of them have no idea what working in a particular career looks like here in the U.S. Loads of them are making choices based on where they think they can find jobs, or on what their friends or family tell them to do rather than on any real knowledge."

"I suppose that could lead to some unhappy, unsuccessful students," Gemi said.

"Exactly. And a lot of dropouts, when they get a sense of what's involved to reach their professed goals."

"So this program of yours might be a solution."

"A start, anyway. The idea would be to find employers in different fields willing to allow some carefully placed job shadowing. I'd like to start with nursing."

"Why?" Gemi asked.

"A few years ago the college started a nursing program. Now it seems everybody wants to be a nurse. Maybe some of them will be great nurses. Others, I think, might be happier in other careers. I want them to have the chance to get some real-world experience." I blew on my tea and took a sip. "And because I know you."

Gemi smiled.

"We could do a pilot. I place one student with you. You let her tag along for as many hours as you're willing to put up with her. I suppose we'll need to establish a certain number of required credit hours and all that, but for now I only need to know if you're open to the idea."

"I see no reason why not, my friend. Who knows, perhaps I might find myself an assistant or two and expand my business."

"That's the spirit," I said.

"I'm guessing you might already have a student in mind for this pilot?"

"I sure do. Remember the student I told you about, the one who reminds me of Antonia?"

"Indeed."

"Turns out she's working as a certified nursing assistant and wants to get into the licensed practical nursing program here. She'll probably be a great candidate, but somehow I'm not sure it's the best choice for her."

"Why might that be?"

"She's a natural teacher. I've watched how she breaks things down and explains them to her classmates when I give them group projects. She's become the go-to person whenever anyone has a question. At break time there's always a few students asking her for help."

"So she says she is interested in nursing, but you believe she should consider teaching?"

"Something like that."

"And you would like me to show her the world of home healthcare?"

"Right."

"To convince her it is not for her."

"No, not at all Gemi. I just want her to see what nursing is all about. Maybe she already knows. Maybe she doesn't. But before she spends two or three years of her life and way too much of her money to earn a degree, I'd like her to be certain her heart is in it. Does that make sense?"

"Absolutely, my dear friend. And I would be more than happy to meet with this student of yours and sort out a job shadow schedule."

"Thank you, Gemi."

"You are passionate about your work with these students," Gemi said, her voice little more than a whisper.

"Passionate? I don't seem to feel much passion for anything these days, but yes, they're still my life," I said. "Sorry. That's a bit melodramatic."

"No apology necessary, I assure you."

We ate lunch and outlined a job shadowing plan that involved a student spending a few hours once or twice a week with Gemi, watching and journaling about her experiences.

I walked Gemi to her car after lunch. "I'll talk to Carmen tomorrow and find out if she's interested. If so, I'll have her call you before the end of the quarter. Does that sound okay?"

"That would be fine."

"Thanks for agreeing to try this with me, Gemi. I truly appreciate it."

"My pleasure," she said. "Shall we walk this afternoon?"

"Sounds good," I said. "See you later."

Twenty-Four

THE PASSENGER VAN stopped at the mall entrance on a gloomy gray December day. Antonia and Mehret stood at the foot of the steps, hands extended to each of the dozen elders who wobbled and hobbled down at a snail's pace, some with canes, others with folded walkers in tow. Under the striped awning outside the double doors, they clustered in a tight group, permed white hair, festive red and green holiday sweaters, walkers and canes decorated with ribbons and bells. They hadn't come to shop. Today they were here on a mission and they were ready.

Preparations had begun the day after Thanksgiving, an idea hatched in the break room when Antonia asked Mehret about her holiday plans and schedule for December. Both would be working. Neither could afford time off for the holidays. Somehow the conversation wandered to family customs, foods, music. They talked of the American tradition of Christmas caroling, how much they both enjoyed singing, how few songs either of them knew in English.

"They will teach us if we ask," Antonia said.

"You're right. They are always teaching us," Mehret said.

"They love to teach us," Antonia added. The women laughed, both having fallen victim to the tactless grammar and pronunciation corrections provided by the residents.

"We can put together a collection of songs and ask Mrs. Farley if she will accompany us," Mehret suggested.

"Mrs. Farley is a retired music teacher, isn't she? I'm sure she'll help us."

"We can invite everybody to sing. Then we can find out who wants to go mall caroling."

"What?" Antonia said. "Mall caroling?"

"Sure. Mall caroling. We'll drive the van to the mall and take a group caroling," Mehret said.

"*De veras?*"

"Sure. Come on Carmen, it'll be fun."

Neither Antonia nor Mehret ever looked forward to the responsibility of supervising outings, too much could go wrong. But the residents loved to go out, so they did their best to make every field trip an adventure. This time took more planning than usual. They photocopied a number of holiday songs and asked Mrs. Farley to lead the group at the piano. Then they asked the residents to teach them the songs. Everyone was thrilled with the daily practices and they loved teaching Antonia and Mehret, as well as correcting each other whenever someone forgot a word here or there or went off key. The halls and mealtimes filled with humming and laughter.

One day about two weeks into the daily practice routine, Mehret suggested a trip to the mall for caroling.

"Can we do some shopping, too?" one woman asked.

"Can our friends come?" asked a man with a non-resident lady friend.

"But how can we sing without the piano?" asked a third.

That stopped them. But Mrs. Farley showed them her pitch pipe, blew a note, and they all broke into a rowdy rendition of "Deck the Halls." When the song, the laughter, the clapping ended, she said, "That is how we do it," in the voice of a middle-school music teacher, and the deal was sealed.

Now a group clustered in front of the mall entrance, nervous, excited, and ready. The mall door slid open and they began the slow progression. A brilliant excess of flowing garlands, gigantic wreaths and sparkling trees greeted them at every turn. In front of each tree, they sang. At each intersection of hallways, they sang. In front of each large store, they sang. They sang with all their might to the gathered shoppers, from tiny children to parents, grandparents, and babysitters. Even the vendors looked up and listened to the colorful group of elderly singers.

Antonia watched and laughed and sang until her throat felt raspy. When they reached the food court, they all collapsed into plastic chairs, exhausted and happy. The mall vendors offered complimentary coffee and tea and the residents glowed like celebrities.

Rested, Antonia and Mehret gathered the group for the walk back to the van. They moved through the mall side by side, tracking the residents. "It's good none of them is quick," Mehret said. "Imagine doing this if they were as active as three-year-olds."

Antonia gave a small laugh, her eyes alert, her surveillance keen despite her distraction.

"You're thinking about something else." Mehret gave her a slight nudge with her shoulder as though trying to redirect her attention.

"I'm sorry," Antonia said. "Yes, I am thinking about my final composition. I must turn it in on Friday."

"For Carolyn?"

Antonia nodded.

"Do you have a topic yet?"

"That's the thing," Antonia said. "Oh, *un momento*. Mr. Jones, let's not go into Victoria Secret today." She jogged a few steps to steer the old man and his walker past the bright pink awning and lingerie-clad mannequins. Then she turned back to Mehret as though the conversation had not been interrupted at all. "I'm thinking about writing the truth."

"The truth that you are the Antonia she once knew in Los Arboles?"

"Yes. The truth that I am Antonia Carmen Santiago Meléndez." It was almost a whisper, the chanting of a name that carried the weight of generations. "And maybe I will tell her more."

"Why now?"

"She's been good to me—both then and now. Did I tell you about the job shadow she set up for me?"

"The what?" Mehret asked.

"Job shadow. Carolina arranged for me to spend a few days with a home healthcare provider. A woman named Gemila Kemmal."

"An Ethiopian like me."

"Yes, I think so, but she has many years here and she has her own business taking care of people in their homes. I'll learn by watching how she works."

"And someday you'll have your own business and you'll give me a better job," Mehret said.

"*Seguramente,*" Antonia said with a laugh. "But first I need to write this composition and tell Carolina the truth. I want to say thank you so much to her. And I do not want to lie to this Gemila when I meet her on Monday. I do not like the lies."

They reached the mall entrance and the waiting van. Mehret and Antonia helped each of their elders to a seat. The ride back was quiet, everyone exhausted. Antonia and Mehret spoke quietly together in a shared seat at the back.

"It is good," Mehret said picking up their conversation again. "Write your truth for your teacher friend and you will feel better."

"Thank you, Mehret. I will write the first draft tonight after my son goes to bed. But I am very nervous to tell my story, to put it all on paper. Maybe she will show someone. Maybe she will get me in trouble."

"She won't! From what you tell me, she will do nothing to harm you."

Twenty-Five

I SAT IN MY CAMPUS OFFICE, a teacup to the right, a stack of student papers to the left, determined to get through the last bunch of final compositions before heading home for the weekend. I played games with myself, organizing the papers based on assumptions formed through a quarter of reading weekly compositions. I wanted a sequence of difficult-easy-difficult-easy. I didn't want to read all the easy papers first and then find myself struggling through an endless pile of difficult ones when I was tired. Easy? Easy to read, few grammatical errors, some originality, a clear voice. Difficult? Full of grammatical errors and typos, frustrating to correct or even to decipher the student's intended meaning.

My computer was open to Engrade, the online grade book I used for record keeping and grade reports. The chair beside my overcrowded desk held the short stack of papers I'd already finished.

I clicked in another grade, stood and stretched, arms high to the ceiling then down to the floor. Not even halfway yet and already 4:32 p.m. Another late night at the office. I wasn't about to take these papers home, and I'd promised the students they could stop by my office on Monday to pick them up along with their final grade for the quarter. I'd decided years before that I wouldn't take work home. I needed the separation. I didn't want a home office like Gemi. I needed to leave work at work even if it meant a few late nights and a few Saturdays on campus.

I sat back down and lifted the next paper from the top of the stack. Carmen's–an easy paper. Pen in hand I settled.

You do not remember me, but I always remember you. You helped me when I was alone and had no home ...

I dropped my pen, all thought of editing gone. I read of that time long ago, of the broken teapot, of the migration north.

... but maybe you do remember. Maybe you are still mad at me, but I want to say thank you for then and for now.

"But I was never angry with you," I told the composition. "I was never mad." I sat and stared at the paper. How could I not have known? Eleven weeks she kept her secret and I was too stupid to figure it out.

I flipped open the folder that held the questionnaires I'd asked the students to fill out on the first day of the quarter and flipped through to find Antonia's. I scanned for a phone number, an email address, even a street address—all either missing or incomplete in one way or another. I glanced at the clock and punched in the phone number for the department office. "I need contact info on a student."

"Sure. Do you have an ID number?"

I read the number from the top of the paper, glad I always required both name and student ID number in the heading. Names can so easily be confused. One quarter I had four students, all with the name Nguyen. From that moment forward, I used ID numbers as a backup.

"Sorry, Carolyn," the student worker said. "There's no email and the phone number is missing a digit. The mailing address is a postal box. Would you like that?"

"Thanks anyway," I said and hung up. Antonia made it impossible for anyone to track her. Brilliant. But now what do I do? I grabbed the phone again.

"You've reached Gemila Kemmal. Please leave a message."

"Crap," I muttered again before the click. "Call me as soon as you can, Gemi. Thanks."

I stood, stretched again, tried to clear my mind. I can deal with this later, I told myself. Gemi will have contact information if Antonia's called her about job shadowing. If not, I'll have to wait until she comes in next week. If she comes in next week.

I've got to finish these damn papers. I coaxed myself back into my desk chair and was correcting the last composition when my cell rang. I saw Gemi's name.

"You're not going to believe this, Gemi."

"And hello to you as well, my friend," Gemi said.

"It was her all along."

"Her?"

"Her. Antonia. Carmen is Antonia."

"I'm sorry, Carolyn, but it's been a long day. Let's slow down and start again."

I took a breath and explained what happened.

"Oh, my. You had your suspicions, didn't you?" Gemi said.

"Yeah, can you believe it? Carmen is her middle name. After years of migratory field work, she bought a false ID using her mother's maiden name."

"Oh my, poor child."

"She recognized me right away, but she was afraid to say anything to me."

"Why would she be afraid?"

"Because of the damn broken teapot. I need to talk to her. Today was our last class, so if she doesn't stop by Monday to pick up her papers, I'm afraid I won't see her again. I tried to get her contact information, but it isn't on file with the college. Do you know how to reach her?"

"I am afraid I do not. She said she did not have a cell phone or a landline. I thought it odd, but we made arrangements to meet on Monday anyway. I'll be picking her up in front of the college at 11:00 a.m."

"Oh no, I have to be available to meet with students from nine to noon."

"Perhaps that's just as well, Carolyn. Let me have a chance to meet the young woman alone, allow the job shadow to follow its course. I'll see what I can find out about her and I'll make a plan for another day of job shadowing. That way if she doesn't meet with you before I see her on Monday and if she doesn't come to campus to see you on Tuesday, we will still have another opportunity."

"I don't want to interrupt your plans, but I really want to talk to her."

"You've waited a long time, a bit more won't hurt, will it my friend?"

I looked at the finished papers on my chair. "Lord, what am I going to do all weekend to distract myself?" I said.

"We can think of something. Certainly a walk tomorrow. Maybe a movie?"

"What would I do without you, Gemi?" I hung up the phone, smiling. It would be hard to wait. I'd waited so long.

Twenty-Six

SHE COULD DO IT TOMORROW. She was too nervous to stop by and pick up her grades from Carolina today. She accompanied her son to school like she always did and then went to the campus library. Gemila had told her she'd pick her up in front of the college, to be out front at the bus stop at eleven.

At quarter to eleven, Antonia found a restroom. She dabbed on more concealer to hide the bruise on the left side of her face. It didn't help.

As soon as she climbed into the car, Gemila noticed. "What happened, Carmen?"

"Nothing," Antonia said. "My son. It was an accident."

Antonia feared Gemila saw right through her boldfaced *mentira*. She didn't want to lie to this wonderful woman who was offering her such an opportunity. She knew that by job shadowing Gemila, she could gain both the experience and the recommendation she needed to get into the college nursing program. She wasn't sure if home health was the direction she wanted her career to take, but Gemila was giving her the chance to find out. If it turned out well, she might even get a job offer. But now she'd lied. Two lies–her name and her face.

As they drove across town, Gemila briefed her on the first client they'd be visiting: a wheel-chair bound, elderly woman. The work involved supervised bathing and physical therapy exercises, some light housework and cooking. "And a whole lot of visiting," Gemila said. "Many of my clients need someone to talk with. They're alone. They insist they want to stay in their own homes, but in many cases their children are living at some distance, or as in the case of Mrs. Newbury, there were no children, and now there is no family at all."

"So sad," Antonia said.

"Yes. That is why we provide the needed services, including much visiting and listening. At the same time we must have open eyes. We watch for changes, for possible problems that could arise."

Gemila did not see herself as a hospice nurse. It was true her services allowed her clients to remain in their own homes beyond the bounds of solitary safety. But she didn't limit her practice to end-of-life care. As she explained to Antonia, she also provided in-home care for those who needed assistance during the post-surgical rehabilitation period when the most basic tasks of bathing, cooking, and cleaning were impossibilities.

Antonia took notes, determined to learn as much as possible from this experienced nurse who was willing to let her tag along.

By the time Gemila parked in front of a hilltop home overlooking Puget Sound, Antonia thought she understood care levels and what would be in store when she was introduced. How wrong she was.

"Here?" Antonia asked, her voice little more than a whisper.

"Yes, here."

"So beautiful." Without thinking, Antonia began to massage her left shoulder. She stopped herself when she caught Gemila's sideways glance.

She hesitated before getting out of the car, feeling suddenly inadequate and fearful. The home that stood before her was so very different from the tiny rundown apartment she shared with her man and son, their neighborhood more akin to a third-world nation.

"It is all right," Gemila said. "It is simply a fancy house and a lonely old woman. Nothing more. Come now. She needs our assistance."

Antonia watched as Gemi lifted a large woven bag from the back seat and followed her to the gracious front door. She was surprised to see the keys Gemila used to enter the house.

"It is easier this way," Gemila said. "Mrs. Newbury has limited mobility. Sometimes I find her in bed. Trust must be established before keys are given."

Antonia cringed. Did Gemila know already what a *mentirosa* she was?

A well-dressed woman in a wheelchair greeted them in the foyer.

"It is a good morning, I see," Gemila said, a broad smile on her face. "I've brought a new assistant with me today. Mrs. Newbury, I'd like to introduce you to Carmen Meléndez. She is a student at the college, and with your permission, she'll be joining me on my visits."

"Come here, girl," Mrs. Newbury said.

Antonia approached.

"Closer," the old woman commanded.

Antonia obeyed until her ankles knocked the footpads of the wheelchair. To her surprise, Mrs. Newbury leaned toward her, grasped her left wrist, and jerked her forward.

"Ouch." It escaped her lips before she could stop it. It escaped her lips in the nanosecond it took for the pain to shoot through her shoulder. It escaped her lips and she pulled back. A reflexive action that only compounded the pain. Tears came to her eyes. Her right hand flew to her left shoulder.

"For goodness sakes, girl, what in tarnation is the matter? Gemi, see to that girl. I'll be in the kitchen when you're finished." With a huff, Mrs. Newbury rolled out of the foyer leaving Antonia alone with Gemila.

"I am sorry," Antonia said. "I'll wait outside." She headed to the door.

Gemila stopped her with a touch on her right shoulder. "This side is all right, is it not?"

"Yes."

"Tell me, child," Gemila said, her voice a quiet mix of gentle concern and stern command. "No lies this time."

"Most times he only hits me or kicks me," Antonia said. "But last night ..." She broke into sobs unable to finish, her head swimming in anguish.

"Come, Carmen," Gemila said and led her into the powder room off the foyer. "Now show me where you are injured."

"Here," Antonia said, pointing to her left shoulder.

When Gemila fingered the spot she indicated, Antonia winced. "Will you let me examine it, child?"

"I think maybe it is dislocated," Antonia said, her tongue stumbling over the syllables of the word she'd learned in one of her CNA classes.

"Will you show me?" Gemila repeated.

Antonia unbuttoned her shirt one slow button at a time, her man's dress shirt, the only thing she was able to put on that morning. She slid the shirt from her left shoulder and stood before the older woman.

"Now I'm going to feel your shoulder, child. I will try not to hurt you." Again pain shot through Antonia's body and stole her breath away as Gemila attempted to finger her shoulder.

"We're going to the hospital." Gemila said. "Now."

"No. I cannot go," Antonia said.

"You must. Your shoulder needs medical attention."

"You can fix it, no?"

"I am not a doctor, Carmen. I believe your shoulder is dislocated and there may be other damage as well. You need a doctor."

"I cannot go," Antonia insisted.

"Do you have medical insurance?" Gemila asked.

"No, only my husband and son have."

"Then we must call your husband."

"No." Antonia didn't mean to scream, but the sound reverberated in the small powder room. She could not call her man. She could not face his rage again, the rage she knew would follow any utterance of agony, any complaint. A hospital visit was impossible. Too many questions, too many forms to fill out, too many bills to pay.

Gemila was quiet. Antonia could feel her eyes, her fingers on the welts, sores, and scars across her back. When she felt Gemi place her shirt back over her shoulders, she began with the top button and worked her way down in silence.

"Come, child. I know a place." Gemila opened the door and Antonia followed her into the kitchen where the old lady was waiting in her wheelchair.

"Well?" she said.

"I apologize for the inconvenience, Mrs. Newbury, but I must take this young woman to see a doctor immediately. Shall I return later this afternoon?"

"A bit unprofessional if you ask me," the old woman huffed.

"Perhaps," Gemila said. "But she is also young and injured. I'll return as soon as possible. In the meantime let's make sure you've taken your meds."

"I can take care of myself. I've been doing it for eighty-seven years. You get that girl to a doctor and make sure whoever's beating her is stopped."

Antonia gasped. "How you know this?" She slapped her hand over her mouth as though trying to push the words back in.

"Ha, I knew it," Mrs. Newbury said. "You don't live as long as I have without learning a few tricks along the way. Now, why in tarnation would a beautiful young woman like you stay with a man who does this to you?"

Antonia looked at the floor, shifting her weight back and forth, left, right, left, right. "*Mi hijo*," she said, unsure how much to tell this stranger. "I have one son."

"Divorce the man. Keep the son. Easy."

"He'll take my son."

"Not if you have proof of physical abuse. Which you'll have today when Gemi gets you in to see a doctor."

"I cannot do this," Antonia said. Tears filled her eyes. Pain? Fear? Gratitude for the concern of these older women who knew nothing about her?

"Come," Gemila said. "First we'll see a doctor. The rest comes later."

"Don't worry about coming back today, Gemi," Mrs. Newbury said. "I'll be fine for one day."

Antonia sat in the passenger seat holding her left shoulder as Gemila drove back across the West Seattle Bridge and into the city. All pretense, all attempts to hide her suffering were gone, all that remained was worry.

"I have no money for a doctor," she said again, this time in little more than a whisper.

"I know a place, child. Do not worry about money," Gemila told her.

"But, *mi esposo*," Antonia said.

"Your husband did this to you."

"You speak Spanish?"

"A lucky guess, child. Now tell me the truth. Has your husband beaten you before?"

"Yes."

"You mentioned a son. Do you have other children?"

"No. Only one son."

"Where is he now?"

"At school. First grade."

"Do you pick him up or does your husband?"

"I get him every day at three-thirty."

"Okay, we will see the doctor first, and then we will decide what to do."

"Do?"

"Yes. Has your husband ever hurt your son, Carmen?" Gemila's voice was calm but firm as though Antonia were on the Aurora Bridge ready to jump.

"No," Antonia said. "*No creo.*"

"*Creo?*"

"I do not think he hurt Carlitos. Sometimes he yells loud and makes him cry. Sometimes he shakes him too much, and I take him away. Then he hits me."

"Carlitos? Like your teacher, Carolyn," Gemila said.

"Yes," Antonia said. Nothing more.

"Carlitos is not safe, Carmen. The violence escalates. Do you understand?"

"Yes. He gets worse day by day."

"That is the way of domestic violence, child. Carlitos is not safe. You are not safe."

The sign on the front of a small building read Community Clinic.

"Come, Carmen," Gemila said. "I know the doctors here. They will help you."

At 3:30 p.m. Gemila wedged her car among a line of others crowded in front of an elementary school. She turned to face Carmen, her left arm now taped tightly to her body in a protective sling.

"Act normal, child. Pick up your son as you do every day. Say nothing at all. If anyone asks about your arm, tell them you had an accident at work. No details. Just get Carlitos and his things. All of his things. Do you understand?"

"Yes, Gemila. I understand."

"We become what we believe ourselves to be, child," Gemila told her as she turned to get out of the car.

But Gemila didn't know, Antonia thought as she walked into Carlitos's school. Gemila didn't understand a life of secrets and lies. Gemila didn't live with Antonia's man.

Five minutes later Antonia walked back to the car holding hands with a curly haired little boy with bright brown eyes clutching a stuffed puppy to his tiny chest. She opened the back door and helped Carlitos climb into the booster seat Gemila had borrowed from the Community Clinic. Antonia introduced Carlitos to Gemila and answered the child's questions in a mix of English and Spanish. Introductions complete, Gemila turned the ignition and started to back out of the parking space. Then she stopped and turned off the engine.

Antonia watched as Gemila took another look at a small handwritten card the doctor had given her. Then she twisted around to get a cell phone from the large woven bag on the floor behind the driver's seat.

"I think it best I call first," the older woman said.

"Call where, Gemila?"

"Please call me Gemi, child. Now to answer your question, it is called a safe house."

"A safe house?" Antonia echoed. "What is this, Gemi?"

"It is a place where nobody—most important, your husband—will know where you are."

"But what about my job? My school?"

"You must decide. Do you go home or do you go into hiding? If you go into hiding, I will call the college and your employer. I will tell them you had a family emergency and you will be back as soon as possible, but you must not contact anyone or tell them where you are."

"How long?" Antonia asked.

"I do not know, child. We will need to contact an attorney."

"Attorney?" Antonia asked. "My husband, he is an attorney."

"Yes, but perhaps it is best to find another attorney."

Antonia couldn't help smiling at the sly twinkle in the older woman's eyes.

"Now, first let me call this number and make the arrangements," Gemi said.

Antonia turned to the backseat as best she could and played quietly with her son while Gemi made the call. "Waitlist?" she heard. "My word, so long," she heard. "Thank you," she heard. When Gemi snapped her phone closed, Antonia faced her, her eyebrows raised in question.

"It appears they have no space. They said that without a police report it is highly unlikely we will be able to find a space in any domestic violence shelter in the city. There are not enough beds, it seems."

Antonia remained quiet. She imagined removing her arm from the sling, untaping it from her torso. She figured she could leave her shoulder taped. Her man would not see if she wore a long loose shirt. Maybe she and Carlitos could be sleeping before he got home tonight, maybe he would not be drunk, maybe it would be a good evening. She wasn't aware Gemi had backed out of the parking space and was driving. Was it really the same day, she thought? Could so much have happened, so many secrets have been revealed in only a single day? She glanced at her watch. "Oh, no," she gasped. "If he comes home and there is no food ready he will be mad. Maybe he won't come home tonight."

"Do you want to go home, child?" Gemi asked.

"I have no other place," Antonia said.

"I would like you and Carlitos to come home with me," Gemi said. "Would you like to do that?"

"Why do you do this for me, for us?" Antonia asked. "Why are you so good person?"

"You need help, child. We all need help at different times in our lives. Long ago, a wonderful nurse helped me see that life was worth living even when I had lost all I cherished. It is my turn to help you. Would you like my help?"

"Yes," Antonia said. "Yes, please."

"All right, but you must make one promise."

"Yes?" Antonia asked.

"You must promise me you will not tell your husband where you are or who you are with. You must give him no information that would enable him to find us. Do you understand?"

"Yes."

"Do you promise, child?"

"Yes, Gemi. I promise I will tell no one."

"Okay then, you will use my cell phone. You will call him now and you will tell him you and Carlitos are safe, but you will not be returning home. Tell him you will call again within the week."

Gemi maneuvered into an empty spot at the side of the road and passed Antonia her cell phone from the console between the seats where she'd placed it.

Antonia took the phone from Gemi's outstretched hand and keyed in the numbers. As she left a message, he picked up.

"I told you never to call this number. What in the hell is wrong with you, you stupid bitch?"

Antonia repeated Gemi's words almost verbatim.

Gemi snatched the phone from her as her man's raging voice filled the car. She snapped it shut without a word, dropped it into her large woven basket on the floor of the backseat, and turned on the ignition.

"Let's go home, child," she said.

Twenty-Seven

THE KNOCK STARTLED me from my book. Gemi? I checked the peephole to be sure before swinging the door open wide.

"This is urgent. May I come in?"

"Of course." I stood to the side and gestured Gemi into my living room, a space so different from her own it seemed odd they were both in the same house. Where Gemi had decorated her apartment with deep hues, straw baskets, and tapestries on wall and floor, some would say my lower level wasn't decorated at all. I left the walls white, the hardwood floors bare, and the furniture minimal. My bike stood in the corner next to a tall bookcase. The sofa of pale gray leather and chrome I'd found at a garage sale. But Gemi was as comfortable in my place as I was in hers. She followed me into the kitchen where I flipped on the lights and turned on the kettle.

"Sit. Sit," I told her. "What's going on?"

"A long story, my friend. So much to say I hardly know where to begin."

"What's it about?"

"Carmen," she said as we settled at my Formica kitchen table, another garage sale find.

"Did she do something wrong? Was the job shadow a disaster? Was she a no-show?"

"No, nothing like that. She was waiting at the designated time and place. She was shy, but well-mannered. A bit overwhelmed by Mrs. Newbury and her wealth, I believe."

"I can only imagine," I said with a laugh, well familiar with the type of clients who contracted for Gemi's in-home care. "I think I'd be uncomfortable, too."

"She's a lovely young woman, Carolyn."

"So what's the problem?"

"It's complicated. When I picked up Carmen, or shall I say Antonia, in front of the college, I immediately had my suspicions."

"Suspicions? What do you mean?" I asked.

"Have you never noticed bruises or excess makeup used to cover bruises?"

"I'm not the most observant person, you know that, especially when it comes to things like makeup or hair or clothes. You saw bruises?"

"That's not the half of it, my friend. Antonia is a victim of serious domestic abuse."

In her simple, straightforward tone, Gemi told me about the dislocated shoulder, the bruises and welts over Antonia's back and hips, about waiting at the Community Health Clinic, about the information from the domestic violence safe house. When the tea kettle clicked off, neither of us heard it.

"So you see, I had no choice. I had to bring them home with me," Gemi said.

"Them? What do you mean by them?"

"Antonia has a son. Did you not know this?"

"I had no idea until I read her composition on Friday," I admitted, ashamed at how little I knew, how little I observed. How could I have been so blind, so ignorant?

"Her son is in first grade. His name is Carlitos. Coincidence? I think not," Gemi said, a smile at the corners of her mouth.

"Oh, my," I said. "And you brought them home with you? You mean, they're here in your apartment? Now?" I was on my feet heading for the front door when Gemi dragged me back to the kitchen table.

"Wait. Not tonight. They've had a very hard day, Carolyn. I've put them to bed. Antonia is finally asleep with the help of some pain medication. Let them sleep."

"But I want to see her."

"You have waited fifteen years, my friend. You can wait until tomorrow. We don't want to disturb her tonight. Besides, she doesn't even know you are here or that I know who she is. We need to decide how to tell her this."

The kettle had clicked off so long ago, I clicked it back on and found the chamomile. Gemi watched as I squeezed honey into each cup and dropped in teabags.

"Mama Lucy would be so disappointed to know that you've succumbed to teabags and mugs. I have half a mind to write her a letter."

"You wouldn't dare," I said with a laugh as I filled the cups with hot water, set them on the table and slid back into my chair. "You know I've never been able to replace the teapot she gave me. Each visit she tells me to take one home with me, but I've yet to see one that speaks to me the same way."

"I know, my friend, I know."

"So what should we do about Antonia?" I asked.

"Let her sleep as late as she is able. She's safe. Perhaps for the first time in a long while. Let's not take that from her."

I nodded.

"When she and the child are awake, I will feed them a good breakfast, and then I will tell her you are both my friend and my neighbor."

"So she doesn't know anything?"

"No, I did not tell her. I only had her call her husband after promising me she would not reveal her whereabouts. There was no energy for anything more. Tomorrow is another day."

"I have to be in my office at eight tomorrow to meet with students. I won't be able to get out of there before ten."

"That should work well. Just give me a call when you leave campus. I'm sure you two will have much to talk about."

"It's going to be weird, you know. It's been so long," I said. "What else did you find out about this husband of hers? Couldn't you get her to call the cops? What about a restraining order?"

"I do not know much. Only that she is very frightened. She said he would have her deported. Didn't you once tell me when you met years ago you suspected she was undocumented?"

"It's amazing, but she's lived here all these years illegally. She told me in her composition. What a life. I wonder what we can do to help her besides hiding her from an abusive husband?"

"I shall call Antonio tomorrow. He will likely have some suggestions."

"That's right. He's active in immigration reform, isn't he?"

"Yes, he is quite involved. He might have some suggestions, and I believe he will want to meet with her. I'll give him a call while you two are visiting tomorrow. Now it is time we both get some rest." Gemi stood and walked to the door. "Good night, my friend," she said, and I closed the door behind her.

After Gemi left, I was wide awake. I couldn't sleep. Again I tried to remember each class, every interaction I'd had with Antonia over the last eleven weeks. I tried to understand my inability to recognize my old friend. But Gemi was right. I was being unfair to myself. Fifteen years had passed and Antonia was using a different name. Besides a class of thirty students limited individual interaction. What I knew of my students came through their writing and Carmen Meléndez had not revealed anything until that final composition.

It's odd though, I thought. How does one know someone, befriend someone who never really becomes a friend at all? We were friends, weren't we? Or had been? But can you be friends when you share little of yourselves, when you hold secrets? I never opened up either. I never shared my suspicions, my concerns, my heart. I never told Antonia about my past or why I wouldn't call my folks. I shared my home, but not myself.

So where do we go from here?

I lifted my backpack from the wall hook above my bike and took out Antonia's composition. Then I plopped down on the hard sofa and began to read again:

You do not remember me, but I will always remember you. You helped me when I was alone and had no home ...

The silence of night fell across my stark living room. *El Salvador*, I read. Had I walked the streets and visited the neighborhoods she hadn't seen since she was a child? *Undocumented*, I read. So many years living under the radar, of hiding and fear. How many of domestic violence? I learned more about Antonia in that short composition than I'd learned in the summer she'd shared my tiny cottage in Los Arboles, but still she shared nothing of the abuse she and her son were suffering. I shuddered as I put the composition back in my pack and headed to my bedroom. Tomorrow, I told myself. Tomorrow I will see my old friend.

Twenty-Eight

ANTONIA AWOKE WITH A START. "Carlitos? *¿Mi hijito?*" she whispered. Upright in bed, she glanced around the unfamiliar room. She saw her son curled under a fluffy comforter on a small fold-out bed in the corner. Relaxing into her pillow, she retraced the events that led her and her son to this attic bedroom in the home of a woman she had just met. Gemi. A faint smile formed as she took a deep breath and released it slowly. She fingered her shoulder, relieved the pain had eased, relieved she was not lying beside her man, relieved Carlitos was safe. Another breath reminded her of the mornings, the years of mornings, tainted by fear. Each day she had awoken holding her breath and hoping her man would leave before she had to get up and start her day. How long had she been holding her breath? How long had she feared the man whose bed she shared?

She pushed the thoughts from her mind to relish the relief she felt within the four walls of a stranger's apartment. She would never go back. She didn't want to go back, didn't want to put Carlitos or herself in any more danger. But what could she do? Where could she go? Again she shoved the thoughts and fears aside. It was too early to worry and too pleasant to let the fears intrude.

She slid from under the bed covers and tiptoed to the window. The heavy golden curtains slid open without a sound and winter sunlight flooded the room. She gasped at the view of the Cascade Mountains so close, as if she could reach out and grab a handful of snow through the attic window. She scrambled back to the warmth of the bed and watched the horizon as the sun rose over the mountain peaks changing the sky from pale pink to magenta to brilliant blue.

The morning quiet held her in its embrace. Perhaps she dozed. When she opened her eyes again, they met those of her little boy standing at the edge of the bed.

"*¿Donde estamos,* Mami?" the child asked, panic in his young voice.

"It's okay, *mi hijito*. You remember the nice woman who brought us here yesterday, don't you?" Antonia lifted her son into bed and snuggled him tight to her breast. "We're safe here," she murmured into his soft curls.

There were sounds of movement below them, and Carlitos startled. He looked into his mother's eyes, fear in his own. "Papi?" he asked.

"No, Carlitos," Antonia said. "That is Gemi. She's our new friend, okay? *Tu papa* will not come here."

Carlitos clung tight, a grip that told of terror Antonia hadn't perceived, buried as she was in her own fear. With newfound determination, she got them both out of bed. No matter what happened, no matter what she had to do, she would protect Carlitos, and she would never, ever go back to that man.

Wrapped in a bathrobe Gemi had laid out for her the night before, she crept down the attic stairs, Carlitos's hand tight in her own, and opened the attic door to the aroma of fresh coffee.

"Good morning," Gemi said. "I thought I heard you stirring up there."

For a moment Antonia didn't know what to say, how to act, even where to stand. As though able to read her mind, Gemi continued to speak. "Come Carmen, let me show you and Carlitos around. It's not much, but sufficient, I believe. This is the living room, of course. The bathroom, my bedroom, and office are down the hall, and the kitchen is right here. Please sit. Would you like coffee?"

"Yes, please," Antonia said.

"And for Carlitos?" Gemi asked.

"Milk or orange juice, please. I don't drink coffee," the child said, his voice filling the small kitchen with joy. The two women looked at each other and laughter reverberated through the bright room.

"All right then, milk for Carlitos and coffee for Carmen, or perhaps I should say, Antonia," Gemi said, her voice ending in the lilt of a question.

"How do you know this?" Antonia stammered.

"There's a little I know and much I do not know, child. Would you like milk or sugar in your coffee?"

"Milk, please. How you know my other name?"

"*Mi mami* has two names," Carlitos said as he accepted a small glass of milk from Gemi. "But she only uses Carmen. The other name is our secret."

"*Basta*, Carlitos." Antonia silenced her son.

"Other name?" Gemi asked. "What is your full name, child?"

"My name is Antonia Carmen Santiago Meléndez."

Antonia saw Gemi's eyes widen. Misinterpreting the source of surprise, she said, "Yes, it is a big name, no? I use Carmen Meléndez. I am not Kline because he did not marry me."

Carlitos finished his milk and slid from the chair. With eager curiosity, he went exploring.

At the table, Gemi asked Antonia, "Where are you from, child?"

"El Salvador, but my parents and me, we left when I was six years old. I have many years in United States. Most of my life."

"When did you enter the United States?"

"When I was seven years old. I remember because my birthday was in Mexico. Then we came to Texas."

"To Texas?"

"Yes, first Texas, then California. Then they were gone."

"Gone? I do not understand," Gemi said.

"It was an immigration raid. We worked in the fields. Immigration took them all away. All but me. I ran and hid and then I was alone for a long time."

"Until you met Carolyn," Gemi said.

Antonia stared at her. One breath, two, three. "How do you know this, Gemi?" she asked.

"Carolyn is my friend too, Antonia. You know, she arranged your job shadow with me."

Antonia nodded.

"We are friends as well as colleagues. I have known Carolyn for many years. In fact, this is Carolyn's house."

"Carolina's house?" Antonia asked. "I no … I don't understand."

"This house is divided into two apartments. Carolyn lives downstairs and she rents this upstairs apartment to me. We have lived in this manner for over a decade now."

For a few moments the only noise in the apartment was the musical pattering as Carlitos talked his way through Gemi's home.

"Why did you not tell Carolyn who you are, child?" Gemi asked.

"She did not know me. I thought she did not remember. Or maybe she was still mad at me." Antonia paused as though confused with the very words coming from her lips. "I never tell my secrets and now I tell you everything. Why do I do this? Why do I tell you my secrets?" There was something in the woman's gentle voice and manner that caused her secrets to flow like warm maple syrup, and once the flow began, there was no stopping it.

"Antonia," Gemi said, her voice a caress. "Carolyn was never angry with you and she never forgot you. When she saw you the first day of class, she told me how much you reminded her of the Antonia she knew in Los Arboles."

"¿*De veras?* Really?"

"Yes, child, she's told me all about your time together in Los Arboles and the broken yellow teapot. She always assumed you were undocumented. She didn't want to cause trouble for you by trying to find you. She knew there was a large raid in Los Arboles the day you left. She always hoped you had caught word and escaped with her students. Then, fifteen years later, you are sitting in her classroom, but with a different name and an older face. She was confused, but decided if you were Antonia and you wanted her to know, you would tell her. Then you wrote your composition."

Twenty-Nine

ANTONIA AND CAROLINA stood together as though they wanted to inhale the very essence of each other.

"Can I hug you? I don't want to hurt you."

Antonia shifted a bit to protect her shoulder and gave her old friend a long embrace.

"I should've known it was you. I did know, or some part of me knew, but I didn't want to let myself believe it could be true. I'm so sorry." Carolina stepped back and held her at arm's length. "It's you. It's really you."

"I am sorry, too. I did not tell you on the first day of class. I was afraid."

"Afraid! Why afraid? Afraid of what?" Carolina asked.

"Afraid you were still mad at me for leaving with no thank you, no explanation, no goodbye."

"I knew why you left, Antonia. I knew you had to leave. I hoped Juan Luis and his family took you with them. Whatever happened to them?"

"They went back to Mexico."

"And you stayed. Why? All these years and here you are. I can't believe it."

When Antonia thought about it later, replaying the events of the day in her mind as she lay in bed unable to sleep, she knew Gemi had been listening from the kitchen, waiting for the right moment to enter. Gemi walked into the living room with Carlitos at her side. As though planned, Antonia stepped forward, and taking Carlitos's hand in her own, she led him to face Carolina.

"*Hijito*, this is Carolina. This is Mami's friend. ¿*Recuerdas?*"

"*Sí,* Mami. You named me for your friend. Is this the friend you lost, Mami?"

"Yes, Carlitos," Carolina said. "I am your mother's friend, but she never lost me. We just misplaced each other for a while."

"Come, sit down," Gemi said. "Have some tea and biscuits."

"Biscuits?" Carlitos asked.

"Cookies, Carlitos," Carolina explained. "Tea and cookies are Gemi's all-occasion comfort food. Not to be refused. I bet she might even let you help her bake them sometime."

"Will you, Gemi? Please?"

"Of course, little one," Gemi told the child.

"But why do you call cookies biscuits, Gemi?"

"I suppose it is a word I learned long ago from a special person in a faraway place. I have never forgotten the person nor the word. Now come with me and I'll show you my magical oven."

The weak winter sun climbed the sky as Carolina and Antonia sat at the dining table and told their stories, piecing together the years of separation.

Gemi and Carlitos moved like shadows on the periphery. Every now and again Carlitos would come and climb on his mother's lap and wiggle for a bit before he got bored and went in search of Gemi. Once revealed, Antonia's truths–no legal status combined with domestic abuse–could be set aside, at least for a bit, at least long enough for them to reminisce and reconnect.

Antonia told of her years of migratory field work with Juan Luis and the others, of buying a false identity and becoming a certified nursing assistant, of her current job working as Carmen Meléndez with a fake green card.

Carolina spoke of her years traveling and teaching in Central America before settling in Seattle. They wondered at the thought that they might have walked the same sidewalks, seen similar sights and heard similar sounds, eaten the same foods, smelled the same fragrances of a world that remained only as traces buried deep in Antonia's childhood memories. It was a home she was taken from when she was only a bit older than her son, a homeland she'd never been allowed or able to revisit. For how would she get the money?

Even with money, how would she leave the United States without a passport? And where was home anyway? She knew no living soul. She had nothing in the land of her birth. No, America was her home now, even though the U.S. government didn't see it that way. This she explained to Carolina in the mixture of English and Spanish they'd developed years before in the tiny cottage in Los Arboles, though now that they'd both mastered the other's language, they no longer needed the combination.

"So you are good?" Antonia asked. "Good job? Good friends? Good home?"

"Yes, I've been lucky, a whole lot luckier than you, Antonia. I'm sorry."

"It is not your *culpa*. I made bad decisions."

"Your starting gate was set back way too far."

"Starting gate?" Antonia asked.

"You've faced challenges she has never had to face, child," Gemi said as she set a plate of sandwiches on the table between them.

"Right," Carolina said. "I remember back in Los Arboles when we first met I was blown away by the fact that you had survived alone for so long. You're tough, Antonia. You're a survivor. I can't even imagine that kind of strength. You'll get through this mess yet. You'll come out on top. I know it."

"But you forget, Carolina. I am still an illegal alien. That's what they call me. Alien. I must always hide and tell *mentiras*."

"*Mentiras* that harm nobody and keep you and Carlitos safe are good lies."

Antonia felt the tears fill her eyes. She wiped them away, swallowed the hurt, determined to show no weakness despite the bruises on her face, the sling and bandages that held her dislocated shoulder, the welts and scars that tracked her back. She didn't know if this haven would last, if this new friend and this rediscovered friend could keep her safe from Kline's violence or from deportation. What she did know was she would never allow Kline to touch her or her son again, and if she had to disappear and start over once again, she knew how.

They ate sandwiches and cookies, drank tea, and shared stories for hours, only vaguely aware of the passage of time. It was late afternoon when Gemi interrupted them. "Antonia," she said. "I need to tell you about a friend of mine."

"A very special friend," Carolina said, her smile so mischievous Antonia couldn't stop her laughter.

"All right then, I have a boyfriend," Gemi said, which only made Antonia and Carolina laugh harder.

Even Carlitos got into the act, dancing around the room singing "Gemi has a boyfriend. Gemi has a boyfriend."

"The point being, Antonio is an immigration rights attorney. I have taken the liberty of telling him what I know of your situation, child. He is interested in meeting you. I also told him you and Carlitos shall be staying in the attic room for as long as you choose. He'll be over this evening and perhaps he will know what steps are to be taken."

Antonia didn't answer. Faraway in a memory of place and time so remote she struggled to capture the details, a large family dined at a long rustic wood table: candles and white linen and a man who flew her through the air, a zooming airplane in his firm hands. "*Mañana me voy, preciosa. Nunca te olvides tu tío* Antonio."

"Antonia?" Gemi asked. "Are you all right, child?"

With a shake of her head the image was gone. "*Sí*, yes, I'm okay, Gemi. Antonio is the name of your *compañero*, your boyfriend?"

"Yes, would you be willing to speak with him? He might be able to help."

"Yes, thank you," Antonia said. "Thank you very much."

Thirty

WHEN THE DOORBELL RANG, Antonia was in the attic room with Carlitos and Gemi was in her kitchen. "I've got it," I called up to them and then opened the front door to greet Antonio. Cold December drizzle had settled over the city as darkness fell, but at the top of the stairs soft lamp-light filled Gemi's living room. The yellows and reds of the walls glowed.

When Gemi emerged from the kitchen, Antonio gave her a quick kiss on the cheek. "She's upstairs. Shall I call her?" Gemi asked. He nodded.

As Antonia and Carlitos descended the stairs and entered the living room, Antonio froze. His face drained of color. He staggered toward them, one step, two, before righting himself.

"Antonio, this is Antonia and Carlitos," Gemi said.

Antonia extended her hand to the older man, but Antonio hesitated.

"Antonio?" Gemi whispered.

"You look just like ..." he said. He fell silent and shook Antonia's hand. A spell broken, he regained his composure. The articulate, immigrant rights attorney reappeared. "What is your name?" he asked Antonia.

"Antonia Santiago."

"What is your full name?" he asked.

"*Soy* Antonia Carmen Santiago Meléndez."

As I watched, I could've sworn I saw Antonio flinch, as though he would again lose his polished composure. Instead he began a stream of questioning as though in a court room.

"*De* Kline?"

"No, I am not married. My husband calls it common law marriage, but I don't know ..." her voice trailed into silence.

"Gemi told me you are from El Salvador. Is that correct?" Antonio asked.

"Yes. I left San Salvador long ago with my parents, when I was six years old. I remember little of this homeland."

"Where are your parents now?" Antonio asked.

"I do not know. We were working the fields in California when *la migra* came and took them." Antonia's eyes filled with tears. "I was thirteen and all alone. I met Carolina and she helped me."

"Thirteen?" I said. "I thought you were fourteen. We had your *quinceañera* party."

Antonia's eyes dropped to the floor. Then she looked up. Her eyes bored into my own.

"*Otra mentira*," she said.

"Why would you lie about your age?" I asked.

"Because I was afraid you send me away or call the police or ... I do not know. You worried I was too young to be alone, so I made myself older."

I laughed. "You read me like a book."

"Come, sit down, all of you," Gemi said. "It seems you have much to discuss."

She led us to the living room and disappeared into the kitchen. I knew she'd be back in moments. I could already see the tray she'd soon set on the coffee table, heavy with a teapot, cups, and an assortment of the pastries she'd begun buying at the Salvadoran Bakery in West Seattle since the day she met Antonio.

"My apologies, Antonia. I have many more questions. Is that all right?" Antonio said. He scrutinized Antonia's face.

I watched a mystery unfold.

"Gemi said you are a good man and I can trust you. She said maybe you can help me. Is this true?" Antonia asked.

"Yes," he said.

"Okay," she said.

The interview continued. "What do you know about your name?" Antonio said.

"Carmen Meléndez is the name of my mother, and my father is Gustavo Santiago. Jeff Kline is the name of the father of Carlitos."

"Do you know why you carry the name Antonia?" he asked.

"Oh yes," Antonia said, a shy smile flashing across her face. "My mother told me she named me for her older brother. He was Antonio, like you, but I do not remember this person. He left San Salvador when I was very young."

For a moment the two stared at each other, a certain realization crept into Antonia's eyes.

From across the room, I saw the similarities in their faces: the wide forehead, the almond shaped eyes, the small nose.

Gemi entered the silent living room carrying the tray. She set it on the coffee table and looked from one face to the other, Antonio and Antonia unaware of her presence. She turned to me, a question in her eyes. I shrugged.

"I remember a dinner," Antonia said, a dreamlike quality to her voice. She spoke in Spanish, little more than a whisper. "I remember candles and a white table cloth and many people. I remember a man, not my father. He held me in his arms and said goodbye. My mother told me later, when I was older, that the man I remembered was my Tío Antonio. She said I had two names because one was for her brother and the other for her. She only had one brother, you see, and he was very special to her. When we came to America, she said we would find my Tío Antonio."

The unspoken question hung in the air, too fragile to put into words.

"When I walked into this room and you came down the stairs, the breath left my body. You look so very much like my sister Carmen. My apologies. I asked so many questions without properly introducing myself. My name is Antonio Meléndez."

Thirty-One

THE FOLLOWING MORNING, when Antonio returned to Gemi's apartment, Antonia was nervous. More was at stake. She'd spent the night thinking instead of sleeping, imagining possibilities. Perhaps she and Carlitos had family. Perhaps she could become a U.S. citizen. Perhaps she would no longer live in fear.

They settled at the dining table, just the two of them. Gemi stayed in the kitchen. Carolina played with Carlitos. She'd come up to Gemi's prepared with a stack of picture books, paints, an easel, and some small colorful blocks. Antonia smiled at her son's namesake, and turned her attention to the man sitting beside her. He pulled papers from a battered leather briefcase, so different from the one her man carried. Some of the papers were crumpled, yellowed, stamped.

"These, I believe, are your parents' birth certificates," he said. "And this is yours."

He handed her a piece of paper so tattered she feared her touch might reduce it to dust.

"Indeed, my sister named her only daughter after me. The dates coincide. You were born on May 7, 1983, correct?"

Antonia only nodded.

"I am convinced you are my sister's daughter."

Antonia couldn't breathe. "Are you sure?" she whispered.

"As certain as we can be without a DNA test," he said.

And then she asked the question she needed to ask, terrified of the response Antonio was sure to give her. "My parents?"

"I am very sorry, Antonia."

Her worst fears: certain truth. The torture and blood in so many daydreams and countless nightmares: real. "I must know," she said.

"Your parents were deported shortly after the raid that took them from you. The place and time match what you told me yesterday. These are the deportation papers." He showed her two papers.

Terror climbed her spine. "And?" she said. No longer aware of the space around her, she didn't notice Carolina carrying Carlitos to the attic room, or Gemi settling in the chair at her side. She didn't notice Antonio switching back to English.

"They were picked up at the airport. Executed a week later. It involved several trips back home, as well as a number of governmental changes, but I secured the documentation. I am so very sorry." He handed her two death certificates.

"They were tortured for a week." It was a statement, not a question. It was as though Antonia had been there and seen it all: the repeated brutal rapes and electric shocks, the beatings and blood. Antonio's silence confirmed her horror.

Carolina slipped back into the room where they sat in mourning. Antonia knew they waited for her, respecting her loss, allowing her the first word. "Now I know," she said as she dried her eyes with the tissue Gemi offered.

"Yes, child. Knowing the truth can be very powerful."

"Powerful?" Antonia asked.

"Antonio is your uncle, child," Gemi said. "Your family. Indeed, I wondered when I first heard your last name."

She'd been so focused on her parents, she'd forgotten her connection to this man who'd done so much to find his own sister.

"Yes," Antonio said. "You are my sister's daughter. You and Carlitos are my only living relatives. I promise I will do whatever it takes to protect you. There are two issues to be dealt with as soon as possible."

"You do not want the DNA test?" Antonia asked.

"That will not be necessary, Antonia. These papers are sufficient in any court of law. But in my heart—one look at your face told me you were family, my sister's daughter."

"Perhaps this will help too," Carolina said. She offered Antonia a small tattered dictionary. "You left this in Los Arboles."

"You kept it all these years?" Antonia asked.

Antonio leaned back and stared at the ceiling. *"Para mi hermana y su esposo con todo mi amor*, Antonio." He spoke the words slowly, each one carefully enunciated in Spanish as though it were his second language rather than his language of birth.

"Here on the first page." Antonia held out the dictionary to show Antonio.

"I gave them that dictionary the night I left, a joke, nothing more. Then the violence began and we lost contact." He shook his head, trying to relieve his own painful memories. "Now there is much to be done."

Antonia sat in a daze fingering the small dictionary. She tried to follow this new uncle as he outlined the steps he planned to take to put her on the path to citizenship, but it was all too much too fast. Could it be real?

"About the problem of Jeff Kline," he said. "I knew about Kline's work, but I did a bit of research last night. Antonia, Kline is married and has two other children."

Again Antonia's eyes filled with tears. "At first I thought all was beautiful. He loved Carlitos and me. He was good to us, but he did not want to marry me. He said common law was okay." Antonia turned her face to the wall. "I am ashamed."

Gemi patted Antonia's healthy shoulder careful to avoid the sling. "There is no shame, child. You were young, alone and in love. This man offered you security and promised his love. You trusted him. Do not punish yourself."

"And then he got angry. Many days he did not come home at all. Then he came home drunk."

"He did that to you?" It was the first mention of the arm bound to her chest in a tight sling.

"Yes," she said.

"Do you have any medical records?" Antonio asked.

"She has these," Gemi said. Antonia recognized the forms she'd signed at the Community Health Clinic.

"Only when Gemi took me."

Antonio read through the papers and smiled. "This is all we need."

Thirty-Two

I FIRST NOTICED it as I unchained my bike. It wasn't so unusual to see a black sedan in front of the college, but there was something out-of-place about the high gloss wax job and the tinted windows. As I rode home, pondering lesson plans, dinner ideas, and Christmas lists, I thought I saw it again, but reflected in my tiny helmet mirror I couldn't be sure it was the same car. I braked in front of my house. The shiny black sedan pulled to a stop behind me. I'd been followed.

I looked up and down the street. The place where I'd felt safe for years turned suddenly menacing. Houses lined both sides of the street, but I knew at this time of day most lay empty. I guessed who had followed me. The last thing I wanted him to know was which house was mine. I remembered the small Mexican restaurant at the corner. I ate there so often I knew the owner and servers. A place to run for help.

The car door swing open and a man step out. Tall, blond, square-shouldered, in a dark suit and shades, he could have been Secret Service. I almost laughed at the stereotype.

Squaring my own shoulders, I stared at him. "You're following me. Why?"

"Are you Carolyn Bauer?"

"Who's asking? And why?"

"I know who you are. Saw your picture on your class website. You're my wife's teacher."

"Jeff Kline." I stated the fact, nothing more.

"My wife and son are missing. I'm hoping you can help me find them." Kline stepped towards me. "Carmen Kline told me all about her teacher, Carolina, who helped her many years ago in California."

"Carmen?" I stalled, my thoughts flying in multiple directions. Did he realize I'd stopped in front of my own house? Did he already know about Gemi? Did he know that Antonia and Carlitos were inside? My god, I hope they don't look out the windows right now.

"Carmen," Kline said. He took another step towards me.

"If you wanted to find me, why didn't you go to Administrative Services instead of following me like some kind of stalker?"

"Here's my card." With the excuse of handing me the business card, he moved into touching range.

I accepted the card and stepped back, dragging my bike along with me, keeping it between us. "You're an attorney with ICE."

"Yes, and I believe you know where my wife and son are."

"Wife? From what I understand your wife's name is Ginger and you have two daughters. What do you want with Carmen? Need a punching bag? Aren't getting enough of a workout at the gym?" I knew I'd gone too far. I could see his anger rise, a red flush across his white face, a clenching and unclenching of his large fists.

"I want Carmen and I want my son, Ms. Bauer. Abduction is illegal."

I swung my leg over my bike and clipped my foot into the pedal. "As is harboring an undocumented woman to use as a punching bag."

"God damn you. You know where Carmen is, and by god, you're going to tell me." He grabbed my handlebars. I could smell his anger, his sweat, the booze on his breath.

"Or what? You're going to beat the crap out of me like you do to her? This conversation is over. Take your hands off my bike. If you follow me, I'll go straight to the precinct office on 12th Avenue. I'm no attorney, but I know a threat when I hear one, and I know the definition of stalking."

A raging bull, he still gripped my handlebars. "You tell that bitch she can't get away so easy. I'll have her deported so fast she won't know what happened." He spat on the ground inches from my foot and turned back to his car.

I trembled as I rode off, trying to show confidence I didn't feel. I watched my mirror to be sure Jeff Kline drove away in a different direction. I pedaled down the street several blocks, and turned into an alley. I rode a fast, haphazard pattern through the neighborhood checking every few seconds to be sure I wasn't being followed. Convinced I was alone, I veered into a grocery store parking lot. I dug my cell from my backpack and called Gemi.

"Where are you?" I asked as soon as I heard her voice.

"I'm right here in the kitchen."

"And Antonia and Carlitos?"

"They're upstairs. Antonio will be here shortly. Are you okay?"

"Close the curtains, Gemi. Keep them away from the windows."

"What happened, Carolyn?" Gemi asked.

"He found me. He followed me home. Kline."

"Oh, no."

"I don't know if he realized we were right in front of our house. He threatened me and I rode off to make it look like I didn't live there."

"Where are you now, my friend?"

"In the QFC parking lot. I'm okay. He didn't follow me after I told him I'd go straight to the cops, but he's scary, Gemi. I mean, really scary. I'm going to ride in circles a bit to make sure he isn't lurking around somewhere. Keep Antonia and Carlitos away from the windows, but if you see a shiny black sedan with tinted windows parked in front, call me, okay?"

"Shall I come for you?"

"No!" I screamed. "Sorry. But no, stay with them and keep them safe, okay? I can ride home. We need to ask Antonio what to do."

"All right then. Be careful," Gemi said. "We'll talk more as soon as both of you are here."

I looped Capitol Hill, back and forth between Volunteer Park and the college, on major streets and tight alleys until certain Kline had left the neighborhood. Then I headed back to the house through a maze of my own making and went in the back door.

"Antonia, we should start legal processing as soon as possible. You may need to testify against Kline regarding the abuse. Are you willing to appear in court?" Antonio asked later that evening.

"Testify in court?"

"Yes. Just talk to a judge. We may also need to file for legal custody for Carlitos. Do you have a birth certificate?" Antonio asked.

"At the apartment," Antonia said.

"No, that won't do. I don't want you going back there. Not until this is settled."

"Maybe we could go," I said. "You could tell us where to look, Antonia, and we could find it."

We sat at Gemi's table, drinking our after-dinner coffee. I had given Antonio a rundown on Kline's threats while Gemi put Carlitos to bed.

"No, it might not be safe for either of you to go there yet. Antonia, was Carlitos born in Seattle?" he asked. I could almost see his wheels turning.

Antonia nodded.

"Okay, I should be able to get a copy from Public Records. Do you know if Kline's name is on it?"

"No. He did not want his name on any legal paper."

"Good. That's good. If he didn't claim his paternal rights then, it will be harder for him to claim them in the future," Antonio said.

"So what do I do?" Antonia asked.

"You state your life is in danger. The court will grant a temporary restraining order against Kline so he cannot come near you or Carlitos. It won't necessarily keep him away from you or keep you and Carlitos safe," Antonio explained. "It's a paper trail, a series of procedures we need to start. First the restraining order, and then we'll file for temporary residency under the Violence Against Women Act."

"What's that?" Antonia asked.

"It's a type of visa the U.S. government grants to victims of abuse. But to qualify for this visa, we will need evidence. That's why the restraining order is important. Your medical report from the Community Clinic will help too."

"Okay, Tío Antonio. I understand," she said.

Thirty-Three

SHE STOOD BEFORE the judge, her arm still in a sling, her face free of concealer to hide the bruises. With Tío Antonio at her side, she spoke the necessary words: "My life is in danger." The judge set the "show-of-cause" hearing. For two weeks, Antonia must wait, worry, and wonder if Jeff Kline would appear in court to defend himself.

Tío Antonio explained they needed more evidence to strengthen both the restraining order as well as her visa application. All they had was the medical report and Gemi's testimony. Antonia refused to even consider putting her son on the stand to testify against his father, and her uncle agreed.

Now, as he drove her back to Gemi's to pick up Carlitos after the court proceedings, she remembered another person who might be willing to testify on her behalf. "Mehret," she said.

"Excuse me?" Tío Antonio said.

"My co-worker, my friend, her name is Mehret. She saw my back where Kline hit me once before. Another time. Maybe she'll testify for me." She spoke in Spanish. Without discussing it, they decided to speak in Spanish when they were alone, in English in the presence of anyone else, including Gemi or Carolina.

"Excellent, Antonia. How can we find Mehret?"

"Can I call her? Gemi and Carolina told me not to call anybody at all. They said nobody could know where I am. I promised."

"Do you trust this friend?"

"Oh yes," Antonia said.

"Then call her. Here, use my phone. Do not tell her where you are living now. Only ask her if she's willing to make a written statement for you. Ask her if we can meet for lunch. I'll take you both out, okay?"

Antonia made the call and gave the phone back to her uncle, a wide smile on her face as she lapsed into the comfort of her first language. "She is off tomorrow at three. Is a late lunch okay?"

"Perfect. Now let's enjoy the rest of this wonderful day."

They stopped at the house for Carlitos and then headed to West Seattle. Tío Antonio had invited them to his home, and Antonia was excited but also a bit nervous. She rubbed her damp palms on her jeans and turned to smile at Carlitos chattering to himself in the new car seat in the back of Tío Antonio's car. She only half listened as her uncle pointed out the sights. After they crossed what he called the West Seattle Bridge, he talked of the Port of Seattle.

"See those big orange cranes and huge boxes, Carlitos? The boxes are called shipping containers, and the cranes pick them up and load them onto the big trucks and trains." He parked at the side of the road for the boy to observe the waterfront activity.

Antonia watched her uncle watch her son watch the cranes, both sets of eyes full of admiration. *¿Mi tío?* She thought and a smile spread across her face. I have an uncle.

"Are we ready to go?" he asked Carlitos.

"Okay," the boy chirped.

Apart from going to court that morning, this was their first outing and Antonia didn't know how to act, what to say, how to connect with this uncle she could only just remember from dreamlike images. They'd put the past together, understood the facts and details of each other's lives as she and Carolina had done. But now they needed to take the next step. They needed to build a present and a future together. She felt inadequate, nothing more than an uneducated farm worker/nursing assistant, living in poverty and abuse. And here was this well-educated uncle with his nice clothes and comfortable car. Yes, he wore jeans, carried a tattered briefcase and drove a simple car, but still she felt awkward with him.

"You're quiet, Antonia. Is everything okay?" he asked.

"It's so much," she said.

"Your life is changing. Is this what you want? Are you ready?"

"I am ready, but I ... I know nothing. You are educated and have a good life like Carolina and Gemi. I am nothing."

To her right lay the beach and across the water stood the majestic Seattle skyline. It was too beautiful to hold. She felt the car angle to a stop in the line of cars parked along the sidewalk.

"Look at me, Antonia. Never say you are nothing. In El Salvador your mother and father were like me. We were educated, middle-class people. Your parents risked everything to make our country a better place while I did nothing at all. I am the one who is nothing. I am the one with a debt to pay. I promise to help you and Carlitos find a better life here in America or back in El Salvador."

"Not El Salvador."

"You don't want to go back?"

She shook her head.

"Not even for a visit some day?"

"Maybe a visit. But this is my home. This is what I know."

"Okay, maybe a visit some day when everything is in order. What about school? Do you want to go to school?"

"Yes, more than anything," she said. She took a deep breath and shared her dream. "I want to get my GED."

"And then?"

"Maybe I could be a teacher. I love small children. Or, I could be a nurse like Gemi."

"You could do either, Antonia." Tío Antonio smiled and started the ignition. "She's pretty special, isn't she?"

"And you love her."

"I do indeed."

"Will you marry her?"

"As soon as she's ready."

A few minutes later he passed a small Statue of Liberty and stopped for the third time. Carlitos clapped his hands in excitement.

"This is Alki Beach," Tío Antonio said. "In the summer this place is full of people. As soon as it gets warm, we'll dig in the sand and build castles, okay Carlitos?"

"Swim," he said. "I want to swim."

"Too cold, little man. You'd freeze out there. Come. I'll show you and your *mami* my condo and the place I met Gemi."

He led them into a brick building across the street from the beach and into the elevator. When the door slid open, he pointed across the hall. "A young woman named Chris lives there. Gemi helped her after a bad car accident and they became friends. They were painting her condo when I moved in. That's how we met. And here, this is my place."

It was a bare, boring place with white walls and non-descript furniture. It looked a bit like the fancy hotel room Kline took her to once before the violence, before she had told him her secrets. She pushed the thought from her mind. "Maybe you need Gemi to help you paint," she said.

Tío Antonio let out a hearty laugh. "True. But in my defense, it's a rental. A furnished rental at that. Nothing here is mine."

"But you've lived here a long time?"

"No, only a couple of years."

"Does Gemi like it here?"

"Yes. The location anyway. She loves to walk Alki beach. She walks for miles. I can hardly keep up." Again that laughter. "Now let's see what we have here." He led Carlitos to a corner of the living room near a sliding glass door. On the floor was a large pile of smooth wooden blocks of different shapes and sizes.

"Mami, look," Carlitos squealed. "Like at school. Can I build something?" He looked from one to the other, pleading permission.

Tío Antonio looked to Antonia and she nodded. "Go for it," he said as he ruffled the boy's hair.

Antonia motioned towards the door. "May I?"

"Of course." He stood and slid the door open.

She stepped onto the balcony and filled her lungs with salt air. She watched the waves lap the shore and the Seattle skyline sparkle in the distance. "It's so beautiful," she whispered.

"It reminds me a bit of home. More so in the summer when it's sunny and warm."

"Do you miss it?"

"El Salvador? Yes, sometimes. But life is good here and I'm doing important work. Like you, I've lived here so long this is home. I wasn't as young as you were when you entered, but I was barely twenty so I've lived more than half my life in this country. This is home now."

Antonia shivered as a cold wind blew her long curls across her face.

"Come. Let's find something warm to drink." He led Antonia to the kitchen at the opposite end of the large room. "Espresso or Americano?" he asked.

"What do you drink?" she asked.

"In the afternoon, decaf espresso and some chocolate. Does that sound okay?"

"Perfect," she said.

Thirty-Four

"WE'VE GOT A TREE, lights, and decorations. The task at hand is to put them all together. What do you think, Carlitos? Ready to help?" Carolina said.

"Oh, yes," the child said. "I've never made my very own Christmas tree."

"This year will be a first for both of us. How does that sound, child?" Gemi said.

They were gathered in Carolina's minimalist living room where a tall, dense tree stood bare and beautiful, filling the front window. Neither Gemi nor Carolina had ever bothered with a Christmas tree, but for Carlitos they decided to make an exception this year.

Since Antonia and her son had moved into Gemi's attic room, all four of them seemed to flow through the house as though the divisions between upper and lower apartments had never been constructed. With the exterior front door for security, they now kept their apartment doors, Carolina's at the base of the stairs and Gemi's at the top, wide open. Antonia loved following her son up and down the stairs between the two apartments. Because Carolina had fewer furnishings and more empty space, her living room was the logical choice for the Christmas tree.

The three women stood around the dining room table fingering the pile of bags and boxes Gemi had brought home along with the tree.

"This stuff is awful tacky looking," Carolina said.

"It will be okay on the tree," Antonia said. "You will see."

"Right then, where do we begin?" Gemi asked.

"Lights, lights, lights," Carlitos said. He danced in front of the tree unable to contain his excitement.

"The child's brilliant," Carolina said. "When I was a kid at home, Dad always put the lights on first. Then Mom and I added glass balls. These aren't exactly glass, are they?"

"Do not worry, my friend," Gemi told her with a wink at Antonia. "Our tree will be beautiful."

Gemi opened the first package of lights and walked over to the tree. "Do you recall exactly where your father started?" she asked.

"At the top. To light the angel," Carolina said.

"Angel?" Gemi asked.

In confused surprise, Antonia watched as her two friends doubled over with laughter. They laughed until tears came to their eyes. "What is so funny?" she finally asked.

"Oh, child, how can we explain? I am a non-practicing Ethiopian Muslim and our friend, Carolina, is a staunch agnostic. Neither of us are Christians, you see, but here we are trying to decorate this gorgeous evergreen for Carlitos when the two of you probably know more about Christmas trees than either of us do."

"Come on, Antonia," Carolina said as she wiped the tears from her eyes. "Show us how this is done."

Both Antonia and Carlitos joined in the laughter. The women looked at each other and then at the happy little boy only to start laughing all over again. Antonia moved a chair from the table and climbed up to string the lights in a circular pattern around the tree as Carolina and Gemi watched. Halfway down the tree she tensed, her hands froze in mid-air. "Oh, no," she said.

"What's wrong?" Carolina asked.

Antonia jumped from the chair and grabbed Carlitos, hauling him to the far side of the room away from the window.

"It's him, is it not?" Gemi asked.

Antonia nodded.

Carolina walked to the window at the edge of the tree and stood in full view. It was late afternoon, but enough winter light still remained to see the car clearly. And for the driver to see her. She drew the tall vertical blinds tight to the edges of the tree as the car sped away.

"All clear," she said.

"He knows you live here now," Antonia said, releasing the boy from her tight embrace.

"Yeah, but I don't think he knows you're here, Antonia. Not yet anyway. I don't think he could see you through the tree."

"I worry."

"Me too, child," Gemi said.

"Lights. Lights. Lights." Carlitos jumped up and down unaware of what had happened.

"For now, let's just have some fun, okay?" Carolina said. "That's what matters tonight."

Antonia and Gemi nodded in agreement, none of them wanting to spoil the fun for Carlitos. Carolina moved the chair away from the tree and continued to string the lights, the mood subdued despite their determination to keep up their happy chatter.

"Do you have Christmas music, Carolina?" Antonia asked as she watched her friend struggling with what had somehow become a tangle of lights.

"What a nice idea, child. Shall I take a look upstairs, Carolina?"

"Here. See if you can figure out this mess. I'll get the music." She handed Gemi the string of lights. Then she fiddled with the iPod setting in a dock almost hidden between piles of books in the floor-to-ceiling bookshelves that filled the far wall of the living room. What Carolina lacked in furniture, she made up for in books and music. Antonia had often seen her walking around campus and riding home from work, earphones in her ears, wires connecting her head to her backpack, listening to music. When Antonia asked Carolina if it was safe to bike with music in her ears, Carolina had laughed and admitted it probably wasn't the best idea, but insisted she kept the volume low enough so she could still hear the traffic sounds around her.

Now the volume was not low. Carolina cranked it up until Antonia worried the neighbors would complain. But as "Deck the Halls" blared through the house, they all began singing along at the tops of their lungs and abandoned their concern. With her patient touch, Gemi managed to untangle the mess Carolina had made of the lights and the tree glowed in twinkling color.

"Carolina is tallest. She decorates the top. Gemi does the middle and Carlitos the bottom. Okay?" Antonia told them.

"And you, miss bossy art director?"

"I put hooks on." She held up a glittering ball and a tiny wire hook to demonstrate.

"Then you'll move everything around once we're done, right?" Carolina said.

"*Quizás*," Antonia agreed with a wide grin on her face. "Perhaps."

Antonia knew both Carolina and Gemi had noticed her eye for detail, the little ways she moved things around to make each of their homes a bit more comfortable, as she had once done in the cottage in Los Arboles. And although it was still winter and much of Seattle's wild foliage stood dormant, she still managed to put together some kind of simple floral arrangement from alley weeds on the walks they'd taken before Kline showed up.

The tree decorated, Gemi made herself at home in Carolina's kitchen. She clicked on the tea kettle and steamed a pot of milk on the stove. Since Carlitos had moved in, Gemi expanded her repertoire of comfort drinks beyond tea and perfected her hot chocolate recipe.

"Antonia, stand right there by the tree. No, better yet, walk back and forth. Yeah, like that. Now keep doing that and I'll be right back." Carolina took a coat from the rack in the entry and banged the outside door behind her. Antonia could just make out her figure through the dense tree. Then she was gone from sight.

"I looked in from the sidewalk and from across the street, coming and going from each direction," Carolina said as she burst back into the living room. "You can't see a thing through the tree. We'll check again tomorrow in the daylight to be sure, but I think it'll be fine. Now you can redecorate to your heart's content, Antonia. Just stay on this side of the tree. You too, Carlitos. Don't go behind the tree, okay?"

"I like it right here," the boy said from his spot, smack in front of the tree. "I can see the whole, big tree."

"*Perfecto, mi hijito*. That's your special place," Antonia said. She knew exactly what Carolina was telling her: Kline couldn't see them as long as they stayed away from the window. If they stayed inside with the doors locked, they'd be safe. But for how long?

Thirty-Five

WE SIPPED OUR TEA with Antonio in front of the glorious tree. Carlitos lay on the floor sound asleep where he and his great-uncle had spent an hour reading Christmas stories together. Since Carlitos insisted on being as close as possible to the tree and since we didn't want him going anywhere near the window, I'd borrowed an area rug and some pillows from Gemi and put them right in his favorite place in front of the tree. I had to admit the place looked a lot warmer and more inviting with the colorful fabrics.

"I need to go to Mound City for a short visit. I told my folks I'd go this weekend since I won't be there for Christmas. Why don't you all come with me? There's no point in hanging around here with Kline lurking about," I said.

"That's a great idea," Antonio said. "I'll keep an eye on the place and see if he comes back. You can enjoy a weekend of fresh air and snow."

"Snow?" Gemi and Antonia said in unison.

"No snow. Come on you two, you won't freeze. I checked the weather forecast this morning. It'll be cold and clear, but the sun will be shining."

"Why not, child?" Gemi said to Antonia. "I'm sure Carlitos would have fun on the farm."

The drive over Snoqualmie Pass through the mountains separating the coastal area of the Pacific Northwest with the agricultural lands of Eastern Washington stayed clear and dry. I drove, Antonia was beside me and Gemi sat in back reading softly to Carlitos. The butterflies were going crazy in my gut. I rarely visited my folks, but it was always the same, always the nerves, the discomfort, the awkwardness. My family didn't know how to talk together perhaps because we had no history of sharing. I never knew what to mention, what to tiptoe around, what to avoid. I'd been trying to see them more often since the onset of Mom's blindness, but I still never managed more than one trip each quarter. I judged time by academic quarters after so many years in the educational system—the rhythm of my life. I saw my parents when classes were adjourned.

I expected the butterflies as I climbed the mountains and dropped into the arid rolling hills of Eastern Washington, sometimes driving Gemi's car, other times traveling courtesy of Greyhound. But this time was different. I'd told my folks I was bringing a few friends, but nothing more. I didn't mention Gemi was an Ethiopian refugee or Antonia could possibly have once stayed in the workers' huts and scaled the ladders in my father's orchard. I hadn't asked Antonia if she would be comfortable returning to an Eastern Washington orchard. Maybe I should've. Maybe she felt as nervous as I did. I glanced to my left, but she faced the side window so I could read nothing.

"How you doing, Antonia?" I asked. "Are you okay with all this?"

"I'm okay," she said. I heard the tone of finality that told me she had nothing more to say.

I dropped back into wondering and worrying. Worst-case scenario, Dad won't let them into the house. Lord, that would be awful.

"Perhaps you might slow down a bit, my friend. We wouldn't want to be stopped, would we?" Gemi said from the backseat.

"Yeah, sorry. They've got those damn radar airplanes overhead around here, don't they? I was distracted."

"Anything serious?"

"I'm hoping my dad isn't a total monster when we get there. You know, there aren't too many Ethiopians in Mound City, or in the entire valley for that matter, and I don't think any non-white has ever set foot in his house."

"And you didn't think to mention this yesterday, my friend?"

"What do we do if he is angry?" I could hear the worry in Antonia's voice.

"Look," I said with as much calm as I could muster. "I'm sure it'll be fine. If there's a problem, I'll get us a couple of hotel rooms for the night and we'll come home tomorrow. I'm sorry. I suppose I should've said something, but I wanted an adventure together. A road trip, you know?"

"Adventure, indeed," Gemi said.

Antonia said nothing. For a long while all I heard was the sound of rubber eating asphalt.

We stopped at a supermarket in the late afternoon, but the early winter dusk and the long hours in the car made it feel a lot later. "I want to get a few things for dinner," I told them. "Come on let's wander and stretch our legs a bit."

"Procrastinating, perhaps?" Gemi said with a wink to Antonia.

What I really wanted was a few bottles of wine to appease my father and to calm my own nerves. Along with the wine, I bought fixings for a simple supper of spaghetti and salad.

It was a short drive from town to my parents' house. When I parked and turned off the ignition, I couldn't move. Darkness had fallen around us. Only a few lights shone, one above the front door, another above the barn door, and, off in the distance, a few strung between the workers' huts, mostly empty at this time of the year. For a moment, just a brief moment, absolute silence held us.

"Are we here? Are we finally here? Can I see the farm now? I've never seen a real farm. Only book farms."

"The farm will have to wait for tomorrow, child. Now we shall meet Carolyn's parents. Are you ready?" Gemi told the boy, but I knew her words were for me as well.

"Okay," I said. "Let's do this."

We gathered our overnight totes and grocery bags from the trunk, and I knocked on the front door. It swung open as though someone had been waiting on the other side. A tall man with wavy gray hair and hunched shoulders supported himself on a cane as gnarled as the fingers of his large hands. "Carolyn?" he said.

"Yes, Dad. It's me."

"About time you got here. Expected you hours ago."

"It's a long drive, Dad."

"Well, get on in here. Your mother's been fretting about you all day."

I stepped to one side instead of following him into the house and ushered the others inside. "These are my friends, Dad."

"Come on in, all of you. Let's not heat the whole orchard." Without so much as a glance, he stomped down the hallway.

I shrugged my shoulders and followed him into the house. We dropped our bags at the landing of the staircase to the second floor bedrooms. Groceries in hand, I led them into the living room.

My mother stood in the middle of the room holding her white cane, an eager smile of welcome on her face. She was a petite woman, a good six inches shorter than me, with gray hair pulled back in a severe bun at the nape of her neck. She'd heard our voices, stood from her easy chair in front of the blazing fire and walked towards us within the sphere of her dark comfort.

"Hi, Mom," I said as I leaned down to kiss her on the cheek. "I've brought a few friends to meet you this time."

"These are your friends?" my father said, his words laced with disbelief.

"Oh, it's wonderful to have you home, and your friends are most welcome," my mother said, coating my father's words with her own. "Will you introduce us?"

I could feel my father's heat behind me as he leaned against the door jamb. I could feel his dagger eyes boring into me and the sneer on his lips. I could feel his hatred, but I chose to ignore it.

"This is Gemi," I told my mother. "She and I share the house in Seattle. Remember I told you I rented the upstairs to a nurse."

"You didn't happen to mention she was black," my father mumbled just loud enough for everyone to hear.

"Her name is Gemila Kemmal, but everybody calls her Gemi. She was born in Ethiopia, but she's lived in Seattle longer than I have."

I rattled on trying to bury my father's hateful words, but Gemi saved the day. She stepped forward and took my mother's hands in her own. "It is a pleasure to finally meet you, Mrs. Bauer. I have heard of you for many years now and I know how important you are to my dear friend Carolyn."

"Call me Edith," my mother said. "Any friend of my daughter's is a friend of mine, Gemi. It's a pleasure to meet you. And you are an African?"

"Indeed. I was born in Addis Abba, Ethiopia."

"Wonderful. I've always wanted to learn more about Africa. Perhaps you will tell me all about it."

"It would be my pleasure, Edith," Gemi said.

"I'm not sure I believe one god damn bit of this," my father scorned from the shadows.

"Now, Norman, that's no way to talk in front of Carolyn's friends," my mother said. "Carolyn, introduce me to your other friends."

"This is Antonia Santiago and her son, Carlitos," I said. "Antonia was born in El Salvador, but she's lived most of her life here in the States and Carlitos was born in Seattle."

"I want to see the farm. I've never seen a real farm," Carlitos said. "Do you have cows?"

"Only a few cows and chickens and pigs. Norman can show them to you tomorrow in the daylight."

"Will you? Please, Mr. Bauer?" Carlitos looked directly into my father's face, oblivious to the rage only partially buried there. If Antonia hadn't been holding him, he might well have run over and started tugging on my father's pant leg in his excitement.

"Humph," my father grunted.

"You can call the old man, Norman. No formalities around here, please," my mother said. "Now come here you two."

Antonia held my mother's hand as Gemi had done, but Mom's other hand went to Carlitos. "What beautiful curls you have, child. How old are you?"

"I'm six. I'm in first grade and I love school, but I didn't go last week and now we are staying in Gemi's house and I don't get to see my daddy, and ..."

"So, we'd like to stay for the weekend. Is that all right with you and Dad?" I asked, interrupting the child's revealing rambles.

"Of course it's all right, Carolyn. You don't even need to ask such a silly question. This is your home and always will be. Now Carlitos, will you tell a blind old lady what you look like?"

"I'm a big boy and I have blue eyes and white skin like my father, and I have curly black hair like my mother."

"And do you speak both English and Spanish?"

"Sí, yo puedo hablar y leer en los dos idiomas. Me gusta mucho leer."

"Then you will read to me, Carlitos, because I can no longer read for myself. How does that sound? Of course, if that's all right with your mother."

"Oh yes, Mrs. Bauer. Carlitos can read to you in English or in Spanish."

"English only in this house," my father grumbled from the corner.

"I think we still have some story books somewhere upstairs. Do you remember, Carolyn? The bilingual books we used to read when you were a child?"

"What books?" my father demanded.

"Never mind, Norman," she said. "Do you remember, Carolyn?"

"Yes, I remember. I'll take a look later."

"And you, young lady, please call me Edith, okay? And with your mother's permission, we'll do some reading later, Carlitos. Now we really must think about dinner."

"Don't worry, Mom, I've got fixings for dinner. We'll settle in the upstairs, and I'll be down in a few minutes to make it."

"That woman who comes left us dinner," my father grumbled.

Apparently he'd finally decided to call the home care providers I'd suggested. He hadn't bothered to mention it, but that didn't matter. I was glad he wasn't doing everything himself anymore.

"You can save that for lunch tomorrow. Tonight we'll have a spaghetti special. We stopped and picked up everything we need. I even got a few bottles of your favorite red, Dad."

I passed him a bottle from one of the grocery bags, and he headed off to the kitchen for a corkscrew, his cane abandoned in the corner.

"We'll be right back, Mom," I said and motioned for the others to follow.

Upstairs, I opened three bedroom doors and then headed to the hallway linen closet for sheets and towels. "I have no idea when any of these rooms were last used," I said. "Could you guys make up the beds and maybe open the windows for a few minutes to air them out, if you want, while I go down and start dinner? Carlitos, will you come with me?"

I led him into the room that had once been mine and dug through the bookcase. Nothing had changed, everything remained as I'd left it years before. A few minutes later, I handed a stack of books to the little boy.

"Do you want to read these to my mother?" I asked him.

"Oh yes," he said. "I'm a good reader."

"She used to read all the time, but now she can't see anymore."

"I can read to her," he said.

I led him back downstairs and set him on a chair beside my mother. Then I went into the kitchen to face my father. When I saw the hefty dent in the bottle of wine, I knew it would be okay. Dad mellowed after a few glasses.

In the end, Carlitos won over my father. For years my parents had been pestering me about marriage and grandchildren. Now this beautiful, bubbly little boy stole their hearts even though he wasn't a grandson at all. After three days of visiting the animals and riding on farm equipment with Dad, baking and cooking with Mom and Gemi, and reading to Mom in the evenings, Carlitos gave them each a tight hug before climbing into the car to leave and begged to come back for another visit.

"Of course," my father said. "You come back and bring that wayward daughter of mine with you, okay?"

"Okay," Carlitos said. "What does wayward mean?"

"Come back soon," Mom told him as she hugged each of us goodbye.

Thirty-Six

THE TRIP HOME was as quiet as the drive over, each woman settled into her own thoughts. Antonia remembered Carolina's reluctance to call her parents when she graduated from university so many years before in Los Arboles. She remembered Juan Luis, his mother and sister, and all of the others whose lives had touched her own. And she remembered the long miserable hours of field and orchard work in blistering summer heat.

She relived the visit, starting with her son's words: *Are we here? Are we finally here?* She remembered unloading the trunk and watching Carolina and Gemi walk to the door. She held back, her son's hand tight in her own. She didn't think she recognized the house or the outbuildings, but she knew the area, recognized the slope of the land, the smell of the orchards even in the winter cold. She knew the apple presses ran long hours late into the year. Cider making was a sweet, sticky process of tedious work. The smell filled her nostrils and she glanced around her, the looming shape of a huge barn off in the distance, a cider shed to one side.

On the long drive back to Seattle, she knew she had never worked or lived at the orchard she'd just visited, but still it had been odd, no, terrifying, to put one foot before the other and walk into an owner's home, especially so because at that moment she still didn't know if it was *his* house. She wasn't certain until she stood in the living room staring into the face of the man in the shadows. Only then was she certain he wasn't the one from so long ago. It wasn't *el patron*'s house she had entered.

"You're mine," *el patron* had told her so long ago. "My little *puta*, and this is what I do to pretty little *putas* who don't pick enough to pay their keep. This is how you pay for the roof over your pretty head. Or would you rather I called *la migra*?" These words had come in gulps of swallowed air as he dragged her into an empty area of the orchard, an area already picked clean, an area where she'd worked for the last several days.

At first she'd thought he only wanted her to do some final cleanup. "You," he'd said, pointing up at her where she stood on a ladder. "You up there, follow me. I've got some work for you." She hadn't noticed the glances between the older women, the whispers of concern. She was too new to know what they already knew.

She remembered that day as though it were yesterday and no matter how many times she tried to push it away, it often floated back to haunt her, to remind her she was nothing more than a dirty *puta*.

The return to Eastern Washington felt like a trip back in time. She'd spent hours alone, walking the orchard and exploring the workers' huts. She knew she had never been on this land, but it was all so similar, each orchard a copy of the next. It could have happened, she was certain it did happen, to many young pickers in any of the orchards rolling over these beautiful hills.

In the isolated orchard, under the shade of a hundred trees, the sky hot blue above, he had grabbed her wrist. She screamed as he tugged her through the trees, but already he was far enough away that nobody heard her, and if they had, what? Would they have risked deportation to save her honor?

She remembered how he slapped her hard across the face and then clamped his large, calloused hand so tight over her mouth and nose she thought she would pass out. She remembered how he shoved her to the ground and climbed on top of her, one hand still clamped to her mouth, the other tearing off her jeans. And she remembered how the pain ripped through her small body and the blood flowed between her slender thighs.

"Oh, sweet little virgin, this one. I'll teach you a few things, my sweet little virgin."

When he had used her until he could use her no more, he stood over her and urinated on her bleeding young body like a dog marking his territory. With a final kick, as though scattering a pile of rotten apples, he was gone. She was alone and bleeding under a blue sky that had lost all luster, sobbing, and shivering in the Eastern Washington heat.

She couldn't move, didn't know what to do or where to go. Her shame cut deep. A ruined *puta*. When the day ended, when *el patron* had returned to his big house behind the picket fence and the pickers had returned to their huts and begun taking turns in the communal showers to wash away the sweat and ache of the day's labor, Jose Luis's mother found her. She said nothing at all, only wrapped her in a mother's embrace and rocked her until her tears dried.

"Come now," she said, her voice the melodic Spanish of northern Mexico. "The showers will be empty now. Let me help you."

They walked through the orchard, Antonia stumbling along supported by the larger, older woman. Now, over a decade later, Antonia still remembered the woman's touch as she washed the blood, urine, and semen from her body. "You will heal. You will heal." But had she? Or had she simply continued to be that worthless *puta*?

Later in the darkness of her lower bunk in the tiny hut, she heard Jose Luis ask about her, concern in his voice.

"A bit of a cold," his mother told him. "She'll be okay in a day or two."

In a day or two they moved on, away from that orchard, to another and then another. For a long time Jose Luis still lavished her with attention, treated her with his special kind of care, something between that of a boyfriend and big brother. But she knew she was no longer good enough for him. She was dirty, used, bad, as though it had all been her fault. A *puta*. She knew he knew and that was why they had left before the harvest was finished. She knew he'd caught wind, someone had whispered through the rustle of the branches, "*El patron*, he took her."

The distance between them became insurmountable because Jose Luis was as helpless as she to change life as they knew it. They moved on, found more work, other farms, and soon Jose Luis began to talk of going home, back to Mexico. Antonia knew once again she would be alone, for despite their insistence she go with them, she had to free Jose Luis from any obligation towards her. She was a ruined woman, a *puta*, and she knew it.

How naive she had been, she now realized, how much she blamed herself for something she could not possibly be held responsible for, and yet she'd felt dirty and worthless for years. Why else would she have allowed Kline to treat her as though she were what that *patron* had called her after he had stolen her innocence? She wrapped herself in a forgiving hug.

Carolina glanced at her from the driver's seat. "Are you okay?" Her friend spoke softly so as not to disturb Carlitos and Gemi dozing together in the back seat.

"*Sí*, Carolina. I'm okay now. Long story. Someday I'll tell you." To distract her friend, and perhaps herself, she kept talking. "I am remembering so many things. Now you visit your parents. Before you did not want to talk to them. Much has changed, no?"

"I suppose we all mellowed with age. Mom's blind now and so fearful she hardly moves from her living room chair. Dad's exhausted himself trying to care for her and is none too healthy himself anymore. But you heard them, they refuse to even consider leaving the orchard. What can I say? They got old and I relaxed a bit."

"That's good," Antonia said.

Later that evening, after the long drive home, Carlitos asleep in the attic bedroom, the three women sat in the glow of Christmas tree lights.

"I can't believe it was only Dad all these years. Mom was a perfect angel. How can that be?"

"I don't know, my friend. Maybe she felt she needed to be loyal to her husband. She lived with him and you were far away," Gemi said.

"Is that why? Is racism why you never wanted to call them or talk to them before?" Antonia asked.

"There was always such a line drawn between us and them."

"Them?"

"The migratory workers."

"Like me. And Juan Luis and all the others."

Carolina nodded and said nothing.

"They are good people, Carolina, and they love Carlitos. We will visit again."

The force of Antonia's words made Gemi and Carolina burst out laughing. A few minutes later, Antonia spoke again. "Something is missing here."

"Gifts," Carolina said.

"I must have gifts for Carlitos. Christmas is this week and I have nothing."

"You're right," Carolina said. "We probably should've shopped on the way home, but I didn't think of it."

"Antonio said there's been no sign of Kline," Gemi said.

"Hopefully we've seen the last of him," Carolina said.

"We'll have to go shopping here," Antonia said.

"Are you sure?" Gemi asked.

"*Sí.*"

"Where shall we go?"

"Downtown," Carolina and Antonia said in unison.

"No malls, I presume," Gemi said.

"No malls," Carolina said. "Let's take Carlitos on the Christmas Carousel at Westlake Center."

"And a carriage ride?" Gemi suggested.

"And hot chocolate at the old Olympic Hotel. What's it called now?" Carolina said.

"Oh, no. It is too much."

"Come on, Antonia. It's our first Christmas together and our first Christmas with Carlitos. We want to have some fun, too." Carolina whined and teased until Antonia nodded her consent.

Thirty-Seven

WE PILED INTO Gemi's car and headed down the hill in the morning rain. I wanted to bus it, but Gemi thought it best to have the car nearby, not knowing how Carlitos would react to so much activity and excitement. Anyway, that's the excuse she gave, but maybe she knew. Maybe her sixth sense told her to be prepared.

We shopped until noon, taking turns distracting Carlitos while the other two shopped for Christmas surprises. For lunch, we headed to Pike Place Market. Carlitos giggled with delight on the back of the life-sized bronze piggy bank at the entrance.

Later I realized he must have been following us throughout the day, must have seen us leave the house, must have trailed us, waiting for the opportunity and calculating the risk. How else would he have found us among the multitude of downtown Christmas shoppers?

He made his move in the market among the dense crowd watching the fish mongers throwing large Northwest salmon over the heads of delighted tourists and residents alike, everybody looking up, nobody looking down at a small child. By this time we were loaded with shopping bags, all but Antonia who kept one hand free for her son. But there was that one moment when she let go, when she needed to shift the weight of her load. He must have been watching for that precise moment: a tiny lapse of caution, a throng of people, and a clear escape route.

I didn't know any of this at the time, only later when I thought about what happened could I put the pieces together. In the moment, I didn't think about anything at all, I just heard the distinct tone of Carlitos's happy squeal. The voice of an innocent child seeing his father in a busy public market, the father he loved and missed, despite the violence he feared.

"Papi! Papi!" the child shouted.

I pivoted toward the sound and from the corner of my eye, I saw Kline sweep Carlitos into his arms and retreat. Without thinking, I started after him screaming at the top of my lungs trying to make my voice heard above the din of the noisy market. "Stop him! Stop that man! He's stealing a child! Stop him!"

I screamed and pushed with Antonia and Gemi screaming and pushing behind me, bags flailing in every direction. But it was Carlitos's screams that caught the attention of the distracted Christmas shoppers.

"Mami! Mami! I want my *mami!*"

A group of young men stood at the top of the stairway to the lower market as Jeff Kline headed down. As though in choreographed slow motion, they spread apart and blocked his way. Kline cursed, turning in every direction, clinging to his son, searching for escape. A trapped animal.

"Is this the guy you're after?" one of the men asked as I slid to a stop.

"Yes. Thank you so much. Please, don't let him go," I said.

"Come, *mi hijito,*" Antonia said. As she approached Kline, he tried to bolt, but the men held him.

"Give the boy to his mother," one of the men said in a tone that held a threat Kline did not ignore. He passed Carlitos to Antonia as a pair of Seattle police officers approached.

"What seems to be the problem here?" one of the officers asked.

"No problem," Antonia said. "A misunderstanding."

"What ...?" I started to say something, but Gemi put a hand on my back.

The officer turned to the group of men. They released Kline and shrugged their shoulders.

"We heard yelling to stop this guy, so we did," one of them said.

"The boy was crying for his mother," said another.

"We didn't hurt him or anything," said the third.

"And what about you?" the officer asked Kline.

"As the lady said, it was just a misunderstanding," he said.

"So nobody here has any complaints or problems?" the officer said.

Silence.

"Well, here's my card." He handed it to Antonia. "Feel free to call me if you decide there's a problem you'd like to report. Now let's move along, all of you."

Before the officer said another word, Kline disappeared. Antonia led the way in the opposite direction, Carlitos tight in her arms, speaking softly to him in Spanish.

A few blocks away from the market, I stopped. "What the hell was that all about, Antonia? What's the point of a restraining order if you're not going to use it? He should've been arrested."

"And me? What about me, Carolina? What happens to me and Carlitos if I talk to the police now?"

In a flash I understood.

"Let's not discuss this here," Gemi said.

Antonia wasn't ready yet. True to his word, her uncle had guided her through the filing procedure for temporary residency under the Violence Against Women Act, but the process was slow and there were no guarantees. She needed to know she could not be deported before she filed a complaint with any uniformed officers even if they weren't with the dreaded Immigration and Customs Enforcement.

Gemi was putting Carlitos to bed when Antonio arrived. I'd never seen him steaming, his handsome face distorted by frustration and anger. And I'd never seen the determination, the steel that held Antonia together, as clearly as I saw in their short exchange.

"Why didn't you tell the officer, Antonia? That's the whole point of filing a restraining order. It must be enforced. You need to make the call. Now." Antonio began without so much as a hello. He railed in Spanish so fast I struggled to follow.

"No, Tío Antonio. I will not call."

"Why in the world not? Do you want to risk your safety? Carlitos's safety?"

"Can you guarantee I will not be deported?"

Silence filled Gemi's living room.

"I thought not," she said, her Spanish formal, distant.

"You know the temporary residency application has been filed," he told her.

"But it has not been granted, has it?"

"No," he admitted.

"So I could still be deported."

"Technically, yes."

"Technically? I will not take that risk. I will not be separated from Carlitos and I will not be deported. I've survived in this country too long."

"My god, you sound like your mother. The same determination. The same stubborn fight."

"Thank you, Tío Antonio. Thank you for the compliment and for the concern and for all the legal paperwork you are doing for me. But I must be certain I cannot be deported or I will not make that phone call."

I think that was the first time I really understood Antonia's strength, the strength that had allowed a thirteen-year-old girl to survive alone, to grow into womanhood undocumented and unwanted in a foreign land with nowhere to go and nobody to turn to for help.

Thirty-Eight

CHRISTMAS WAS A JOYOUS AFFAIR. Antonio showed up, loaded with gifts, late on Christmas Eve after Carlitos was in bed.

Antonia wasn't certain where her uncle had spent the night, but she was happy to see him at Gemi's side on the sofa, reading the newspaper and sipping coffee when she raced Carlitos down the attic stairs Christmas morning.

"Can we go down to the Christmas tree, Mami, please, please? Can we see if Santa Claus came?"

"Go down and see if Carolina's door is open, and ..." Before she had a chance to finish her instructions, the boy was flying down to the first floor.

"It's open, Mami," he hollered up the stairs.

Antonia looked at Gemi and her uncle and laughed. "What can I do?"

"Get yourself a cup of coffee, child, and we'll head down," Gemi told her.

Together, they walked down the stairs and found Carlitos dancing from one gift to the next, reading name tags, and guessing contents.

"Santa Claus came. See, Mami, I told you. Santa Claus came this year. Can we open them? Can we open them?"

"Shall we wait for Carolina, child?" Gemi said. She laughed at the disappointment that crossed the boy's bright face. "I'm sure she'll be awake soon."

A few minutes later Carlitos rushed toward the sound of Carolina's bedroom door opening. "Are you awake now, Carolina? We're waiting for you. Are you awake now?"

Antonia handed Carolina a cup of steaming coffee and an apology.

"Just give me a few minutes to wake up, okay Carlitos? Do you think you could do me a favor? Could you run up to the attic and get me, get me—"

"—the quilt on the small bed. Carolina is a little chilly this morning."

"Nice save, Antonia. Thanks," Carolina said as Carlitos darted off to the top of the house.

Hardly a moment passed before boy and quilt came tumbling down the stairs. "Here, Carolina," he said, shoving the quilt into her lap. He looked at the four adults sitting and drinking their coffee in front of the tree. "Now?"

"Now," the adults said.

Kline's absence at the hearing two weeks later felt like another Christmas present. Almost. Antonia was convinced the restraining order meant little to him. After all, they knew he'd already violated it at least twice. How many other times had he trailed her? Had he followed them at a distance when they walked to the park the day after Christmas? Had he watched them take down the Christmas tree on New Year's Day?

She was relieved Kline didn't show, relieved she didn't have to stand in the impersonal court room with him, relieved she didn't have to hear any excuses for his violence. But her feelings were irrelevant. Kline didn't show up for his day in court and his opportunity to defend himself. As a result, the judge automatically ruled for a one-year extension of the restraining order. She and Antonio were on their way.

"What good does it do, Tío?" Antonia asked as they left the building. "He ignores it. What will stop him next time?"

"Nothing will stop him unless you call the police. Next time, you must talk to the police and tell them he is violating a restraining order so they can arrest him. All of these steps—the restraining order, the extension, and an arrest if he violates again—will strengthen your visa application. That's why we must do it. And that's why you must call the police if you see Kline again."

Antonia understood, and she knew she'd have to make that phone call whether or not she felt comfortable talking with the police. But she was tired. Tired of telling and retelling her story, tired of signing papers, tired of hiding under Gemi's and Carolina's protective wings. She had hated standing before the judge and saying those words her uncle had coached her to say: "My life is in danger." She had counted the days, dreading the return to court, but when the day arrived without Kline and the restraining order was automatically extended to a full year, she was a confused mess.

Most of all she felt sad. She couldn't help but remember the good times with the man she once loved, the man who fathered her beloved Carlitos, the man whose blue eyes and cocky smile hooked her heart and never let go. Not completely. Despite the drunkenness and beatings, the lies and threats of deportation. Despite the fear for her son and herself, she had given some part of herself to him and now she knew it was gone forever. To save herself and to protect her son, she had to testify not only against Kline but also against the part of herself that remained his.

She mourned this loss. Though she knew Carolina, Gemi, and Tío Antonio supported her, perhaps even loved her, she also knew she had to let go of all she had been during her life with Kline and even during the many years before Kline. Now was a time of adjustment, of change, of reflection, of long hours alone, or with Carlitos, in the attic room remembering — the good and the bad — and of imagining a new future for herself and her child.

She had not returned to work and neither she nor Carlitos had returned to school. They were in hiding and she had no idea how long life would be this way. Carolina and Gemi had a large, fenced backyard, so Carlitos had a place to get some exercise, to play his games with his imaginary friends, to build a snowman when a rare snow storm hit Seattle — all hidden from the eyes of the world around them. But it wasn't enough, it wasn't a life. "Patience," they told her. "*Paciencia*," she told herself. But still, it wasn't enough.

Thirty-Nine

EARLY MORNING ON New Year's Day, Antonia unlocked the front door of the apartment. Carolina and her uncle followed her inside, arms loaded with collapsed packing boxes. She told them she had very little to pack, but they had insisted on coming prepared with boxes and bags.

The apartment was small, cold, and clearly abandoned.

"He has not come back," she said.

"Good," Antonio said. "Now where should we begin? Take only what's yours and of that, only what you want to keep. Everything else stays for Kline to deal with, okay?"

They started in the kitchen taking only a pressure cooker and a few of Carlitos's favorite dishes and cups. The cupboards and the refrigerator were almost empty.

"I'm wrong," Antonia said. "He came back a few times. He ate all the food and left the dishes dirty."

She no longer saw any humor in Kline's slovenly behavior, in his expectations, in his demands for care and attention. Now she only saw him as an abuser and she wanted to be as far from him and this place she had shared with him, as possible. She could feel her heart beat in her chest. She saw herself sitting in that chair in the corner waiting for her tormentor to return, hoping it would be a good night. Over time those good nights became few and far between.

She shuddered and felt Carolina's hand on her shoulder.

"You okay?" her friend asked.

"This place," she said. "I want to leave fast."

A knock on the front door interrupted them. They all spun to face it.

"He wouldn't knock," Tío Antonio said. When he opened the door, a gray-haired man in worn blue overalls stood before them.

"Mr. James?" Antonia said.

"Thought I heard someone in here. Rent for December is long overdue. January is due now. Moving out? No notice?"

"I'm sorry, Mr. James," she said.

"I'm an attorney representing Ms. Santiago," Tío Antonio said. "I understand the rental contract is in the name of Jeff Kline. Is that correct?"

"Yeah, but I ain't got an address for Kline and the number he gave me don't work."

"I'll be happy to provide you with both his office and home information. Ms. Santiago and her son are vacating the premises. Any further dealings will need to be with Jeff Kline."

Tío Antonio pulled a small notebook and pen from his coat pocket and scribbled Kline's information on a slip of paper. Handing it to the building manager, he escorted him to the door and locked it behind him. The manager gone, the three sorted quickly through the apartment taking clothes, toys, a few books, and little more.

"Are you sure that's everything?" Carolina called from the living room. She walked into the kitchen and found Antonia dumping the contents of a large canister of sugar into a paper bag. "What are you doing? We don't need sugar, and I'm sure Gemi doesn't need it either."

"This," Antonia said. Triumphantly, she shook the sugar from a small plastic baggie and showed it to Carolina. "He did not find my money. See."

Carolina laughed. "That's quite the banking system you've got there. How much are you hoarding anyway?"

"Oh, not so much. My savings from all my work, even before I met Kline. Four thousand, I think. I only make minimum, so I did not save a lot."

"I'm impressed."

"Okay you two, let's get out of here." Tío Antonio stopped when he saw the bag of money. "Tell me that's not drug money," he said.

"Drug money? Really? You think I sell drugs?" Antonia was laughing as she looped her arm through her uncle's. "Come on, Tío Antonio. *Vámonos de aquí.*"

Forty

ANTONIA KNEW IT was time for Carlitos to return to school. She wasn't ready to go back herself, but she knew her young son needed the routines and the companionship of other kids. Despite the legal guarantees of the restraining order and the assurances of the principal at the local elementary school a half dozen blocks from the house, Antonia wasn't comfortable leaving Carlitos alone at the school. She didn't trust the school's ability to protect him from Kline.

"How about being a classroom volunteer?" Carolina suggested when the two of them met with the principal. "Would that be possible? Could Antonia stay here at school and help out each day?"

The principal and teacher were both only too happy to have extra help in the classroom, so on the first day of school after the winter holidays, Gemi dropped Antonia and Carlitos off at school together. The women had a plan. None of them were comfortable with Antonia and Carlitos being out and about alone, so they decided Gemi would drive them to school each morning on her way to work, and Carolina would meet them after school to walk home together. But some days Carolina would be tied up with students and wouldn't be able to meet them.

"Keep your cell phone handy. You know he could show up anywhere."

"We don't want to frighten you, child," Gemi added, "but you need to be alert, you must be careful. If you see him, call 911."

"Even if he does not come too close?" Antonia asked. She knew Kline could only come within one hundred feet of her or Carlitos.

"If you see him, call 911," Carolina said. "Tell them you're frightened. Tell them exactly where you are. There's the Starbucks, that Italian Bistro, Tully's, the pharmacy. You know all the places along the way. If you see Kline, go inside. Stay close to other people and call 911. Then call Antonio, Gemi, or me."

A month passed without incident. Antonia was happy, truly happy, happier than she'd ever been working at the retirement home, and she'd loved that job. There was something special about being with children, so much hope and joy in their small bodies. It was like being surrounded by thirty variations of her own son, and nothing made her more content than Carlitos.

"I love all the little ones," she told Carolina one day on the walk home. "They are all so eager and full of energy, and they want so much to learn."

"Have you ever thought about going into education instead of nursing?" Carolina asked.

"*Sí*," Antonia said. She dropped her eyes.

"So? What's the problem?"

"Gemi. I do not want to tell Gemi."

Carolina laughed. "Don't worry about Gemi. If you decide to be a teacher, Gemi would be just as thrilled as she would be if you continue in nursing. She only wants you to follow your heart. And so do I."

"But I am too old."

Again, Carolina laughed. "Do you know what the average age at the college is?"

Antonia shook her head.

"Thirty-one. You're not too old, Antonia. You're not even thirty. Sure, you're getting a later start than some, but you're bilingual and you have more life experience than most teachers. If you want to be a teacher, go for it."

"But it will take a long time. And money."

"True. You'll need to get your AA degree and then transfer to a four-year university. Once your residency's in order, there's financial aid. In the meantime, we're all here to help. You just have to decide it's what you truly want."

"But my English is not perfect."

"Antonia, you will always have your beautiful accent and you may always make a few mistakes, but your grammar is improving, and you'll keep working on it. English will not be a barrier. Determination and money are the factors that hold most students back."

The conversation flowed in and out of Antonia's mind for weeks as she volunteered in the classroom, listening to children read, helping with their arithmetic problems, leading art projects. When Carlitos's teacher asked her if she'd like to teach the class a Spanish lesson a few days each week, she jumped at the chance. Already other teachers were approaching her to see if she'd be willing to come into their classes to teach Spanish as well. With each passing week, Antonia became more convinced teaching was her calling.

Forty-One

A FEW NEIGHBORING GROWERS, some church folks, and the orchard foreman, Manuel, were the only locals willing to face the heavy snow storm to attend my father's funeral. We took Gemi's car and drove over the pass as soon as Mom called and told me paramedics had rushed Dad to the hospital. Gemi offered to come, but I convinced her to mind her clients. I had Antonia to help, and Carlitos would be a good distraction for my mom. I didn't think there'd be much to do but keep her company and wait until Dad's condition improved. I didn't understand there would be no improvement until I spoke with the doctors. Gemi and Antonio joined us as soon as I called with the news of Dad's death.

"The real work will begin after the funeral," I told Gemi when I called. "What am I going to do with my mother?"

"I suppose she will need to come home with you," Gemi said.

"That's what Antonia said, but I doubt she'll agree to that," I said.

"You won't know until you ask. She certainly can't stay alone, can she now?"

"Nope, but I dread the struggle of convincing her of the obvious."

We hosted a small reception in the living room following the church service. After my disappointment when Manuel refused my invitation to attend, the startled looks and quiet comments when I introduced my friends didn't much surprise me.

"Why in the hell are they here?" a belligerent grower whispered loudly after too many drinks. "Norman must be turning in his grave about now. Not even cold and look who's waltzing right into his front room."

"What's that?" Mom asked.

"Mr. Granger's insulting my choice of friends, Mom," I said.

"Well you tell him any friend of yours is a friend of mine."

Mr. Granger slammed his drink on the coffee table and stomped out of the room, his wife murmuring apologies in his wake.

"Thanks, Mom" I said. "I think he heard you."

Hours later, after the last person had left, I found myself alone with my mother. Antonia put Carlitos to bed upstairs while Gemi and Antonio washed dishes together in the large, old-fashioned kitchen.

"So what was old man Granger going on about, Carolyn?" The directness of the question startled me. "You've always been honest with me. Let's not change that now."

"He didn't like my friends."

"I figured as much. Now let me guess. Antonia and her uncle are dark-skinned Central Americans. And Gemi is a black-skinned African."

"Yes, but you already knew that, right Mom? I mean I thought it was clear when we came over at Christmas. I'm sure Dad had plenty to say to you about it."

"He sure did," Mom said and laughed. "So Harry Granger didn't think Norman would want them in his sitting room. Well, I suppose he was right about that."

"What about you, Mom?"

"I don't care who you choose as friends, Carolyn, as long as they're good people who treat you well. I just want a bit more of you in my life while I'm still walking this earth."

"Really?"

"Of course. You don't think I agreed with everything that old goat believed, do you? Don't get me wrong. I loved your father heart and soul, but he sure could make me mad with some of his racist attitudes."

"Why didn't you ever tell me how you felt?"

For a few moments my mother was quiet, as though she were gathering her thoughts like she'd learned to gather flowers in her glorious summer garden–by touch and scent instead of by sight.

"Early on, when you were young, I thought it would be disloyal to your father. And then, in a flash, you were gone. First off to university in California and then all those years of travel and work abroad. You never came home, never seemed to have time for a phone call or letter. I was angry, hurt. When the blindness came on, I became so dependent, I feared upsetting Norman. What would I have done without him? Until you visited at Christmas, I wasn't sure ... I'm so glad you came."

"I'm glad I did too, Mom. And I'm glad I wasn't such a chicken about bringing my friends. You know, when I was driving over here that first time, I wasn't so sure Dad would even let Gemi and Antonia into the house."

"Oh, did we ever have a fight that night." Mom chuckled softly as I watched in amazement. She seemed a feisty white-haired stranger, like a character on some evening sitcom or something. Certainly not the mother I remembered.

Earlier, on the drive over, Antonia and I had talked about my mom's options if Dad couldn't care for her any longer. Like Gemi, Antonia had suggested Mom move to Seattle and offered to help care for her until she adjusted to her new surroundings. I insisted she accept payment, but Antonia refused. We went around in circles for a while, getting nowhere. The only definite was that bringing Mom to Seattle made absolute sense, if she'd only agree.

As though reading my thoughts, Mom brought up the subject. "So what do we do now? I know I can't stay here alone, though it will break my heart to leave the old place. I suppose you'll be wanting to put me in St. Francis."

"Is that what you want, Mom?"

"Well, no ..."

"But you know my job is in Seattle. I mean, I could come over during the summer and even quarter breaks, but not during the school year." I let my thoughts flow, let myself imagine operating a summer orchard with well-paid, happy workers, climbing and picking as I'd done in my youth, retiring from teaching and moving back to the orchard. I realized my mother had been saying something and I wasn't listening. "Sorry, Mom. What was that?"

"I was wondering how big your house is. You know I've never even seen it properly. Only those pictures years ago."

"Big, plenty big," I said, snagging the end of the string my mother trailed for me. "Will you come home with me, Mom? We can try living together and see if we like it. You'd be alone while Gemi and I are at work and Antonia is at school with Carlitos. But we'll find a way to manage it, at least until you learn your way around."

"Doesn't Antonia have a job?"

"Long story. But for now, no. Anyway, the point is, somehow, we can make this work if you want to give it a try. What do you think?"

"I think it would be a grand adventure," my mother said.

As I walked towards her, she stood and we wrapped each other in a tight embrace.

It was several weeks before Mom was ready to leave her home of fifty-some years. I knew there wouldn't be enough time to finish before my bereavement leave ended, and I had to get back to Seattle to finish winter quarter. Antonia offered to stay behind to help Mom sort and pack. Carlitos missed following my dad around, but Manuel took the boy under his wing. Missing a week or two of first grade wasn't going to be a problem.

Grades submitted, I headed back to Mound City in a rental van to load up my mother's necessities and a few pieces of furniture, including her favorite wingback chair, the chair in which she once sat to nurse me.

The day finally arrived when I locked the front door of the old farmhouse confident the place could be left in Manuel's capable hands. I'd known him since childhood, and I even remembered his father, the orchard foreman in whose footsteps he followed. I was determined the orchard would continue operation, at least for the upcoming year. I asked Manuel for a monthly accounting of needs and expenses. I told him I wanted to learn the business, and if it made sense, if we could make it thrive, we'd do it together. I assured him I'd bring my mother back after spring quarter so I could spend the summer working the orchard. Manuel was happy to keep his job with the possibility of expanded responsibilities and increased pay. "Who knows?" I said. "Maybe we could even try making hard cider."

Forty-Two

THE SUN HAD ALREADY set when the school door closed behind Antonia and Carlitos. They'd stayed a bit later than normal making large, illustrated word cards for Spanish lessons the following week. It was Friday and Antonia hadn't wanted to carry the posters home with her. Carolina was sick, and Antonia told her to stay home with her mother. They could walk home alone. After all it wasn't really so late, it's just that darkness fell early in wintertime Seattle. Still, she wished they'd left earlier.

She heaved her backpack over her shoulders and took Carlitos's hand in her own. "*Vámonos, hijito*. Let's go home," she said.

"It's so dark, Mami," Carlitos said.

"*Sí*, it's a bit late. But you did good work. Thank you for helping with the vocabulary cards."

"*De nada*, Mami. I like to help you. My *mami* is a teacher, now." Carlitos skipped along with joy in his young voice.

They were still three long blocks from home when she saw him. He was standing in the shadows of a bar on the far side of the street. She held Carlitos closer. The door to the nearest coffee shop lay a half block away.

"*Ven aca*, Carlitos," she said. "I need a cup of coffee. Do you want hot chocolate?" Glancing over her shoulder, she saw Kline push off from the wall and follow them. Drunk. She could tell by the walk. She opened the coffee shop door and shoved Carlitos towards a booth as far from the door as possible. With her back to her son, she made the phone calls. First 911, then Carolina. She got Carlitos started with the crayons on the paper placemat and went to the counter. "I'm being followed," she told the barista. "I just called the police. I have a restraining order."

"Okay," the barista said. "Can you see him from here?"

"Yes," Antonia said. "That man crossing the street now. He is drunk."

"Tell me what to bring you and stay in your booth out of sight," he said. "If that guy comes near the door, I'll lock it."

Tears of relief and gratitude filled her eyes. "Thank you," she said.

"What's wrong, Mami?" Carlitos tugged on her sleeve as she slid into the booth. "Is Daddy going to get us?"

"No." It was almost a shout. "No, *mi hijito*. No one is going to hurt us. Never. Ever. Now let's get started on your homework, okay?" She made certain her son's back was to the window and she had a broad view of Kline. He'd crossed the street and was now in clear violation of the restraining order. She watched with one eye, the other on Carlitos and his arithmetic worksheet.

Kline must have heard the police sirens before she did. She watched in frustration as he hopped into a cab and left the moment the cruiser pulled up to the curb outside the coffee shop.

"What's happening, Mami?" Carlitos asked.

"*Nada, hijito*. Do your homework," Antonia told him.

When the officers entered the coffee shop, Antonia stood and walked towards them. As if on cue, the barista walked to the booth and distracted Carlitos with more crayons and a coloring book.

"I am Antonia Santiago. I called 911. I do not want my son to hear this conversation, please."

"Okay," one of the officers said. "Do you have the restraining order with you?"

"Yes, but you are too late. He heard or saw you and took a taxi away."

"And you've been here in the booth since you made the 911 call?"

"Yes."

At that moment, Tío Antonio rushed through the coffee shop door. "Tío? How did you know?" Antonia asked.

"I was almost to the house when Carolina called. Officer, I am Antonio Meléndez. I am Antonia's uncle and attorney. Did you get him?"

"Not this time," the officer said.

FORTY-THREE

YOU CAN'T GET YOUR GED by taking a single test. Instead, you have to pass a battery of five individual tests in reading, writing, social studies, math, and science. Truth be told, I wasn't sure I could pass all five. They were tough, far tougher than graduating from most public high schools. But I knew Antonia was determined to earn her GED, and I was equally as determined to do what I could to help her. I stopped by a colleague's office and borrowed a stack of books and practice tests in each of the subject areas.

Later that afternoon, I dropped my heavy backpack on my coffee table and watched Antonia's eyes widen as I took out the books, one at a time.

"All this is for me to use, Carolina?"

"Sure is, *amiga*. Time to start studying. You love to read, right?" I said.

"Yes," Antonia said. "Now that I spend only mornings at school with Carlitos and afternoons here with Edith, I can study in the evenings."

"What do you mean by that, young lady?" My mother sat listening to our conversation in her favorite old chair with late winter sunshine streaming through the front window. "We finish lunch by one o'clock. Seems to me there're two good study hours before Carolyn gets home and you two need to scurry off to get that boy of yours. I won't be wasting your time or distracting you from your studies, and I certainly do not need a babysitter. I'm blind. I'm not stupid. I don't suppose my daughter told you I was once a high school math teacher."

"*De veras*? Really? I'm horrible in math and science."

"Well, it's a good thing I'm not."

"Will you, is it okay, can you help me?"

"It would be my pleasure, Antonia," my mother said. "You make me lunch and help me learn my way around this big house and I'll help you earn your GED. Is that a deal?"

"Oh yes," Antonia said. "But how ..."

"How will I read the book? I won't. You'll read it to me aloud and we'll figure out the problems together."

"Sounds like you two have a plan. Now let's go get Carlitos." I knew Antonia wanted to be early, to be at the classroom door before the bell rang. Leave Kline no room to approach. We didn't think he'd have the guts to come near with the two of us together. We didn't yet realize how wrong we were.

Although never formally educated, Antonia read avidly in both Spanish and English. Within a week, she'd finished the GED reading test prep books and practice tests. When she showed me her scores, I knew she was ready.

"What have you been doing, studying all night?" I asked. "I'll check the ..."

Before I could finish my sentence, Antonia showed me the college testing schedule with several dates highlighted.

"I can take it next Tuesday morning," she said. "I tell Carlitos's teacher I won't be there on my test day."

"Told. You told ..." Carolina corrected. "Wow, always two steps ahead of me, aren't you?"

Antonia laughed. "But I am nervous to take this test."

"You'll do fine," I said and turned to the sound of Carlitos's happy chatter as he walked down the stairs from Gemi's place, my mother in tow.

"Slow down, little one. You don't want to make a blind old lady fall, do you?" Mom scolded.

"Sorry Abuelita Edith," Carlitos said.

"¿*Abuelita?*" I said. "Now she's your grandma?"

"Why not, Carolyn?" Mom said.

"Why not, Carolina?" Antonia said. "We are almost sisters, no? And Carlitos wants *una abuela*."

"Okay, Carlitos," I said. "But if you want a grandma, you need to slow down and be careful, okay?"

"Okay, Carolina. I have a grandma and a student now," the boy said as he danced around the three of us in the landing.

"A student?" I asked.

"Yes," he squealed. "I'm going to teach Abuelita Edith to speak Spanish. She will teach Mami math and I will teach her Spanish. I'm a teacher now, just like my *mami*."

"Oh, my," Gemi said from the top of the stairs. "What have we created here?"

Antonia breezed through social studies and writing next. By spring she only had math and science left.

"Almost there," I told her.

"But I'm terrible at math," Antonia said. "I'm lucky your mother is a good teacher like you. But I have much to learn. Those two tests will take longer to prepare."

We were sitting at the kitchen table, a pile of study materials between us. Carlitos was already in bed, Gemi was upstairs at her desk, and my mother was knitting in her chair, eavesdropping.

"You're not so terrible at math or science, young lady," Mom said. "You've got a good head on your shoulders. We'll get you through the last two tests before you know it, you'll see."

Forty-Four

"WHEN WILL YOU STOP fooling yourself, my friend?" Gemi said. "We both know why you have chosen to make a spring-break trip to Los Arboles."

"Mama Lucy took a fall. Thank goodness she didn't break any bones, but she's getting fragile. She's almost ninety. I need to see her," I said.

"And who else do you need to see?"

We were all gathered around Gemi's table where we'd just finished a traditional Ethiopian dinner, dirty dinner dishes scattered between us, bits of *injera* still on the shared platter.

"Okay already, I've got finals to grade," I said.

"Who will you see in Los Arboles?" Antonia asked.

"Did you ever meet Mama Lucy, child?" Gemi asked.

"The potter? The one who made the teapot? No, but Carolina told me about her."

"That's the one. Did she also tell you Mama Lucy has a grandson named Jason who happens to be exactly the right age for our Carolyn?" Gemi asked, her dark eyes blazing with mischief.

"No, she did not tell me about this Jason. Why did you not tell me, Carolina?"

"Oh, for heaven's sake. Look, Jason was in school in Oregon when you and I met, Antonia. I only knew Mama Lucy and her son, Henry. He was Jason's father. Mama Lucy is my friend, more than a friend. She became a grandma to me. Kind of like Carlitos and my mother. I've gone back almost every summer, sometimes more often, to visit her. Jason married, got a teaching position, and stayed in Oregon. I've seen him off and on through the years. Then, after his dad's death, he started spending more time in Los Arboles to help Mama Lucy. Apparently, his wife wasn't crazy about that and divorced him."

"So now he is single? How do you say? Available?"

"Yes, child, Jason is available and our dear friend, Carolyn, seems to be making more frequent trips to Los Arboles. Will he be meeting you at the airport again this time?"

"Why should I rent a car if he's free to pick me up? Look, I'll only be gone a few days. It's no big deal. I just want to see Mama Lucy."

"Jason lives in Los Arboles now?" Antonia asked.

"Yes," I said. "He's living in the old house with Mama Lucy."

"And you will stay with Mama Lucy, too?"

"Yes. But it's not what you think. We're only friends."

Antonia looked at Gemi and they both started laughing. Before long Carlitos, clueless, joined in and they laughed even harder.

"Whatever you say, my dear friend," Gemi said. "You have a nice trip and enjoy your visit with Mama Lucy."

"I will," I said. "As long as all of you can manage while I'm gone. What about you, Mom?"

"Of course I'm okay with it, Carolyn."

"But you've been so quiet."

"I'm only wondering who this mama is."

"Everybody calls her that, Mom. She's more like a grandma really, an old, hippie grandma."

"All these years you've gone to visit her. More than you visited your father and me."

The room was silent.

"It's true, Mom. It's like I ran away to Los Arboles to try to make a new life for myself. In fact, I met Mama Lucy the same day I met Antonia. Jason's always been part of that world. I've never forgotten Mama Lucy. She's still important to me. I've known her since I was a student. I couldn't agree with the way Dad ran the orchard or treated the workers. I couldn't accept his racism, Mom. I lost you because I rejected him."

"But then you came back."

"I came back."

"So why, pray tell, haven't you and Jason gotten together sooner?" Mom asked.

"Let's see. When I met Mama Lucy, Jason was going to school in Portland. He got a job there right after graduation. Oh yeah, then his girlfriend got pregnant and he married her."

"Ouch."

"Not so much at the time. I mean, we were just friends. I still had a lot to learn about myself and the world. Mama Lucy encouraged me to head to Latin America, so I did."

"So I have her to thank for all that worry."

"I suppose so. Anyway, his wife miscarried. They stayed married for a while, but it didn't last. Then, like I said, when his dad died, he moved back to Los Arboles to keep an eye on Mama Lucy."

"And his mother?"

"She died when he was young. Mama Lucy is the only family he has."

"It sounds like this Mama Lucy is lucky to have both of you in her life," my mother said. "I never knew how much you needed a grandmother, or even a mother, all those years ago. I am very grateful to Mama Lucy for being there for you, Carolyn. Of course you need to go to her now. Antonia and Carlitos can take care of me, and with Gemi's help, we'll all be fine. I have no doubt you'd be on a plane even without the additional enticement of young Jason."

Again the room filled with laughter, and I couldn't help but laugh right along with them.

Later, when I opened my closet doors to start packing, frustration got the better of me. Boring, boring, boring. Khakis and cords all hung in neat rows on clip hangers, all varying shades of the same. The tops offered little visual relief, the only variation was sleeve length. Sure, I had a range of colors, but every single shirt could be worn with every pair of pants. That interchangeable. That monotonous.

I'd built this uniform-of-sorts over years of teaching to make my life easier. Every morning I could reach for any pair of pants, any top, a pair of loafers. The only decision required was short or long sleeves. It made the rush to early morning classes that much quicker. It made biking to work possible. But it sure didn't make for an interesting wardrobe. Being interesting had never been important to me. Until now.

I turned from the open closet and snatched my bathrobe from its hook over the full-length mirror on the back of the bedroom door.

The mirror I almost never used. I raked my fingers through my blond hair, tugged at the corners of my eyes, at the early creases around my mouth. "Not too bad, I suppose, but what am I going to pack?"

Packing had never been a problem before. In fact, I never thought much about what I threw into my backpack when I traveled. Count the days. Throw in the same number of tops and *chones* and half the number of pants. *Chones*. Mexican slang. Funny how I'd held onto that word. I never thought of them as panties or underwear. I never thought of them much at all, so why was I thinking about them now?

I slumped on the edge of my bed. "Damn. Maybe they're right. Maybe I am going to see Jason." All these years. There'd been other men but they never seemed to stick. Never meant much. Not like Jason.

I remembered the first summer we met, the way the sun hit his auburn hair, the way his smile lit up a room, the way my heart skipped a beat when he stood close, when his hand brushed mine as we loaded pottery into Henry's old truck or washed dinner dishes in Mama Lucy's vast kitchen.

It was hard to get to know someone I'd already heard so much about—and who'd heard so much about me. We were both aware Mama Lucy believed we were destined for each other, but by then Jason's girlfriend was planning their wedding. We kept our distance through the years. I came back to the States, I accepted the teaching position in Seattle, I began my summer sojourns to California, and still we maintained that distance. The friendship grew, but nothing more. Then he got divorced and moved back to Los Arboles.

Last summer the ground shifted between us. We were awkward in a way we'd never been before. And now I was flying down again and it wasn't even summer. I shook my head at my own denial.

Standing, I stretched and took another look at my clothes. I dug through the short sleeve tops and pulled out the V-necks, those that fit best, the few I sometimes wondered about. Were they appropriate for class? I looked for the pants I thought fit best, didn't stretch out too much, made me feel good.

"My *chones* are pathetic," I groaned as I pawed through a drawer full of plain cotton underwear. "But I'm getting ahead of myself. Maybe I'm reading this all wrong. Maybe he's already found someone new. Maybe he never cared at all."

I zipped my bag shut with unnecessary force, cursing myself for allowing my imagination to get the better of me, and headed up to Gemi's for an evening cup of tea.

"I'll have to go shopping," I told Gemi. "Problem is, I'm a lousy shopper and I don't know what to buy."

"Can I give you some advice, my friend?" Gemi said.

"Sure."

"You recall how awful I used to dress, don't you?"

"And Mrs. Newbury told you to do something about your appearance."

"Indeed," Gemi said. "The gall of that woman."

"So you went shopping, right?"

"Yes. I went into Nordstrom and looked at the saleswomen until I found one I thought might understand what I needed. Then I asked her for help."

"So you're saying you think I need a personal shopper? But Jason already knows I'm a slob."

"No need to throw it in his face, dear Carolyn. Maybe this time you might show him a bit of your sparkle."

"Lord, my mother said the same thing."

"Smart woman."

"All right, all right. I'll go shopping when I get there. I sure can't do it tonight."

High above the Pacific I let my imagination wander. I felt his arms around me, his lips on my own for the first time. Damn, I thought. I almost wish he weren't picking me up. I could use some shopping time. Maybe Gemi's right. Ever since she first entered Nordstrom and found someone to help her change her look, she was certain I'd have fun if I gave it a chance. But I'd always argued I didn't need a fancy wardrobe. I was an ESL teacher in a run-down urban community college. Why did I need to look attractive? And besides, I rode a bike everywhere. I'd shut myself down, denied my femininity, my sexuality. I'd decided I was the proverbial old maid and dressed for the role.

But now was different, I was different, and, by god, I was determined to find out if Jason cared even a tiny bit about me.

Jason Cabot. I loved his name. I loved our shared interests in teaching and pottery. I loved that he lived with Mama Lucy and made pottery. Of course he claimed Mama Lucy did the work, but I knew better. I knew most of what had been coming out of Mama Lucy's pottery shed for the past year were Jason's creations. Sure they went to the shed together, but Jason worked the wheel and threw the pots while Mama Lucy sat on her stool chatting. I knew he'd also landed a post at Los Arboles high school teaching history and pottery classes. But was he dating anyone? If honest with myself, I'd been afraid to find out, afraid to allow myself to think about the possibilities.

I gazed at the fluffy white clouds out the plane window, at the deep blue Pacific below and tried to relax. I'd find time to shop, I decided. There were plenty of great boutiques in Los Arboles. I think I dozed off with a smile on my face.

I felt the descent, the landing gear activating, the touchdown. I rubbed my eyes and tousled my hair. Make-up, I thought. Maybe I should try a bit of eye make-up or lipstick. I barely had time to dig for a breath mint before we'd taxied to a stop and people filled the narrow aisle, pushing for escape from the claustrophobia of modern travel.

I remained seated next to the window finger-combing my hair and trying to calm the butterflies that seemed to have moved in permanently. The plane was almost empty as I stood, pulled my backpack from the overhead compartment, and made my way down the aisle.

I walked through the airport to the exit and there he was, waiting for me at curbside, leaning against Henry's battered old pickup in jeans and cowboy boots, his face California-tan, his auburn hair shining in the morning sun. How could I not be attracted? When he kissed my cheek in greeting, I could've sworn there was electricity in the air.

Forty-Five

WHEN GEMI RETURNED home after dropping Carolina at the airport, her kitchen was warm and bright, the spring sunlight dancing shadows across the table where Antonia sat, her head in her hands, a cup of steaming black coffee and a plate of toast in front of her.

"What is it, child? Is Carlitos all right?" Concern colored Gemi's words.

Always concern, I always worry them, Antonia thought. I need to get on with my life and not depend on them so much. But I need them. I need their help. I need Carolina. She gave a shake of her head, a shrug of her shoulders.

"Tell me, child. You know I can read your face like a roadmap. What's worrying you? Is Carlitos all right?"

"Yes, Carlitos is at school."

"Where's Edith?"

"She's listening to her music."

"So what has got you sitting here so glum, child?"

"*Nada*. I am being self-thinking ... what is the word?"

"Selfish?"

"*Sí*. Yes. Selfish."

"And why, might I ask, do you call yourself selfish?"

"Because I am afraid. Carolina goes to California. She has a friend, a man there. Maybe she will not come back."

"My dear, Antonia, your Carolina has had a foot in both states for a very long time. Has she told you much about Mama Lucy?"

Antonia shook her head.

"You already know Carolyn and her parents didn't always have the best relationship. When Carolyn was at school in California—"

"When we met?"

"Yes, when the two of you met, that was a real low point for Carolyn. By a strange coincidence she met Mama Lucy and you on the very same day."

"Mama Lucy gave her the teapot. And I broke it."

"And then you disappeared. By the way, Carolyn broke that teapot just as much as you did, so you must stop blaming yourself." Gemi stood to fill the tea kettle and then continued. "So after you left, I think Mama Lucy became friend, grandmother, confidant, I'm not sure what you would call it, maybe all of those things. What I do know is that she filled a hole in Carolyn's heart."

"Now she goes back," Antonia said.

"She's gone back once or twice a year for as long as I've known her. She spends the better part of every summer in California."

"Really?"

"Yes. And now there's Jason. All these years something has stood between them ..."

They both turned to the sound of Edith's cane on the stairs, one by one, as she made her way up.

"There you are," she said as she walked through the open door. "I thought I heard voices up here. What am I missing?"

"Would you like a cup of tea, Edith?" Gemi asked.

"That would be nice, but the gossip would be even better."

"Antonia is concerned your daughter might decide to stay in California with Mama Lucy's grandson, Jason," Gemi explained.

"Well, that would be a disappointment, wouldn't it?" Edith said.

"Exactly," Antonia said.

"You both want time with Carolyn. We all do. There is nothing wrong with that. I am certain Carolyn wants the same."

"I don't know, Gemi. I worry. Do you think Carolina will decide to live in Los Arboles again?"

"I do not know, child. But what I do know is our friend could use some love in her life and, if Jason's the one, she would be wise to find out instead of wasting her life waiting on a dream of something that does not exist."

"Yes," Antonia said. "But I do not want her to move to Los Arboles."

"One step at a time. Perhaps, if they choose to be together, Jason will come to Seattle. Or to Mound City. Or maybe they are not right for each other at all. Time shall tell."

"Carolina loves him," Antonia said. "I see it in her eyes."

"But does Jason feel the same?" Edith asked. "I suppose that's the question."

The women nodded in agreement.

FORTY-SIX

EARLY EVENING DUSK settled over the Los Arboles hills, the air pungent with eucalyptus. Mama Lucy was already in bed for the night.

"Come on," Jason told me. "I want to show you something."

We walked to the pottery shed behind the house. When he switched on the light, I was stunned. The shelves I expected to see depleted of Mama Lucy's large collection, were instead lined with new work. The colors were intense, the forms novel. Teapots, cups and saucers, cream and sugar sets of every size and shape imaginable marched along the shelves like characters from *Beauty and the Beast*.

"Yours," I said.

He nodded.

"They're beautiful," I told him.

"You're beautiful." He moved towards me. "I've wanted to do this for years." He ran his index finger down my bare arm and I quivered.

"May I?" he asked.

I nodded, unable to speak a single word.

He pulled me towards him. The touch of his lips on mine took my breath away. He tasted of cinnamon and pottery dust and eucalyptus. He tasted better than in any of my very best fantasies.

"It's been too long," he said.

"A lifetime," I agreed.

He looked around as though trying to find a spot to settle like a dog circling three times before lying down. I grasped his hand and moved towards the large house, the house we'd both known for years. My room, the room I used every summer, was on the lower level at the rear of the house. The farthest from where Mama Lucy now slept.

We both knew this, knew where we were headed, the decision we were making, the path we were taking.

In the dark of my room, we undressed each other, button by button, kiss by kiss. I couldn't stop smiling, all concern about new *chones* forgotten.

"I need to see you," he whispered as we stood naked in front of each other. "Can we turn on a light?"

"Here." I reached for a small lamp on the corner of the antique dresser.

"Perfect. You're perfect."

He moved his hands over my bare body, like a sculptor over stone, a potter over clay, but unlike the sculptor or the potter, I knew he was not trying to reshape a single thing about me. As our bodies melded into one, I knew I was home.

The following morning Mama Lucy was already in the kitchen when we staggered in looking for coffee. I squirmed like a naughty teenager under Mama Lucy's long look. She gazed from one to the other, back and forth, before a wide grin deepened her wrinkles. "It's about time you two got together. No need to sneak around. We're all adults here. Besides I've been waiting years for this."

I looked at Jason, and he looked at his grandmother. "Really?" he said.

"Of course," Mama Lucy said. "You never should've married that girl in Oregon. Thank goodness you've finally gotten that mess all straightened out. Now it's time for you two to start making babies."

"Babies?" I gasped. "Aren't you moving a bit fast, Mama Lucy?"

"You're no spring chick, honey. Besides, it'd be nice to see my great-grandchild before I kick the bucket. What's holding you up?"

The large kitchen filled with laughter. "She'll never change," Jason said.

"Thank goodness." I leaned over to plant a kiss on the old potter's cheek.

Forty-Seven

SPRINGTIME IN SEATTLE: daffodils, spring cleaning, and garage sales. Carolina and Antonia were on their Sunday morning walk. Gemi had conjured the routine. "She just wants Carlitos all to herself," Carolina told Antonia as they strolled along in the shade of the leafing sweet gums.

"To bake cookies," Antonia added with a laugh.

"We need a serious workout so we don't feel guilty about all the calories when we get back."

"Because Gemi will make us eat many."

When they saw the sale, Antonia insisted they stop. It was one of those huge neighborhood garage sales, stuff seeming to spill from the stately old homes as though the houses themselves could no longer hold the excess. The kind of collective sale that flowed out over the sidewalks threatening to block traffic as cars squeezed between the rows of vehicles parked on both sides.

Carolina saw it first: bright sunshine yellow, leaning against the frame of the open garage door. It drew her forward with an invisible string, and she dragged Antonia along with her.

"Look," Carolina said. "It's a beauty.

"Same as the teapot."

"And exactly the right size."

"But you have a nice *bicicleta*, no?"

"Not for me. For you. This one's too small for me anyway."

"Ah, no, Carolina."

"You can do it. Come on. It'll be fun."

"It belonged to my daughter," said an elderly man, his gray-blue eyes bright under his heavy white brows. "She moved back east and has no use for it now. I almost hate to see it go. So many memories, you know. Why not give it a whirl, young lady?"

"Because I do not know how to ride a bicycle," Antonia said.

"You rode as a kid, didn't you?" Carolina said.

"Yes, but that was a long time ago."

Carolina grabbed Antonia's arm as she backed away. "Come on, Antonia. You did it then, you can do it now."

"Your friend's right," the old man said. "It's a skill once learned, never forgotten. Give it a try. The road's flat. You'll be okay. Here, you'll need this." He handed Antonia a bright yellow helmet that matched the bike.

Carolina pushed the bike to the curb and Antonia trailed behind her adjusting the helmet strap under her chin. For some reason this was important to her friend, so she figured she could give it her best shot.

"So you've got two brakes, here and here, but only use the one on the right for now, okay?"

Antonia nodded.

"And these are the gears."

"Gears?"

"They make it easier to get up the hills. Don't worry about them right now either. Let's see if you can find your balance, okay?"

Antonia reached for the bike and stepped over the low center bar.

"I'll hold the back of the seat, okay?"

They both looked up and down the street to be sure it was clear of traffic. Then Antonia nodded, stepped down on the right pedal and took off with Carolina running behind her. Within seconds, she found her balance, Carolina let go, and Antonia wobbled off down the block. She rode back and forth, up and down the street. Once she was comfortable with the brakes, first the back and then the front, Antonia played with the gears until she understood how they worked. When she finally rode back into the yard, she glowed.

"Happy trails," the old man told her as he walked away pocketing Carolina's money.

"So you know how," Carolina said.

"It was a long time ago," Antonia said.

"Let's go home and get mine so we can ride together."

"No, I cannot."

"What? Buy it? It's already done. Don't worry about that. It's yours now."

"No, Carolina. You do too much for me. You cannot buy me *bicicleta*."

"I didn't buy it for you. I bought it for my own selfish reasons," Carolina said.

"What are these reasons?" Antonia demanded.

"I need a riding partner. Gemi refuses to ride and sometimes it would be fun to have someone to ride with. Are you okay with that?"

"But you are a good rider and I am a beginner."

"There's nothing to it, Antonia. You're in good shape. We'll start slow, okay?"

"Could we ride along the path on Alki Beach? It's so beautiful there."

"Where Antonio and Gemi's friend, Chris live? It's a long ride, but it's possible. The challenge is biking uphill to get home. It's tough."

"Harder than the hill you rode up in Los Arboles?" Antonia asked, a sly grin creeping across her face.

"I was a lot younger then," Carolyn said. "Come on. Let's go get my bike and start with something easier today, okay? We can go down to the lake. We'll still have to bike uphill, but it won't be such a long ride. Riding Alki will be an all-day event."

When they got back to the house, Gemi and Edith were still in their bathrobes sharing their morning coffee in Carolina's apartment. Carlitos stretched on the living room rug and pillows, the comics spread in front of him.

"Come and look at what we found," Carolina told them as she lifted her own bike from the hooks on the wall. "We're going for a ride. We'll be back in an hour or so. Is that okay with everybody?"

They gathered in the entry, the front door open wide. Gemi looked at the bike, looked at Antonia and looked back at the bike. "Are you certain about this, child?" she said. "Will your shoulder be all right?"

"It's okay," Antonia said. "Remember, the doctor said it healed good. No more problems."

"Just don't fall off that thing," Gemi said.

"Oh, make your cookies with Carlitos and stop worrying like an old lady," Carolina told her as she swung her leg over her bike and rode off. "You go first, Antonia. Set the pace. I'll stay right behind you."

"The same way we walk?"

"Yup. Down the hill. But remember, be gentle with the left brake. Gemi will never speak to me again if you brake too hard and go over your handlebars."

Antonia laughed and took off as though she'd been riding forever. She hadn't told her friend about the old rickety bikes she'd used here and there throughout her years of field and orchard work. There always seemed to be a rusty bike that belonged to no one and nobody was interested in using propped against the wall of one of the workers' huts. She would ride off by herself whenever the opportunity presented itself. Those rides gave her freedom. This pretty yellow bike was like riding on air by comparison.

She headed down the narrow, curvy street with Carolina right behind her. At the bottom of the hill, they rode the lakeside trail, flat and fast. The spring sun sparkled on the blue water as they circled the small peninsula of Seward Park, and then headed back the way they'd come.

Seattle is a city of hills so no matter where you ride, if you're out for more than a few miles, you'll be going up or down. And if you go down, you have to go back up to return to your start point. Warm despite the spring chill clinging to the morning air, they stopped at the base of the hill to catch their breaths before attacking the climb.

"Like the hill in Los Arboles, but not so long," Antonia said.

"To the cottage," Carolina said.

"Where we met."

"I'll never forget."

It was a short steep hill with a sharp curve halfway to the top. Antonia felt the burn in her thighs. She shifted to her lowest gear, the one that makes you feel you're pedaling in place. Too low, too slow, and you wobble. Balance on an uphill standstill is tough. Finding the right gear, enough tension to maintain stability while lessening the muscle burn, is also tough. She shifted her gears up the hill, struggling.

"Watch out. you son-of-a-bitch!"

She heard Carolina's scream behind her and glanced over her left shoulder. She saw the black sedan in the corner of her eye. Too close.

"Ride, Antonia. Keep moving. Don't stop," she heard.

The car edged in slowly on Antonia's left side, so close she could've touched it if she'd been able to keep her balance with only one hand on the handlebars. But she didn't want to touch it. She didn't want it near her. But it inched closer at a snail's pace up the steep, isolated curve. She veered to the right, dropped off the pavement and into the rough gravel at the edge of the narrow street. The car continued to inch towards her. She struggled to pump the pedals.

"Keep pedaling," Carolina yelled. "Don't stop."

She kept going, her breath coming in gasps, her quads burning hot.

The car window on the passenger side opened. Kline leaned across the empty seat towards her. "Hey *puta*, where's my son? I bet I can find him back at the house with that black bitch. I think I'll go for a little visit now. Wanna race?"

"No!" Antonia screamed.

Kline gunned the engine and sped up the hill spraying both Antonia and Carolina with sharp gravel. Antonia ducked and swerved. The narrow tires couldn't handle the uneven terrain. The bike slid out from under her.

Her legs hit gravel. Her head hit asphalt, first her helmet, then her chin. Sprawled in a twisted heap, she felt like she couldn't breathe at all.

A moment later, Carolina knelt over her. "Slow, shallow breaths. You'll be okay. You got the wind knocked out of you. Take your time."

Antonia struggled to roll onto her back, to draw air into her lungs. She felt Carolina unwrap the bike from between her legs and move it off her. She felt her touch on her legs, her arms, her shoulders. "Does anything feel broken?"

"Call Gemi," Antonia gasped as soon as she could get the words out. She fought the pain and nausea, desperate to protect her son. She heard Carolina on the phone: "Call 911 ... Hide Carlitos ... Don't open ... She's okay."

"Can you sit up now?" her friend asked.

Antonia nodded. She sat. Blood dripped from a gash on her chin that her helmet had been unable to shield. Gravel and dirt coated her palms, her pants were shredded, and her left hip screamed, but none of it mattered. Carlitos mattered.

They sat forever in the gravel at the side of the road, but only long enough for Antonia to catch her breath. Then they hiked the remaining grade to the top, pushing their bikes. There, Carolina got the chain back on the sprockets and checked Antonia's brakes before they rode the remaining few blocks home.

A police cruiser was parked behind her uncle's car when they approached. An officer was walking up the front steps towards Tío Antonio and Gemi as they braked to a stop.

"Where is he?" Antonia screamed, her face a bloody mess.

"With Edith," Gemi said.

"*Gracias a Dios*," Antonia said.

"Kline got away," Tío Antonio said.

"Are you Antonia Santiago?" the cop asked.

"Yes," Antonia told the officer.

"Are you all right?" Gemi asked. "Your shoulder?"

"I'm okay. Where are Carlitos and Edith?"

"They are upstairs, child. Carlitos is safe. Come with me," Gemi said. "We must remove the gravel and stop that bleeding. Looks like a butterfly bandage will be needed. You too, Carolyn. You both need some medical attention."

"I'm fine," Carolina said. "I'll be right in."

"Definitely a restraining order violation, but technically not a hit and run," Antonia heard as Gemi closed the door behind them.

Mound City, Washington
2012

FORTY-EIGHT

I TAPPED MY FINGERS on the steering wheel of Gemi's old sedan. I needed to break down and buy a car. I never wanted one before, all I ever needed was my bike, but now was different. Now I was borrowing Gemi's car more often than I should, more often than even the best of friendships permitted.

I wondered what Jason knew about cars. Maybe we could take a look at Craigslist together. On my laptop. In bed. Under my new sheets. I felt the smile creep across my face just as Jason walked through the wide sliding glass doors from SeaTac arrivals.

"Love that smile," he said as I jumped out to greet him. We stuffed his bags into the trunk and made our way out of the airport and into the tail end of evening rush hour traffic.

"It's going to take a bit of time," I said.

"I'm sorry," he said. "I wasn't thinking. Look at this traffic."

"I'm not complaining. I'm glad you took off as soon as you could get away. More time together this way." I chattered on, non-stop, pointing out sights like a tourist guide on steroids.

"Carolyn, it's okay," he said. "I'm nervous, too. But I want to be here with you. I want to see where you live. I want to meet your family of friends and your mother. I want to be with you. So let's take a great big breath and try to relax, okay?"

We both inhaled long and slow, and then I exhaled with as much noise and show as I could muster.

"How very Zen of you," I said.

"Feel better now?"

"Foolish. Ridiculous. But, yes, better. It's weird, you know. I mean, I've known your world, at least your Los Arboles world, for years. But you know nothing of mine. I guess I'm afraid you won't like what you see."

"Do you want me to like what I see?"

"Of course I do."

"And why would that be?"

"I suppose because I want you to come back for a second visit, maybe a third or fourth. Who knows?"

He reached over and gave my shoulder a squeeze. "I can't wait to see your place. Any chance we'll be alone for a while?"

"I think that can be arranged."

But I was wrong. Everyone seemed to want a bit of Jason when we got to the house, even Antonio came over to meet him. The two of them talked about everything from Central American history to pottery production and sales. As the hour grew late, they finally headed to bed, first Carlitos to the attic room, then my mother to her downstairs bedroom. It was midnight before Antonio stood and stretched. He extended his hand, "A pleasure, Jason. I hope to see more of you."

"I passed the test?" Jason asked, his eyes bright with jest.

"That you did, my friend." Antonio gave him a slap on the back and turned to Gemi. "I hope you don't have an early client tomorrow."

She looped her arm through his and walked him down the stairs to the front door. Antonia gave Jason a shy hug and disappeared up the stairs to join her sleeping son. When I heard the front door close, I looped my arm through Jason's. "Time for bed," I whispered.

"Good night," Gemi said as we passed on the stairs.

"See you later, alligator," I said.

I felt Jason's presence, smelled his essence, before I opened my eyes. But when I reached out to hold him, to feel the warmth of his skin under my fingertips, the bed was empty. I bolted upright and searched the room in the morning light filtering in along the edges of the blinds.

"Afraid I left?" he chuckled from the far corner of my large bedroom. "I wouldn't do that, you know." He came towards me with what looked like a ball of newspaper the size of a basketball in his hands. "I wanted to get this," he murmured in my ear.

"A ball of newspaper?"

"A gift."

"For me?"

"For you. Sorry about the wrapping job. I'm not too good at wrapping and Mama Lucy's no better."

"Mama Lucy?"

"It's from both of us. Go ahead. Open it."

I lifted the ball into my lap and began unwrapping layer after layer of newspaper. When the first gleam of sunflower yellow caught my eye, I stopped and looked at Jason.

"Mama Lucy told me to tell you she's been trying to reproduce that pot for years, tried time and time again, but it was never right. Then the day after your last visit ..."

"You're blushing," I teased.

"Anyway, after you left, she insisted I take her to the shed. She told me what to do, walked me through the throw, the shaping, the glaze. When it came out of the kiln, she shouted with joy. She claimed the only reason it finally came out right was because you and me, well, you know, we finally ..."

"The teapot," I whispered.

"The teapot," he repeated.

"So she told you that story, too?"

"She told me lots of your stories. And I'm sure she told you a few about me."

"A few," I admitted as I finished unwrapping the teapot. "My god, I think it's an exact replica. How could she possibly remember?"

"It's probably not that exact."

"It is," I said. I reached for my robe on the floor as I scrambled out of the tangled sheets.

"I like the view better without the robe," he said.

I leaned across the bed to kiss him, long and deep. Pulling away I went to the bedroom closet and reached toward the top shelf buried in the corner of the large old house.

"Look at this." Triumphant, I emerged with the broken yellow teapot.

"An exact match. She's quite a potter."

"She couldn't have done it without you." I set the broken pot on the bedside table beside the new one. "Thank you," I said as I wrapped him in my arms.

"Mama Lucy told me I had to leave and let you and Antonia have tea alone together."

"Later," I told him as I let my bathrobe slip to the floor.

"Later," he agreed as he beckoned me back into bed.

Alone in my kitchen, I poured hot water over Mama Lucy's loose tea leaves at the bottom of the new teapot. I loaded a tray with two cups, the new teapot, and a plate of cookies, and carried it into the living room. There I set the tray on the dining table in front of Antonia and her pile of books. I sat down across from her.

"This time I won't move," she said.

"This time I'll be more careful," I said.

Antonia ran the tip of her index finger along the plump curves of the sunflower teapot. "It is the same, the very same teapot."

"A very exact reproduction."

"How did she do this, your Mama Lucy?"

"Mama Lucy and Jason did it together."

"Jason." Antonia's voice was a jealous whisper.

"He can be your friend, can't he?"

"Yes. He is a nice man."

"So what's the problem?"

Antonia stared at her hands.

"Come on, Antonia. Don't give me the silent treatment. I want to know what's going on. Gemi says you're worried about something, but she won't tell me anything else. She's up there keeping Mom and Carlitos and Jason busy so we can inaugurate the teapot alone together. Her word: inaugurate. So out with it. What's bugging you?"

"Okay. Okay. I am selfish and *celosa*."

"¿*Celosa?* Jealous? Of what?"

"Jason."

"What?"

"I am afraid you will go live in California with Jason and Mama Lucy and I will lose my friend again."

"So that's what this is all about. You might be jealous, but I'm just plain dense." I leaned forward and looked directly into Antonia's eyes. "Look, *mi querida amiga*, I am not moving to California. I love Mama Lucy and I hope to spend as much time with her as I can. Her days are numbered and I will miss her horribly when she's gone, but she's lived a long and fulfilling life."

"But what about Jason?" Antonia asked.

"Jason."

"You are in love. You will leave and go live in California."

"Yes, I'm in love. No, I won't live in California. Antonia, if Jason and I decide to be together, he'll have to move here and join this big crazy family of ours. But all of this is too soon to even talk about. For now we're getting to know each other. So let's flow with it, okay?"

"*Sí*, okay, *está bien*," Antonia said.

I reached forward and poured two cups of tea. I passed one to Antonia and leaned back with a cup in one hand and a cookie in the other. "Yum. Gemi and Carlitos sure do know how to make cookies."

Antonia laughed, but I saw the shadow cross her face. I waited.

"Carolina, do you think he is a good man, your Jason?" I said nothing and waited for her to continue. "At first I thought Jeff was a good man and then the trouble started. He drank and he hit me. How do you know Jason is a good man?"

"You were young and alone, Antonia. You didn't have a lot of choices. Maybe you weren't seeing as clearly as you would given the same situation today. I think Jason is a good man. But if I'm proven wrong, I have no doubt you and Gemi and Mom will take care of him."

We clinked our cups of tea and laughter filled the room.

FORTY-NINE

"**BUT I STILL DO NOT** understand why I got this one wrong, Edith. It is a simple percentage, no?"

"No, I don't believe it is, Antonia. Read it to me again and let's break it down."

They sat at Carolina's table, books and tests spread between them. Carlitos was in school, Gemi was at work, and Carolina and Jason had gone in search of a new car. Edith and Antonia continued to plow their way through the practice test, examining each incorrect response, figuring out where Antonia had gone wrong.

"We've been at this for a while now, Antonia. Have you checked the time?" Edith asked.

"*Ey, no,*" Antonia said. "I must go now. Right now."

"But where's Gemi? She's supposed to be driving you today, isn't she?"

"She called. There was an emergency and she went to Harborview Hospital with a client. I told her I can go alone." She put on a sweater and grabbed her backpack as she spoke. "I will ride my bike."

"Are you sure?"

"*Sí.* Yes. It's much faster." She took her dented helmet from the hook where it had hung next to Carolina's since her run-in with Kline. She knew she needed a new one but hadn't found the time to shop. "We will be back soon, okay?" She gave Edith a kiss on the cheek, got her bike from its place in the entry, and pushed it out the front door.

"I'll be fine. You be careful on that thing. You have a phone, right?" Edith hollered behind her.

"Lock the door, Edith," Antonia yelled back as she rode off.

She glanced at her watch. Already ten minutes late. Carlitos would be waiting outside in front of the school. Kids would be finding their buses. Parents would be picking up. Teachers would be trying their best to keep some semblance of order in the chaos. She pedaled faster weaving her way through the alleys to avoid cars and traffic lights.

She approached the school just as the buses were moving away from the curb. As the last bus drove off she saw it in the distance, parked on the corner of the cross street: Kline's black sedan. Frantic, she scanned the front steps, the lawn spreading wide on both sides of the walkway.

There he was, a tiny first grader, inching his way across the grass towards the father he loved and feared.

"No, Carlitos!" she screamed.

"Go back inside!" she screamed.

"Find Ms. Clark!" she screamed.

She screamed in loud, clear Spanish, and her young son heard her. He turned from his father, the well-dressed, handsome man coaxing him away from the school and towards his car.

"Run!" she screamed. "Run, Carlitos!"

And then she ran. She dropped her bike on the lawn and ran interception as Kline too ran to snatch the boy. Her small body blocked Kline and he swung at her with all the force of his worst drunken rages. Before she fell she saw the school door close behind her son. Safe. Safe was the last thought she remembered before the pain, for Kline too had seen his son slip again from his grasp. He exploded in rage, pounding Antonia, kicking her, cursing her. But they were not alone in a rundown apartment this time. The teachers, the principal, the parents closed in on them. Later they told her it took two male teachers, a father, and the custodian to drag Kline off her and hold him until the police arrived and cuffed him.

She opened her eyes in a hospital bed, Tío Antonio at her side. "Carlitos? Where ...?"

"Shush," her uncle told her. "Carlitos is safe at home with Gemi and Edith. Kline is in custody. You'll be okay."

"Okay? I do not feel okay," she said.

"The doctor says you'll be sore for some time. You have a broken rib and a lot of bruises, but you'll be okay, thank god."

"Can I go home now?"

"Not yet. The doctors must do a few more tests."

Internal bleeding, Antonia thought. They will check for bleeding and organ damage before they let me go. This she knew from her medical training.

"What happens next?" she asked.

"Kline?"

"*Sí*," she said as they spoke in hushed Spanish.

"We will add the hospital and police reports to your petition for residency. Kline might get a little jail time. He's definitely out of a government job. We'll have to figure out some tighter safety measures when he gets out. For now, let's just focus on getting you strong again."

The door opened and Carolina rushed in, Jason behind her. "Antonia, I'm so sorry. It's all my fault. I should've been there. I should've given you a ride."

"No," Antonia said. "It was my fault. I was late. I was studying and forgot the time. It was not your fault."

"Still, you shouldn't be riding or walking alone," Carolina said.

"You do not need to babysit me, Carolina. Carlitos is my responsibility, not yours. I must not be late ever. And I must learn to drive."

"I'll teach you as soon as you're up to it," Jason said. "I used to teach high school kids. We'll use the car Carolyn bought."

"And I'll help," Tío Antonio said. "There should always be an extra car available. I'll buy another."

"No, she can use mine," Carolyn insisted. "I don't need it for work. It will always be there."

"Unless you are on the other side of the mountains," Antonia said. "No, I have money. I will buy a car. But first I need a license."

"No, I'll buy a car," Tío Antonio insisted.

"I'll buy one too, then it'll be like a used car lot in front of the house," Jason said.

"Ouch. Do not make me laugh. It hurts," Antonia said.

Hours later, Antonia was released and Carolina insisted on driving her home in her new car, leaving Jason to ride home with Tío Antonio.

Gemi and Carolina helped Antonia upstairs, while Edith and the men tactfully distracted her young son in the downstairs apartment. Carlitos had not seen the beating his father gave his mother, but he'd seen enough other beatings in his short life to know what had happened and to fear the worst. He was inconsolable. It wasn't until Antonia, now settled on Gemi's sofa under a pile of comforters, insisted he be allowed upstairs that the child stopped crying.

"You were a good boy," she told him in a mother's quiet Spanish. "A very, very good boy. You listened to me and you were safe."

"But not you, Mami. You were not safe. Papi hurt you. He hurt you bad this time," the boy whimpered.

"I'm okay, *mi hijito*. My rib bone is sore. Right here." She took his hand in hers and touched her side. "I won't be able to play very much for a week or so, but I'm okay. I just look bad, that's all. Is Mami ugly now?"

"No, Mami. You are never ugly," the boy insisted.

FIFTY

I NEVER CRIED, couldn't remember the last time I'd shed tears. Had I even cried at Dad's funeral? Now I was bawling like a baby. "It's not fair. I wasn't there. I wasn't with her. It happened so fast I didn't even get to say goodbye," I sobbed. "Two funerals in less than six months. It isn't right, damn it."

We'd just finished birthday cake and opened presents. We'd just run out to the back alley to ooh and aah about the car Antonio had given Antonia for her birthday. We'd just come back into the house when I got the call.

"*El novio,*" Antonia said to Gemi and Edith as I headed to my bedroom.

"Jason?" Gemi asked.

"Yes, *novio* is boyfriend. You really do need to learn some Spanish, Gemi," I heard my mother say as I closed the door behind me.

"She's gone," Jason said.

"Gone? Where?" I asked.

"Mama Lucy died."

"What? Mama Lucy? No. It can't be."

"I'm sorry, Carolyn. She died sometime this afternoon. I thought she was napping so I held dinner for her. I finally decided to wake her, but when I went into her room, she was already gone. I could feel it, Carolyn. I could feel she was gone."

"Gone?" It didn't register, wouldn't sink in.

"Yes. Mama Lucy is gone," he repeated.

"How? Stroke? Heart attack?"

"Old age, I guess. Peacefully. In her sleep. I'm here with her now. You're my first call. I've got to call the Neptune Society. Can I call you right back?"

"Of course." I wiped my tears and walked out to tell the others. A few minutes later the phone rang and I returned to the bedroom.

"They said they'll be here within the hour, maybe sooner," he said.

"She prearranged everything," I said.

"Yeah, it's weird. She gave me her attorney's name and number a few weeks ago. It's like she knew her time was near."

"Weird to think she even had an attorney."

"And a will, too, apparently."

"But you're her only family, right? Is there anyone else you need to call?"

"No other family. I'll call the attorney as soon as they come for her. I can call the market association and her friends tomorrow. I suppose I'll put an obit out."

"How can I help? What about a funeral?"

"There won't be one. She told me she didn't want any ceremony at all. Just spread her ashes someplace meaningful."

"Meaningful?"

"Yeah."

"To whom?"

"I don't know. Maybe there'll be some details in her will," Jason said. "I dread going to meet the attorney. I don't know why. It feels so final, I guess."

"Would some company help? I could take a personal day and fly down tonight if you want."

"That would be great."

I heard the relief in his voice. It felt good to be able to comfort him. I could almost see him there in the old frumpy chair in Mama Lucy's bedroom, her body still warm in the bed beside him.

"I keep expecting her to wake up."

"I'm so sorry. I wish I could be there with you right now. I've got my laptop open. There's a flight that gets in around eleven tonight. Would that be okay?"

"Perfect," he said.

I booked the flight while we talked.

When the people from the Neptune Society knocked on the front door, he said goodbye.

I started throwing things into my overnight bag. It was Wednesday night. I'd only miss one day of classes since I didn't teach Fridays, but what about Carlitos?

I went out to the dining room and filled them in on my plans. "Are you comfortable picking Carlitos up alone, Antonia?"

"Of course. Or maybe Edith will want to come with me. Now I will drive my pretty new car, so you don't have to worry about yours." Antonia dangled the car keys in front of me, laughter in her eyes, teasing me about all the fussing I'd done over her learning to drive in the car I'd bought the month before.

Jason started teaching Antonia to drive right after Kline's attack at school landed her in the hospital. When he left, Antonio continued the practice, taking his niece out for a drive every afternoon. Antonia had taken the driving test and gotten her license a few days before. And now, thanks to her uncle and the convenient timing of her birthday, she had her own car, a bright red used Jetta everyone at Carlitos's school, and even the neighborhood cops would soon recognize. All part of Antonio's personal protection plan, I figured.

"I'm sure you're as good as your uncle claims you are behind the wheel," I teased. "Seriously though, will you all be able to manage if I'm gone for four or five days? Do you feel safe with the drop-offs and pick-ups and all?" I was careful not to mention Kline's name. We'd developed a code of sorts when Carlitos was around.

"Go," Antonia, Gemi, and Edith said in unison.

"We'll be fine," Gemi said.

"You need to be with Jason now," Mom said.

"He needs you," Antonia said.

"Don't worry, Carolina," Carlitos said. "I'll take care of everyone."

"That settles it. Carlitos is in charge. Gemi, can you drive me to the airport?"

"I'll take you," Antonia said, an impish smile on her face.

"I don't think so," I said. "Too far. Too dark."

"Carolyn's right," Antonio said. "You might want to stick to the neighborhood for a while, okay?"

The house was empty and sad without Mama Lucy's vivacious presence, her loud voice, her keen eye. I didn't want to leave him. After checking with Gemi and Antonia, I requested two more personal days and booked a flight home late Tuesday night. It was awful to imagine Jason there alone. I guess he was feeling the same because he suggested coming to Seattle as soon as school let out in June. Knowing I'd see him again soon made getting on the plane a little bit easier.

"I told Jason all about the orchard," I said to Gemi in the drive from the airport. "He'll be here next month to see it."

"To see the orchard?" Gemi asked.

"Well, I suppose he's coming to see me too. But you know, if he likes it, maybe we could spend the summer in Mound City. I could take Mom back for a long visit. Antonia and Carlitos could come too, if they want. And you and Antonio could come over whenever you have some time."

"Sounds like a lovely plan, my friend," Gemi said.

Fifty-One

THE KNOCK AT THE DOOR caught Antonia and Carolina off guard. They weren't expecting anyone. Not yet. Later Tío Antonio and Gemi would be coming for Friday dinner, but it was too early, and they wouldn't knock anyway.

Antonia froze. "It's him," she said.

Carolina put a hand on her shoulder before walking to the door to look through the peep hole.

"So early?" Antonia heard her ask as she swung the door open.

"Have you heard the news?" Tío Antonio asked as he lunged into the entry.

"News? No. What news?"

"Where's Antonia?"

"I'm here. ¿Que pasa?" Antonia came out of the kitchen with Carlitos at her side. "Why did you come so early, Tío Antonio? La cena no está lista."

"Forget the dinner," Tío Antonio said. He picked Carlitos up and swung him around the room. He passed him to Carolina and hugged Antonia. "There's big news. Huge news." He danced her around the room in some combination of a waltz and the Texas two-step.

"What's up, Antonio?" Carolina asked. "Come on. Explain yourself."

"Turn on the television. Hear what our wonderful president has done. It's not enough. It's not all that is needed, but it's a first step. And best of all, it solves our problems."

Carolina turned on the television and flipped through the channels landing on a 24-hour news station. For a moment they stood in silence and listened to the discussion of President Obama's executive order.

"What does it mean, Tío?" Antonia asked.

"It means ICE can no longer deport undocumented immigrants if they meet certain requirements," Antonio explained.

"What requirements?"

"You must have been brought into the country before your sixteenth birthday."

"I was only seven years old!"

"You must have a high school diploma, GED or be attending school."

"I am. Or at least I was. And I almost have my GED!"

"You must be under thirty-one years of age."

"I am twenty-nine!"

"Precisely, my dear." Tío Antonio held her at arm's length. "Precisely. You qualify for a deferment. It does not allow you citizenship. Not yet. But you cannot be deported."

Antonia turned to Carolina and saw the tears of joy in her friend's eyes. "Is it true?" she asked.

"Seems so," Carolina said.

"After so much trouble for you, Tío Antonio. All those papers and appointments for the visa. So much effort."

"It was our only option, but it might have taken years before you were granted permanent residency and a green card. Now, with one signature of Barak Obama's pen, you are safe from deportation. We will continue the other process as a back-up plan, a security measure. Who knows what might happen if politics change, but for now, *mi querida sobrina*, you are protected, or at least you will be as soon as I file the paperwork Monday morning."

Antonia was stunned. Her thoughts spun as fast as one of those stationary bikes at the YMCA where she wanted to take Carlitos for swimming lessons. She could not believe the words she heard, and yet she knew her uncle would not lie to her, she knew the president of the United States was not lying on national television, but still she could not believe it was true. She had lived in hiding her entire adult life, longer. Even as a young child crossing the Rio Grande in her father's arms, she knew she was in hiding. Fearful, always fearful that she would be caught, that she would be deported like so many others. The years since Carlitos's birth had been the worst. She lived with the fear that Kline would turn her in, exert his paternal rights, and steal her son by simply arranging her deportation. She'd lived in terror and endured Kline's brutality, knowing she could not fight back without risking what she cherished most of all: Carlitos. But now this president had made her dream come true. Now she would be a legal resident in the only country she considered her home.

She looked back and forth between Carolina and Tío Antonio. "Is it real? Am I safe?" she asked.

"Yes," they told her.

"We have fought many years for these reforms. This is truly a day of celebration," Tío Antonio said. "I shall be a very busy man in the coming weeks and months, but your paperwork will be the first documents I process. That's a promise."

Fifty-Two

ONCE AGAIN I SAT in front of the sliding glass doors at SeaTac arrivals listening to NPR and impatiently drumming my fingers on the steering wheel, this time my own steering wheel, the steering wheel of the first car I'd ever owned. Crazy it took me so long to buy a car. It was so convenient to have one, to not be borrowing from Gemi or taking the bus whenever I needed wheels that moved faster or carried more than my bike. Funny I'd never thought to buy one before–an excuse to not visit my parents maybe. What a horrible daughter. He hadn't been that bad, had he? I mean, I didn't like how he put himself above all the workers, but he never mistreated anyone. And Mom? A gem. I just never knew. Never gave them a chance.

The temptation to drive everywhere was new. Never an option before, I'd always checked the bus routes if I couldn't ride my bike–if it was too far, if I had to carry too much, if the weather was miserable. I was beginning to worry about the pounds I'd be gaining if I didn't keep riding my bike every day when I saw Jason, long and lean, stroll through the exit, a duffle bag slung over his shoulder. The man was never in a hurry, never flustered, without a care in the world. He could've been wearing baggy shorts with a surfboard on his shoulder coming in off the last big wave of the day, his auburn hair long and wet. I jumped from the car and rushed into his open arms, struggling to control my passion for this beautiful man.

"Throw it in next to mine," I told him as I opened the trunk. I saw the confusion in his eyes. "I figured we'd head straight to Mound City rather than spend the night in Seattle. Is that okay with you? We'll miss the traffic and have plenty of time to get there before dinner."

He folded himself into the front seat. "Let's do it. Can't wait to see this place."

"It's funny. As a kid all I wanted to do was to get away. Now it's the opposite. I think I could drop everything and move there tomorrow."

"Everything?" he asked.

"Well, no. Only if I could figure out how to get everybody I love to make the move with me."

"Fair enough."

"And I suppose I have to figure out if the orchard has a viable economic future. Manuel should be able to help us figure that out."

"Us?"

"Well, you're part of this adventure, aren't you?"

"I sure hope so. I suppose that's what I'm here to find out, isn't it? And who's this Manuel?"

"Manuel grew up in the orchard. His father was the foreman before him. If anyone knows the land and the market, it's Manuel."

"And you trust him."

"Totally. He was like a second father to me, or maybe an understanding older brother. I could always go to him and his wife, Elena, whenever I wanted to run away. They'd let me stay long enough to convince me to go home. They only had one daughter who was a few years older than me. At the time, she was the closest thing to a best friend I had, but we could never be together."

"Because of your dad?"

"Yeah. He didn't think I should socialize with the workers."

"But it sounds like Manuel and his family were more than workers."

"To me, we were, but Dad had this invisible line. Was it racism? Was it classism? Maybe a combination. All I know is that it was them and us, and we didn't socialize. Not in his world. It'll be strange to try to redraw those lines now that he's gone."

We were quiet for a bit as I negotiated the freeway off- and on-ramps, heading out of Seattle.

"I love my new car," I said as we settled onto Interstate 90 eastbound towards the Cascade Mountains.

"I didn't think you'd actually buy one, you know. Didn't think you'd ever drive."

"Don't remind me. I was awful. All that crap I gave you about driving back and forth to Oregon. The environment and all that."

"Yeah, you told me I should take Greyhound."

"Sorry. I totally was full of myself back then. Thanks for helping me find this. It's been a godsend."

"Is Antonia driving now?"

"Yup. Antonio bought her a used Jetta for her birthday. Bright red. She's totally independent now. Still fearful and cautious with Kline out there, we're all on high alert, but at least she can't be deported now and she's got legal custody of Carlitos."

"Good," he said. "That's really, really good."

We drove in silence for a long while, the Cascades looming on both sides of the highway, only traces of snow remaining on the upper peaks.

"We're both older and wiser now, right?" he said.

"I suppose. But where'd that come from?"

"Just checking. We're wise enough to avoid all the stupid games couples play?"

"I hope so," I said.

"So, cards on the table. We're headed to Mound City to see if we can build a life together there. To see if I love the place as much as you love it and as much as I love you."

"Do you love me?"

"I love you."

"Okay."

"So we're clear about it," he said with a laugh.

"Right." I struggled to concentrate on the highway in front of me. I tingled. Every molecule, every cell tingled with joy. I was smiling so wide I was certain my lips would crack. A rest stop sign loomed before me, an invitation to stop and I pulled to the side of the highway. I turned off the ignition, unbuckled my seatbelt and leaned into him. "I love you, too," I said.

The kiss was deep and long. We were both breathing hard.

"This place looks abandoned enough," he murmured.

"There's a bunch of trees over there."

We ran from the car like lovesick teenagers. In the wooded darkness, he tugged at my khakis and I tugged at his jeans. He entered me hard and sure, my back against a rough tree trunk. I led him to the ground–a soft, damp cushion of Northwest moss. There we explored each other's bodies until he groaned his pleasure and I screamed my release. Joyously spent and laughing at our own recklessness, we collapsed under the canopy of green overhead.

I'm not sure how long we lay there, a tangle of arms and legs and half discarded clothing. I shivered. He held me tight. "We should go," he whispered.

"Do we have to?" I said.

"Do you want to get to that orchard of yours today?" He stood and lifted me up with him as though we were still connected, as though we were still one. Dressing, we made our way back to the car brushing pine needles and twigs from each other's clothes, picking them from our hair.

"We'll have to remember this rest stop," he said.

I laughed, too happy to say a single word.

It was later than I'd planned when we finally arrived at the old farm house. I'd brought along a few things for dinner, but I wasn't looking forward to cooking.

"That's odd," I said.

"What's odd?"

"Look. The windows are open. I'm sure I closed the curtains when I left, and I know I locked the windows. Even upstairs. That's my bedroom window. It's wide open."

As we got out of the car, Manuel and Elena came around the side of the house and walked toward us.

"Is everything okay?" I asked.

"Oh, yes," they said.

"But the windows are open," I said.

"Your mother didn't tell you," Manuel said. He turned to Elena and added, "So like Mrs. Bauer."

"Tell me what?" I asked.

"Mrs. Bauer called us last week and told us to prepare the house for your arrival. She said you were bringing a special friend."

"Yes, I'm sorry. Manuel and Elena, this is my friend Jason Cabot. Jason these are my old friends, Manuel and Elena Jimenez. Without them this orchard would be nothing but scrub."

After the handshaking and greetings, Elena said, "I think the house is ready, all but a few of the bedrooms. If you need anything, you know where to find us. There's dinner in the refrigerator. Just warm it in the oven. Come on, Manuel." She pushed her husband in the direction of their small house on the far side of the barn.

"Thank you," I called after them. Then, I took Jason's hand and led him in the front door. "Oh my," I exclaimed as we walked through the house. It was brighter and cleaner than I ever remembered it. The bay window sparkled in the setting sun, and there were bouquets of wild flowers on the coffee table in the living room, in the center of the dining room table and even on the kitchen table. The refrigerator was stocked and a few bottles of my favorite wine stood on the counter. Down the hall, the door to my parents' bedroom was closed and I knew without opening it that it hadn't been touched, but the downstairs bathroom shined as bright as the kitchen appliances and windows.

"I can't believe this." I slumped down on the open stairwell to the second floor.

"Elena?"

"No, my mother. I mean yes, Elena must have worked her butt off. But Mom? Why would she do this for me?"

"Because she loves you?"

"I guess so. Amazing."

"Come on. Show me the rest of this beautiful old house. There must be a few bedrooms up here somewhere." He wrapped an arm around me and we climbed the stairs.

At the top, the hallway was lined with four doors, a bathroom and three bedrooms, the rooms Gemi, Antonia, and I used on our last visit. One was my bedroom; the other two had been empty throughout my childhood, sad reminders of the children my parents were never able to conceive. Now only the doors to the bathroom and my bedroom stood slightly ajar. Like my parents' room downstairs, I knew the two extra bedrooms had not received Elena's meticulous attention.

I opened my bedroom door and gasped. My single bed was gone. The faded fluffy bedding and curtains gone. The junky bulletin board and small desk gone. The walls were clean of the posters and glistened with a coat of fresh paint. Even the closet had been emptied. Only my bookcase remained.

The room had been transformed with butter yellow walls and soft white curtains that fluttered at the open windows. A large bed buried under a sunflower comforter stood flanked by white bedside tables. A matching dresser on one wall was crowned with another huge bouquet of wild flowers.

"Oh, my word," was all I managed to say.

"She did all of this?" Jason asked.

"Apparently so. I need to call her." I dug in my backpack to find my phone and dialed the house.

"How did you do it, Mom?"

She sang a line from the Beatles song about getting help from your friends and asked, "Did Elena do a good job?"

"Incredible. It's absolutely beautiful, Mom. But how did you convince her to enter the house? Manuel wouldn't even come in for Dad's funeral."

"I told Manuel that Norman was gone and times were changing. And I told him I needed his and Elena's help. I think that's what did it."

"Well, it sure worked. The place looks fabulous. By the way, what happened to my old bed and desk?"

"I told Elena she could have it for when their sweet little granddaughter comes for a visit. Is that okay?"

"Of course, Mom. I was just curious."

"I asked Elena to box up all your old high school stuff. It should be in the hall closet or one of the other rooms. I'm sure she didn't have time to spiff them all up."

"But the bed and the furniture and everything. How did you pull that off?"

"The delivery people removed the old furniture and installed the new. Amazing what you can do on the Internet these days. Of course, Antonia and Gemi helped me pick it all out and place the order. Do you like it? Are the colors good?"

"I love it, Mom. Yellow and white with a sunflower motif. It couldn't be more perfect. The whole house glows. The flowers are beautiful, the bedroom is gorgeous, and the kitchen is full of good food and drink. Thank you so very, very much."

"Well, I hope Jason likes it too. The bedroom's not too girly, is it? I asked Antonio, but he didn't seem to have much of an opinion."

"Hey Jason," I said. "Mom wants to know if the room is too girly."

"Not at all, Edith," he yelled. "It's stunning."

"So there you have it, Mom." Her happy laughter made me smile.

"Okay, then. Hang up now and feed that man some of Elena's fabulous tamales. Goodbye, sweetie."

"Bye, Mom. I love you so very much."

It was noon by the time we knocked on the Jimenez's front door the next day. When Elena opened it, I startled her with a huge bear hug.

"Thank you," I said. "Everything is incredible. My mother made you do too much. The house has never looked so good. Dinner was wonderful. And the flowers, oh my! Thank you so much."

"It was a pleasure to be part of your mother's surprise, Carolyn. We haven't heard her sound so happy in a very long time. You've been a good change for her."

"We've been good for each other, Elena. I can't wait to bring her back for a visit."

"Will that be soon?" she asked.

"Probably early next month, but we'll see. We're wondering if Manuel could show Jason and me around the place."

"Of course. He's out in the cider shed. Should I call him?"

"That's okay. We'll find him."

We spent the day walking the orchard. The week, learning about the crops, the market, the options. By the time we headed back across the pass, we were both certain of the direction we wanted our lives to take us.

"I hate to go," Jason said when I stopped outside SeaTac departures. "There are so many loose ends to tie up. Once the estate closes, I'll be a free man."

"Do you want to be a free man?" I teased.

"I want you to marry me," he said. "And if that developer wants Mama Lucy's house, we'll be able to invest in the orchard and carry out some of those improvements Manuel suggested."

"Yes," I said.

Fifty-Three

"SURPRISE," ANTONIA YELLED when she opened the front door and entered the house.

"Surprise," Edith echoed as she walked into the entry at Antonia's side.

"Surprise, surprise, surprise," Carlitos chanted as he danced around them both.

"So many surprises?" Gemi asked from the top of the stairs as she wiped her hands on a dish cloth.

Carolina came out of her kitchen, a potato in one hand and a peeler in the other. "What's up?" she asked.

"Edith, you look wonderful," Gemi said.

"Mom?" Carolina said. "My goodness, she's right. You look, I don't know, younger."

"I feel terrific," Edith said. She ran her fingers through her short gray curls.

"I never even knew you had curly hair. You've worn it in that bun for as long as I can remember," Carolina said.

"True. I always loved your short hair, but your father liked mine long, so I never cut it. This morning I told Antonia I was ready for a change, so after we picked up Carlitos, we went to a salon she chose for me. It was wonderful. They treated me like a queen. But enough about me. Antonia and Carlitos have surprises, too. Your turn, Antonia."

"Ta da!" Antonia said as she held up her test results for the GED science exam. "Four down and only one more to go."

"Congratulations," Gemi said.

"President Obama said I need my GED, so I'm getting it," Antonia said with a laugh. "But I'm still worried about math."

"Oh, stop already," Carolina said. "Mom told me you could pass it tomorrow if you wanted to. I'm sure you're ready."

"One more surprise," Carlitos said. He was jumping from one foot to the other, so full of excitement he couldn't contain himself.

"Sorry, Carlitos," Carolina said. "What's your surprise?"

"Ta da!" he said as he held up his spelling test just as he'd seen his mother do only moments before. There was a big, bright star at the top of the page. "Perfect, perfect, perfect," the boy chanted.

"Well done, little man," Carolina said. "I guess all that practice last night helped."

Antonia couldn't contain her smile, the smile of a proud mother. Spelling had been tough for her son, maybe because he'd been bilingual from birth. Carolina had told her not to worry too much about it, but still she was thrilled at Carlitos's newfound success. She'd taken him to the ice cream shop next door to the salon while Edith was getting her hair cut to celebrate with a special treat.

"All right then, Carlitos, let's see if you can make cookies as well as you can spell. Are you ready to help me?" As soon as the words left Gemi's mouth, Carlitos scampered up the stairs.

"I'd better get back to my soup," Carolina said.

"Let's watch the news, Antonia," Edith said. "It's been a busy day. I think I'm a bit worn down."

The local news had already started when Antonia switched on the television. "Now this late breaking news. A man identified as Jeff Kline, a former attorney for the U.S. Immigration and Customs Enforcement was found shot dead in his car this afternoon."

"*Ey no*," Antonia screamed. "*No puede ser.*"

"What is it?" Carolina asked as she ran from the kitchen. She glanced at the television screen. A moment later, she grabbed her cell phone and called Gemi upstairs. "Kline's dead. Turn off the radio and don't let Carlitos watch TV. Keep him up there, okay?"

As with many local broadcasts, this one focused on the gruesome details. High school kids had found the black sedan at the end of a dead end street when they cut afternoon classes. They peeked inside and called 911. A pistol with a silencer was found in the car. Suicide was suspected. There were photographs of a smiling man, his estranged wife, and two young daughters. There were details about a recent arrest on charges of violating a restraining order, but Antonia's name was not mentioned.

Stunned, she sat in between Carolina and Edith. "*No puede ser,*" she mumbled.

Edith wrapped her arm around Antonia and held her tight.

"Here, check a few more channels," Carolina said, passing Antonia the remote. "I'll check online."

Antonia flicked through channels until she found another version of the same story. Then Carolina showed her an online report. The article was small, the picture prominent. A handsome young man with bright blue eyes and blond hair, a man who seemed to hold the world in his hands. "Former ICE Attorney Found Dead. Suicide Suspected," the headline read. The article included more grisly details.

"Why?" Antonia cried. "Why would he do this thing? Why kill himself?"

"Maybe he gave up," Edith said. "Seems to me he was the kind of man who needed power and control. He lost both when you got away from him. Then he got fired because he couldn't control himself, his violent rage, or his excessive drinking. After he lost everything—you, Carlitos, his job, his wife, and daughters, and who knows what else—he was too much of a coward to start over."

"Mom's right, Antonia," Carolina said. "I bet he really hated himself, too. I mean, here he was a successful man with a good career throwing undocumented immigrants out of the country and he meets you. He must have hated himself for falling in love with the enemy."

"I feel bad," Antonia sobbed. "I know it is not true, but I feel it is my *culpa.*"

"Fault? It's not your fault," Carolina said.

"Antonia, Kline chose to end his life because he was a coward, nothing more. You know this. You're a smart young woman. He'd already lost his job and he couldn't face going to court on abuse charges, let alone admit he was harboring an illegal immigrant. He was a coward."

"I know, Edith. I see he is a coward and a very violent man. Was. He was. But I feel bad."

"It'll take time, that's all," Edith.

"It's over," Carolina said. "That's what matters now. It's over and I have to admit I'm glad."

"Glad?" Antonia asked. "A man is dead."

"Yeah, glad. You and Carlitos are finally safe, Antonia. Really, truly safe. You can't be deported and you don't have to worry about Kline attacking you or kidnapping Carlitos every time you leave the house. You don't have to be looking over your shoulder all the time. You're safe. You're a free woman. It's over and I'm glad for that."

"It's over," Antonia said. She burst into tears and curled into a ball, her knees to her chest.

Edith rocked her like a baby until she stopped shaking, then Carolina handed her a box of tissues.

In the attic room that night, with Carlitos snoring his little boy snores, Antonia wasn't so sure. Was it over? Totally and completely over?

She poked through the box she'd brought from the apartment she once shared with Jeff Kline. It contained very little. The newspaper article she'd found on the break-room table that day, the one Mehret had helped her understand. It seemed so long ago. Mehret. Now she could call her old friend, pick her up after work in her own car, take her to lunch, share her whole story. It felt like a lifetime since that lunch with Antonio. She knew now she could begin again. She was safe. She was free. She was legal. It was almost too much to believe.

Antonia leafed through the old school books and papers. She knew someday she'd need to tell her son about his father. She struggled to find the balance between the love and the horror, trying to make sense of who Kline had been. She found what she hadn't realized she was looking for, a small strip of black and white photos. She remembered the day as though it were yesterday. They were at the mall only weeks after Carlitos was born. It was Kline who saw the photo booth, who tucked them inside, who held their tiny baby. She remembered the kiss he planted on her cheek as the camera flashed. A handsome man, a newborn baby in his arms, kissing the smiling cheek of a dark, young beauty, a face she no longer saw when she looked in the mirror. This she would save for Carlitos.

Fifty-Four

WE DECIDED TO make it a super-long weekend. Even Gemi and Antonio decided to stay through Wednesday. Carlitos was thrilled to be heading back to the orchard, but for Mom and Antonia, both reliving whispers of past lives, there was a mix of emotion.

Jason flew up on Friday. He'd have to go back to finalize the sale of Mama Lucy's home and rent a U-Haul to move north–neither of us thought his Dad's old pick-up could make the trip–but he wasn't about to miss the work party or the Fourth of July barbecue. He'd already resigned from his teaching position in Los Arboles, and I'd managed an unpaid leave-of-absence from the college. We wanted to give the orchard life one full year, a trial period to see if we could make a go of it. We figured we might want to make changes over time, but for now the house was fully furnished, so all we needed were our clothes and personal items. I was already guessing Jason's U-Haul would be filled with pottery equipment, and a pottery shed would soon stand out on the hill behind the house with a view of the orchard.

The work party was more a painting party than anything else, and Manuel and his workers had already prepped and painted the front of the house when we caravanned into the yard midmorning on Saturday. As I climbed out of the car, I saw Manuel busy with a spray gun high in the upper reaches under the peaked roof on the south side of the house.

"It's beautiful, Carolyn," Gemi said as she climbed out of the backseat of Antonia's Jetta, Carlitos right behind her. She looped her arm through mine, and we watched the old gray house disappear under the spray of soft, yellow paint.

"Like the big house and your little one behind it in Los Arboles," Antonia said, as she came to stand on my other side.

I smiled at her and our shared memory.

"Looks like you got a running start on us," Jason shouted up to Manuel.

"Couldn't waste the daylight," Manuel said. "At this rate, we'll finish spraying today."

"Can we start on the front trim and porch?" Jason asked.

"Should be dry enough to remove the masking."

"Okay, then," Jason said. "We'll unpack and get started."

We headed into the house with armloads of groceries and overnight bags to change into old clothes. I listened with joy as Gemi and Antonia went on and on about how beautiful the house looked, but the real surprise was upstairs and Carlitos found it first. He came sliding down the stairs hollering, "Mami, Mami, I have my own bed now and it's even got a farm and a tractor on it."

As Antonia and Gemi followed him back upstairs, I explained to my mother that I'd followed her lead and ordered a queen-sized bed and bedding for Gemi and Antonio's room as well as the special comforter for Carlitos. Manuel and Elena had rearranged Antonia's room, moving in the single bed from Gemi's room so Carlitos wouldn't have to sleep on a cot. They'd done their magic again and the upstairs bedrooms were freshly painted and sparkling clean.

I knew I'd need to spend some time with Mom sorting her bedroom, discarding much of what remained in my father's closet and dresser drawers, and reviewing some of the files of old paperwork. We'd talked it over and she was ready, but she was still trying to convince me that Jason and I should have the master bedroom. I insisted it was hers and always would be. Besides, we loved our upstairs room. We loved the view of the orchard, the miles of trees climbing and dropping over rolling hills, a sea of trees in all directions. It felt like we were on top of the world.

I walked Mom into her room. "Nothing's been moved," I told her.

"But it smells different," she said. "Better. Much better."

It was true. Although nothing had been moved, Elena had aired out the room, scrubbed the windows until sunlight sparkled on the mirror above the antique dresser, washed and rehung the curtains, cleaned the carpet, and put fresh linens on the bed.

After I got Mom settled and ran up to put on some ratty old khakis, I headed outside. I cracked up laughing when I saw Gemi on a ladder painting the white trim around the bay windows. She was dressed in beige polyester pants several sizes too big and a baggy tunic top, her long black hair hidden under a twisted headscarf.

"Haven't I seen that ensemble somewhere before?" I asked.

"You didn't think I'd throw it away, did you?"

"Wasn't that how you first impressed Antonio with your beauty?" I teased.

"Indeed. I'd already changed my wardrobe and abandoned the headscarf, but I was wearing my old clothes to help Chris paint her condo," Gemi said.

"And you'd dropped a bunch of weight."

"Yes," Gemi said without an ounce of bragging in her voice. "We were having a painting party a bit like this one."

"I'd only just moved in across the hall," Antonio said from his spot on the front porch where he'd begun the tedious task of painting the railings. "I stopped by to meet my new neighbor ..."

"I was mortified when Antonio came to the door."

"... and my life changed forever."

"Just like that," I said with a snap of my fingers.

"Just like that," he agreed.

"Just like that," Gemi nodded.

We painted and talked and walked the orchard all weekend. The dining room table was crowded with the seven of us at each meal, sometimes nine, when Manuel and Elena joined us. The house was full of conversation and laughter.

Somehow I found time alone with both Gemi and Antonia as well as with my mother. Saturday evening when Mom and I sorted her bedroom, I learned she didn't want to move back to the orchard with Jason and me. She loved her new life in Seattle and hoped I'd be okay if she spent time in both places.

"Whatever you prefer is okay with me, Mom," I told her. "But do we know Antonia's plans?"

"Talk to her, Carolyn," my mother told me.

Antonia had passed the math test and been awarded her GED. In fact, Gemi, Mom and I had already planned a celebration dinner for Sunday evening, but I was still in the dark about her further plans.

I crawled out of bed early Sunday morning without waking Jason and met Antonia in the kitchen for our morning walk–Sunday mornings with Antonia, Wednesday afternoons with Gemi. How life would change when I moved to the orchard. I'd miss our walks. They were our time to focus only on each other, time out of our busy schedules to listen and be heard.

"So what do you think?" I asked as we struck out through the trees. "Could you see yourself here?"

Antonia was quiet for a long while. "It is your dream," she finally said. "You and Jason will be very happy here."

"Not without you and Carlitos," I said.

"We will visit often. For now we will stay in Seattle. I will earn my associate's degree and then transfer to the university. I want to be a teacher."

"Maybe then you could come and start a school here for the migrant children. You know how badly they need the chance to get a decent education."

"Perhaps someday," she said. "Tío Antonio is family. Gemi is my Mama Lucy. I cannot leave them yet. I need to stay and be family, give Carlitos a family."

"I understand," I said. "I'll miss you so much."

"I will miss you, too." She wrapped her thin arms around me in a tight hug.

"Mom says she wants to stay in Seattle too, at least part of the time, probably most of the time."

"Yes, we talked of this."

"Will you be able to continue to care for her? Is that what you want?" I asked.

"Yes. We thought Carlitos and I might move into your bedroom. That way I'll be closer to Edith at night and Gemi and Tío Antonio will have more privacy again."

"That makes sense," I said. "But ..."

"But what about when you come to Seattle? We will clear out the storage room at the back of the house behind the stairs and make another bedroom. We do not use the house as two apartments, so a bedroom there would be good."

"Wow, you guys have given this a lot of thought, haven't you?"

"Tío Antonio said the storage room is bigger than the attic room. We can add a window for daylight."

I laughed. "Again, two steps ahead of me, aren't you?"

"Carolina, I still do not have a job. I cannot pay rent."

"Of course you have a job, Antonia. You're taking care of my mother. You're cooking and cleaning and doing laundry and making sure she's safe and happy. That's a big job. I'll need to pay you."

"No, Carolina. I do not want your money. A home is sufficient. A home for Carlitos with his Abuelita Edith and Gemi–and sometimes Tío Antonio–is perfect."

"Maybe more of Tío Antonio in the house?"

"I hope so," she said.

Later, after dinner and the GED celebration, after the dishes were washed and put away, while Carlitos, Edith, and Antonia read stories together and Antonio, Jason, and Manuel talked about whatever it is men talk about, Gemi and I took a walk, flashlights in hand, through the dark orchard.

"Sounds like you, Antonia, and Mom have been making plans for me," I said.

"Oh, do not be getting touchy, my friend. We all want the best for you and Jason. As long as you hold onto your Seattle house, I think we can make it work. If you decide to sell, we'll need to adjust."

"Oh, Gemi, I have no intention of selling. I love that old house and I can't imagine not having a place in the city. What have you and Antonio discussed? Do you see yourself living together?"

"I've let go of so many of the old traditions with which I was raised," Gemi said. "Perhaps I am letting go of the legal bonds of marriage as well."

"Very liberal of you."

"Perhaps I need more time. Perhaps I am afraid."

"There's no rush, Gemi."
"I know Antonio would love to be closer to Antonia and Carlitos."
"And to you."
"And to me. Do you have objections to Antonio moving in upstairs with me, Carolyn?"
"It's your home, too, Gemi. I long ago stopped thinking of you as a tenant. Of course, it's okay."

That July Fourth was a celebration I will always remember. We set up a long picnic table in the backyard and decided it should be a totally traditional American barbecue. Antonio was in charge of cooking the hamburgers and Antonia arranged the fixings. Jason made Mama Lucy's Potato Salad, Gemi and Carlitos baked apple pies, and I shucked corn until I thought my arms would fall off. Manuel, Elena, and the workers all joined us at the long table, each with a dish to share, and we had a feast with wine, beer, and cider for all.

Jason stood, glass in hand. "A toast," he said. "To my beautiful friend and lover, thank you for inviting me to share my life with you here in this small piece of paradise."

Clapping and laughter filled the evening air.

"And an invitation," he said, wrapping an arm around my waist as I stood beside him.

"We hope all of you will join us again a month from now to bear witness ..." I said.

"... As we exchange our wedding vows on Edith Bauer's front steps," Jason concluded.

Everyone jumped to their feet. "Cheers! Cheers!" they shouted as Jason and I kissed. Tears of happiness streamed down my face as Gemi and Antonia wrapped me in a tight hug. Peering over my shoulder, I saw my mother standing at the head of the table, Carlitos's hand in hers. "I'll be back," I told my friends and I made my way towards her. "I'm so happy, Mom," I whispered in her ear.

"Not as happy as I am, my dear daughter." When she wrapped me in her arms, my tears of overflowed.

We ate and drank, laughed and talked, until shadows fell over the orchard. As if by magic, fireworks lit the night sky in a joyous celebration of new beginnings.

Fifty-Five

I STROLLED THROUGH the autumn orchard, the trees heavy with radiant red apples. In a matter of weeks these trees would be picked clean. Already the workers' cottages were at capacity. Already Manuel was organizing the teams of pickers, sorters, and packers. Already they were preparing the final push.

I walked slowly between the heavy trees, humming softly to myself, my hands clasped over my round belly. Every now and again I reached up to touch a green leaf here, a red apple there. I took a deep breath of the sweet air and remembered the blossoms of spring. I no longer rushed from place to place on my trusty old bike. Slowed by the bulk of new life I carried, I no longer rushed at all. I held my belly and felt the movement of my baby, our baby, the kicks, somersaults, and wiggles of new life.

New life. My due date was two weeks away. In two weeks, in the heat of the harvest, a harvest baby would be born. I couldn't decide if our timing was perfect or a perfect storm, but either way there wasn't a thing to be done about it now, and I was too happy to worry.

New life. My only regret was Mama Lucy was no longer with us to share our joy. She would not see her great-grandchild, would not hold him or her in her gnarled old hands, would not see the contentment on her grandson's face. If only our timing had been a little better. "I'm sorry, Mama Lucy," I whispered to the apple trees and the sky above. "I miss you. I wish you were here with us. Perhaps you will always be with us, won't you?"

New life. Through the rows of trees, high on the slope behind the house, Jason's pottery shed stood as a replica of Mama Lucy's in

Los Arboles but with a new kiln, skylights, and more shelves. Jason divided his time between the hard cider business and throwing pots. We left the day-to-day running of the orchard to Manuel given he knew far more than either of us would ever know. Still, Jason would be on the ladders with the workers as soon as the picking began.

I held my swollen belly and remembered our wedding. I walked down the front stairs of my parents' home and into Jason's arms. Dad was probably rolling in his grave about our guest list. "Get over it, Dad," I whispered in the breeze. "I love you, you old goat, but you were wrong, just plain wrong."

It was later, after we said our vows, after we ate and drank and danced in the moonlight, when my mother looped her arm through mine and asked me to help her to her bedroom. Odd, I thought. She could find her way around this place better than any of the sighted guests, but I walked her into the house and gave her a kiss good-night.

"One more thing," she said.

I felt a twinge of impatience. I wanted to say, but it's my wedding, Mom. I wanted to get back to the party. But I bit my tongue, and later I was so very glad I had this once.

"There's an envelope on the dresser, isn't there?" she said.

"Yes. A large manila envelope."

"It's for you, Carolyn. For you and Jason."

She must have heard me start to open it because she said, "Not now. Take it to your room. Open it later when the others have gone, when you and Jason are alone. Put it in your room now where it is safe."

"Okay," I told her. "Thank you, Mom." Then I kissed her again and did what she asked. I ran the envelope up to our room and went back outside to join the fun.

Hours passed, our guests left for their hotels in town, Manuel and Elena walked home, and the workers returned to their cottages. When Gemi and Antonio closed their bedroom door and Antonia snuck into her room without waking her sleeping son, when Jason and I were alone in our bedroom, I remembered the envelope and handed it to him.

"It's from Mom. Open it," I said as I undressed.

"Now?" He watched as my dress dropped to the floor.

"Mom told me we should open it together after everybody left and we were alone."

"Okay then, come here and sit with me." He patted the bed next to him and slit open the envelope.

"What is it?" I asked.

"The deed," he said.

"Huh?" I asked, too distracted by the happiness of the day to pay much attention.

"It's the deed, Carolyn," my handsome husband told me. "Your mother has signed over the deed to the house and all the land. It's yours."

"No," I said. "It's ours. She said it was for both of us. Look there, clear as day, Jason and Carolyn Cabot."

Now I smiled as I walked through the autumn orchard remembering our stunned joy. So much had happened in only a few months. I held my bulging belly, lovingly caressing the baby within. I suppose I always knew someday the orchard would be left to me, but to be given the deed on our wedding day was the most perfect gift my mother could have conceived, the gift that made it our own.

We'd already begun a number of improvements. Through the trees I caught a glimpse of the latest building project, heard the pounding of hammers and the whine of a table saw. With a full heart, I emerged from the orchard onto the small dirt road leading to the workers' cottages, refurbished with new plumbing, wiring, roofing, and soft yellow paint to match the house.

The building under construction differed only slightly from the other cottages that stood in two neat rows facing a long, green garden, but it was not to be another house like all the others. Instead it would be a community school and library. The side walls would be lined with books and the front would hold a large white board. The tables and chairs would be big enough for adult comfort but small enough for children to use. The windows would be curtained with embroidered white cotton and the door would be open to all.

I was busy writing grants for funds to stock the bookshelves and install a few computers so the workers could easily contact their families and friends in distant lands. With sufficient funding I knew the Orchard School would be able to serve both the adults and their children. Maybe soon I'd be able to offer Antonia a teaching position and lure her to Mound City.

I could almost see her bright yellow bike leaning against the porch railing. I'd walk through the open door to find Antonia at her desk correcting papers, planning classes, prepping for the coming day. Carlitos would be sitting on the sofa in the library corner with a few other children. They'd be reading quietly together in a gentle mix of Spanish and English, pointing to the pictures and teaching each other the words they didn't know.

"Like us," I'd whisper to Antonia. "Just like us in Los Arboles so very long ago."

ACKNOWLEDGMENTS

I am so very grateful ...

To my husband, Thomas Clay Williams, who spent long hours listening and offering insights as I read the entire manuscript of *Biking Uphill* aloud, for his patience and his support as I dedicate my work-free hours to this crazy passion of writing.

To former student and dear friend, Clara Ines Arango, for reading a draft of *Biking Uphill* to make certain my use of the Spanish language has not been totally buried in the recesses of memory.

To Ken Shear and Booktrope for publishing my work, to my wonderful creative team: Pamela Hobart Carter, Loretta Matson, Katrina Randall and Kay Ellington for polishing that work until it shines, and to Adam Bodendieck and Victoria Wolffe for pulling it all together in production. Of course, all errors remain my own.

To each of you who reads my words, thank you.

ALSO BY ARLEEN WILLIAMS

Running Secrets - The Alki Trilogy

Flight attendant Chris Stevens is bent on self-destruction until she meets Gemi Kemmal, an Ethiopian homecare nurse. Gemi and Jake, a paramedic, help Chris heal from and confront her difficult past, and regain a passion for living. In the process, Chris and Gemi forge an unusual friendship that bridges cultural, racial, and age differences. Their friendship gives both women the support each needs. Gemi comes to question restrictive traditions dictating her immigrant life, such as the headscarf she's worn since entering puberty and the celibacy she's practiced since the brutal death of her husband and infant in the violence that destroyed her homeland and family. Chris uncovers family secrets that challenge everything she's ever known to be true. Together, the women learn that racial identity is a choice, self expression is a right, and family is a personal construct.

The Thirty-Ninth Victim - a memoir

The Green River murders were headline news throughout the 1980s. By the time the perpetrator was sentenced in 2003, at least forty-eight young women had met an untimely death at his hands. What started as a string of local killings in Seattle became a national nightmare before it was over. In homes all across America, television news programs and newspapers large and small carried feature stories about the ever-growing list of victims.

Now imagine that during this time, someone you love--your baby sister, a beautiful young woman of 19--suddenly goes missing. The police are at best unhelpful, and at worst, seemingly uninterested in what's happened to her. And then comes word you hoped you'd never receive: your youngest sister's remains have been found. She is yet another victim of the Green River killer.

With amazing candor, Arleen Williams tells the story of her family's journey, before and after the Green River killer murdered her sister Maureen and left her body in a stretch of wilderness off the west side of Highway 18. As insightful as it is heart wrenching, *The Thirty-Ninth Victim* gives you a window into the family dynamics that contributed to this life-altering tragedy. This is a memoir unlike any other. The author set out to tell Maureen's story, but in doing so, she tells bits and pieces of every family's story. You cannot read this profoundly personal and cataclysmic tale and come away unchanged, nor will you ever view your own family in quite the same way.

You will applaud Ms. Williams's courage in sharing this recounting of her family's trauma through one of the most atrocious streaks of serial killings in American history. And like the family, you will never forget *The Thirty-Ninth Victim*.

MORE GREAT READS FROM BOOKTROPE

Dismantle the Sun by **Jim Snowden** (General Fiction) A novel of love and loss, betrayal and second chances. Diagnosed with cancer, Jodie struggles to help her husband Hal learn to live without her. As Hal prepares to say goodbye to his wife, he discovers the possibility of happiness—in the arms of one of his students.

Dove Creek by **Paula Marie Coomer** (General Fiction) After a disastrous and abusive marriage, single mother Patricia draws on her Cherokee roots for courage. She finds her place as a Public Health nurse, but she must constantly prove herself—to patients, coworkers, and family members—in her quest to improve the lives of others.

Holding True by **Emily Dietrich** (Contemporary Fiction / Coming of Age) Born in the hopeful energy of the civil rights movement, Martie struggles to live out the values she inherited by founding the Copper Hill commune, with tragic results.

Lark Eden by **Natalie Symons** (General Fiction) A play chronicling the friendship of three Southern women over seventy-five years. At once a deeply moving and darkly comic look at the fingerprints that we unknowingly leave on the hearts of those we love.

Living and Dying with Dogs by **Duke Miller** (Literary Fiction) Living and Dying with Dogs is a journey from war to epidemic to famine. Your tour guide? A hesitant, unsure narrator with a unique and tragic understanding of refugees, war, sex, the past, and our bloody world.

Thank You For Flying Air Zoe by **Erik Atwell** (Contemporary Women's Fiction) Realizing she needs to awaken her life's tired refrains, Zoe vows to recapture the one chapter of her life that truly mattered—her days as drummer for an all-girl garage band. Will Zoe bring the band back together and give The Flip-Flops a second chance at stardom?

Discover more books and learn about our new approach to publishing at www.booktrope.com

Made in the USA
Middletown, DE
15 March 2015